Came Home for a Killing

A Caleb Cove Mystery

by
Mahrie G. Reid

www.mahriegreid.com

ISBN 978-0-9937022-5-9

This is a work of fiction. All of the characters, organizations, and events portrayed in this novel are either products of the author's imagination or are used fictitiously. Previously issued as Katya Binks Came Home From Away

Cover Design: Lorraine Paton

Copy Editor: Ted Williams

Thanks to Alberta Romance Writers' Association members past and present. Without you this book would never have become a reality. Additional thanks to all the Bingley's, the Nova Scotia branch of my family, for hospitality extended to me during my research phase. Love you all.

CHAPTER ONE

Kelsey twitched the bedspread in a final adjustment and pulled her suit jacket out of the closet. She glanced at the bedside clock. *Half an hour to enjoy a coffee before I leave for work.* She headed toward her small kitchen. The coffee should be...

Burnt coffee odor reached her. *Oh crap. How did I forget the pot?*

The pot sat a foot from the coffee maker. Coffee sizzled on the burner and oozed in ever growing puddles across the counter. She threw the jacket toward a chair and dashed forward. Grabbing a tea towel, she mopped the burner and shoved home the pot in an attempt to stem the flooding mess. Jerking open the drawer, she added more towels to the puddles.

Thump, thump, and thump. Damn, now someone was at the door. *Just what I don't need.*

"Hey, Sis. I know you're still home and I can smell the coffee."
Brock.

"Just a minute," she hollered and soaked up the last puddle. Tossing the towels into the sink, she turned. At the door she flipped the lock letting in the oldest of her three brothers.

"Morning, Sis." He toed off his muddy cowboy boots and set a shoebox and his keys on the small table in the entry. He hung his Stetson on a hook and headed for the coffee pot.

"Wow. What happened here? Is the pot leaking?"

"No," she said. "Small lapse in concentration." A symptom of the disquiet she'd been experiencing lately. "I forgot the pot."

Brock looked back, an irritating grin on his face. "YOU forgot? Has anyone checked to see if Hell has frozen over?"

Kelsey swatted his shoulder. "Never mind your smart remarks. Sit. There should be enough coffee left." She pulled two mugs from the cupboard. "What's up?" she asked glancing from Brock to the box he'd left by the door. Was it for her? "I thought you were moving cattle this morning."

"True," Brock said. "But there were errands to run. And I knew you'd have coffee on." He wrapped his hands around the mug she handed him and raised his gaze to hers. "There are three things, two that you really need to know."

Kelsey laughed. He always had a specific number of topics. She raised an eyebrow though at the need-to-know part. "That sounds serious." At twenty-five, Brock's serious moments were minimal.

"First, it's about Andy."

"My boss?"

"He came by the house last night." Brock ducked his head. "I was kinda napping on the sofa and I could hear him talking to Dad in the office."

Andy talking to Dad? Was there something wrong with the ranch accounting?

"Eavesdropping?" Kelsey raised one finger in a manner she'd adopted while helping raise her younger brothers. "You know better than that."

Brock shifted on his chair. "They got talking before I could get moving. Then it didn't seem smart to speak up."

Kelsey added a frown to the finger wag. "Whatever you heard, if Dad wanted you to know, he'd have invited you to the meeting. To talk about it is gossiping."

"Andy asked Dad, and I quote, for your hand in marriage."

Kelsey spit coffee. "What." Forget the no-gossip rule. This involved her. She grabbed a napkin and wiped up the coffee spatter.

"Figured you might feel like that." Brock grinned. "I know how it is with Becky and me," he said and blushed, "and I never got the idea you and Andy were like that."

"No bloody way," Kelsey said. "We work together. We've gone to company parties and movies. But that's it." She sliced a hand through the air. "Period. End of sentence. End of story." What possessed Andy to think she'd marry him?

Brock snorted. "Well, Andy never did mention love and Dad never asked. They talked about you becoming a partner at the firm and about Andy and you helping run the ranch. The benefits of you two getting married. That type of thing. The conversation held all the charm of selling a prized heifer."

"Thanks," Kelsey said, "for planting that in my head." She slapped both palms on the table and pushed back. The shock dislodged the unease she'd kept at bay for months. She'd raised her three younger brothers because she loved them. She'd taken over the ranch bookkeeping when her Mom died. She'd taken courses to help with the bookkeeping, been good at it and ended up as a Chartered Accountant with the firm that did their taxes. She'd wandered into her life, not chosen it.

And now, without being consulted, she was getting slotted into a role as a wife. *Mrs. Andy—NOT going to happen.* She stood and grabbed her cup. "I need a new life."

"Agreed." Brock stood. "You've been taking care of us far too long. We're big boys now," he said. "We can take care of ourselves. Well, *I* can and I'll ride herd on the young ones."

For once she didn't laugh and correct him. She teased the boys that they'd need her until they found wives. She still went out to the ranch several times a week, filled the freezer with pre-cooked meals and ran the vacuum. Maybe she should stop.

"You could move away. Make us go cold turkey." She looked at Brock who towered over her by almost a foot. Heir apparent to the Maxwell holdings, he'd worked the ranch with their dad since he'd finished high school. But when did he become so muscled, so mature?

"And Dad can learn to cope." Brock voiced the other family issue. "His old-school division of duties needs an overhaul." He paused, sipped his coffee.

"Second," he said, "you know Becky is opening a daycare." She nodded.

"Well, I went up to the attic to check for that long kids' table and chairs we used to have. Remember? Found it and a few other things. Are you okay with me giving them to Becky?"

"Sure. She's almost family." Kelsey teased and watched Brock's face. He was totally enamored.

"Great." He drained his coffee in one long drink. "Look, I have to get going." He retrieved his hat and flipped it onto his head, tapped it once to settle it and headed for his boots. He thunked into them. "Thanks for the coffee."

"Hey, you said three things," Kelsey said. "Don't tell me you got your number wrong." Whatever it was, perhaps it would lighten her now dismal mood.

"Ah, that." Brock picked up the shoebox he'd left on the entry table. So it was for her. It took him long moments to turn back and face her. "When I was in the attic, I found this." He held it sandwiched between his palms even though he could have easily held it in one hand. "I think you'd better have a look before you make any decisions." His forefinger tapped the lid.

She stepped closer, her gaze on his unsmiling face, and put both hands on the box sides. He didn't release it. "I have it, Brock. You can let go."

Brock removed his hands, opened his mouth. Closed it.

"It's, um." He shrugged. "I don't know. But you need to look." He met her gaze, held it and planted a hand on her shoulder. "And by the way, you're the best big sister a guy could ever have." Brock pecked a kiss on her cheek. "Don't ever forget it."

"What ..."

But he was gone, clattering down the stairs. "Call me if you need me." His parting shot echoed in the narrow stairwell.

Kelsey blinked and closed the door. His seriousness, the box and the unexpected compliment didn't leave her with a good feeling. She set the shoebox on the table. Faded lettering, a stain or two and the dust on the cover revealed its age.

Old. She splayed her fingers across its top. Brock's reluctance to let it go took on greater import. Her gut clenched.

She removed the lid and stared at the papers inside. *Documents*? Kelsey poked at them, seized a paper corner with thumb and forefinger and pulled. Government quality paper unfolded under her touch. She spread it flat. It was an expanded Nova Scotia birth certificate for a Katya Binks with the same date of birth as hers. *That's odd.*

She read the parents' names. Wait a minute. Her mother's first name was Susan too. The last name didn't match and the father's name didn't match, but the similarities could not be ignored. A chill wrapped her back and reached her toes. Something was off. Very off.

One by one she laid out the other items from the box. An envelope addressed to Susan Maxwell had Frank Binks in the upper left corner as the sender. A certificate ascertained that Frank Binks had been granted his Red Seal Ticket as a chef. Two photos and a small stuffed mouse covered more legal papers.

Kelsey held the mouse and her memory searched for an elusive name. The photo of a young family, the father holding his daughter, both parents laughing at the camera, wrenched her heart. *It can't be? Could it? Is that me?* She looked closer. The young woman was undoubtedly her mother, Susan. And the child might be her. But the man was not Will Maxwell.

Kelsey looked at the papers remaining in the box. They were legal documents, folded in thirds. One had Adoption stamped on it and the other Legal Change of Name. She backed away from the table. When the wall stopped her progress, she sank down, pulled up her knees and wrapped her arms around them. Staring at the shoebox, she started to shake. The truth eased into her mind. She pressed her eyes closed. The man she'd called Dad for as long as she could remember was not her father. Not her birthfather. Her birthfather was some guy called Frank Binks. And her mother had never mentioned it. Tears swelled behind her closed eyelids.

They lied to me. She blinked, tipped her head back against the wall and stared at the ceiling. *How could they do that to me?* The ticking of the kitchen clock incised the silence. She focused on the rhythm of the clock, the beat of her heart. Every muscle in her body tensed, ready to fight. A short bark of laughter dashed her tears. Her earlier words echoed in the calm gathering in her middle. *I need a new life.*

Damn straight she did. Kelsey scrambled to her feet and stomped back to the table. And she knew just how to get it. She stuffed everything back in the shoebox and rammed on the lid. Looked like travel was on the agenda, but she wasn't headed for Paris. *Nova Scotia here I come.*

· · · · ·

Four days was all it took for Kelsey to put a plan in place. All that remained was to confront her father, correction, her adopted father. Kelsey kept her foot hard-down on the pedal all the way out to the ranch.

Am I going too fast? Probably. Do I care? Not today.

Dust swirled behind her as she sped along the last road. Slowing for the ranch entrance, she glanced up at the sign. *Maxwell.* A name to be proud of in that part of the country. A ranching family with large land holdings, prime cattle and sought-after horses. The name of a man who was a pillar of the church and the community. A name that apparently wasn't her birthright.

She was barely out of the car when her dad flung open the front door and stood looking at her. Arms crossed, chin tucked, he stood there ready to lecture her. She'd locked up her apartment and quit her job that morning. Apparently Andy must have called her dad as soon as she'd left the office. Her knees quivered. She locked them momentarily and when she strode forward the knees cooperated.

She looked up at him from the verandah's bottom step. "Hi, Dad." She'd prepared for this encounter, but her nerves still skittered under her skin. *Nothing like an angry parent to turn me into a chastened child.* She took a breath and mounted the three steps to face him.

"What do you think you are doing?" His low monotone served to make the question ominous.

She'd heard it before, preceding one of his numerous lectures on behavior. She knew better than to challenge the question. Instead she joined him by the door, put her arms around him and gave him a peck on the cheek. "Nice to see you too, Dad."

He snorted and relented, giving her his stiff, back-patting hug.

An elusive memory of other hugs, real hugs, accompanied by laughter flashed through her memory. A fleeting sense of acceptance flared and dissipated plunking her back to reality.

He withdrew from the embrace. "You haven't answered the question." Her father's voice was tight, a voice trying to be neutral and failing. He might strive to be fair, but his inner judgments got in the way. Over the years she often mitigated his tendency to find the one tiny fault in a job otherwise well-done by one of the boys.

Kelsey held his shoulders and his gaze. She took a deep breath. She had her speech ready. She could do it. "You have blue eyes."

"Don't be silly." Another cardinal sin on his list. "You've seen my eyes before. What has that to do with anything?"

"The boys have blue eyes." Her conversation was oblique, but from experience she understood it was the best way to approach an issue with her father.

"Oh, for heaven's sake, Kelsey. Quitting your job, leaving town, babbling about blue eyes."

"Bear with me," she said and dropped her hands from his shoulders. "Mom's eyes were blue too. Right?"

He nodded, and his aforementioned blue eyes deepened to navy. If history was any indicator, a verbal lashing could follow.

"And my eyes?" she asked, her voice soft. "What color are they?"

He opened his mouth. He closed it. The frown faded, his shoulders slumped. Kelsey became acutely aware of the lines around his eyes and the gray at his temples. He'd aged when she wasn't looking. And he understood what she meant.

"What I am doing," she said, "is going searching for the man who gave me these gray-green eyes." She met his gaze. "Unless you can tell me there are grandparents with eyes this color."

"Please don't go there," he said, shaking his head. "Your mother took you away from him for her own reasons."

"Mom's dead." She said, her voice flat. "And I am not. I have the right to make my own decisions. I'm going."

"Please, Kelsey. Stay." That gave her pause. Her Dad rarely asked and never begged. Why now? "Trust me, no good will come of your search," he said.

"How do you know that?" she asked. "Have you information that I should know, information that would give me reason to let it go?"

He shook his head. "Your mother handled everything. She didn't want to tell me details, and I didn't push her." To give him credit, his sagging shoulders and downturned mouth could be from regret.

"I see." *But I don't understand.* He'd called her his daughter, raised her, and as far as she knew, loved her. But he'd also been complicit in a huge lie about her life.

She'd loved him, respected him, tried desperately to please him, and he'd lied to her. Why should she trust him now? A faint notion tickled her. *Mom initiated the lie.*

Her Dad stuck his fingers in his jeans pockets, rocked on his feet and curled his shoulders. Sure signs of tension. "How?" he asked and faltered. But she understood.

"A box in the attic," she said, "filled with papers that should have been destroyed. Maybe mom wasn't so sure she didn't want me to know."

"Will you come home again?"

A tentative question?

She smiled. "Of course, the boys are here." She hesitated "You're here." She touched his arm and waved, encompassing the yard, the fields, the barns and the corral where she'd learned to barrel race. Wherever she'd come from, she'd ended up here and her life was good. Stifled but good. "I grew up here. It's home."

He relaxed and for the first time in her memory, initiated a hug. "Yes, it is. I'd like you to come back." That was as close as he'd ever come to verbalizing emotion. Contrasted with his stern, rule-oriented manner over her lifetime, it took on proportions that warmed her heart. Should she really go? She shook off the doubt. She *needed* to go. There were too many questions.

She returned the hug. In spite of his old-fashioned role assignments and his reserved nature, he wasn't a bad dad. Only demanding and work-oriented. When she'd been barrel racing and working with him in the barn, there were times he'd approved. His relationship with the boys hinged on similar events. It was just the way he was.

"Dad, this raises questions about who I am. It's complicated. But I need to find this man, my birthfather. I need to know what happened."

Brock's truck pulled into the yard. She stepped back and held out her car keys. "Brock's taking me to the airport in Calgary. I'll leave my car here, if that's okay."

First stop Ottawa and the only people she'd been able to find with the same last name as her birthfather. *Frank Binks.* It sounded so unfamiliar. If that didn't work, she'd head to Nova Scotia and some place called Caleb Cove, her birthplace.

She gave her dad a last hug. "Bye, Dad - I'll be in touch." In spite of her decisive actions, her mind roared with confusion. She needed time to sort out how she'd ended up as Kelsey Maxwell instead of Katya Binks.

And why? Don't forget the why. Coming home again might depend on the answers.

She headed to where Brock transferred her cases to the truck. *This is it, ties cut.* The satisfaction of confronting Andy and her dad faded. As necessary as those confrontations were, they didn't answer questions.

But her course was set, the flag dropped and the horse out of the starting gate headed for those barrels. The old mix of fear and excitement raced in her blood. *I haven't felt like this since before Mom died.* Head high, she gave her dad one last wave and climbed into Brock's truck. She'd always stuck the course and taken home the trophy. She tipped her head against the seat and closed her eyes. She could do this too, couldn't she?

CHAPTER TWO

Kelsey parallel parked on the narrow Halifax street, kept the engine running and stared diagonally across at *The Mingle and Touchdown*. Part restaurant, part sports bar, it squatted beside the narrow street like so many buildings on the Halifax Peninsula. A facelift had improved it, lighting and signs enhanced it but there was no hiding that the upscale business lived in an old, old building.

She switched off the engine, wiped the back of her hand upward under her chin. The humidity was stifling. Three thousand miles separated her from home and the dry, windblown heat of the Alberta foothills. Two cities, hundreds of computer searches and dozens of phone calls were behind her. She'd finally located Frank Binks. But now she'd found him, what did she do?

Gut-flutters kicked into action. Sweat dotted her lip. Go in? Wait? Play it safe and run for home? She'd put all her energy into finding the man. What to say to him hadn't been high on her list of priorities.

Hi, I'm your daughter. Or Mr. Binks, I've been looking for you, I think I'm your daughter. Are you the Frank Binks on this birth certificate? Endless possibilities but none seemed quite right. Nausea gripped her. It might be the no-lunch factor. More likely it was stress.

Her stomach action escalated to a near puke level. Kelsey put the car in gear, flicked the turn signal and eased into a break in traffic. She'd come back later, rested, calmed and with a prepared speech. Yes, for sure, a prepared speech.

At 5:30 Kelsey pulled into the parking lot beside *The Mingle and Touchdown* and maneuvered the rental car into a slot. The place was popular. At least there would be lots of people and she could blend in while she cased the place. Casing the place? The shot of humor carried her from the car to the boxy front entry. Two doors flanked the tiny lobby, white stenciling on frosted glass proclaimed *Dining* to the left and *Bar* to the right. She took a deep breath, held it and pushed open the Dining Door on her exhale. No way was she up for a bar.

Quiet music supplanted the thudding pulse in her ears. Wood decor, subtle lighting and plush booths confirmed she'd made the right choice. The woman who greeted Kelsey towered over her, even with her best high heels on.

"Table for one, Miss?" The husky voice carried the East Coast cadence she'd heard around her since she'd got off the plane.

Kelsey nodded, followed the woman past occupied booths to a small end-of-the-row spot. She chose the bench against the wall where she could view the other diners. Mouth-watering odors, artfully plated food and happy patrons filled the room. Frank Binks must be a good cook.

The woman poured the requisite water and provided the menu. "My name is Vi," the woman said. "Our special is the fish and chips and Nick will be your server. Enjoy your meal."

"Thanks," Kelsey said and picked up the menu, more to keep busy than to choose. No matter what the food her stomach would object. When Nick arrived, she ordered the special and a glass of red wine. White might be recommended for fish, but did fish and chips count?

She rested her chin on one hand and surveyed the room. Nick disappeared into a hallway underneath a sign for the washrooms. The kitchen must be somewhere back in that hall. More adrenalin rushed through her. She was so close. In through the nose, hold for seven and out through the mouth. Two calming breaths kept her from bolting for the door. *Kelsey Maxwell, you've come this far, don't chicken out now.*

Her opening line was ready. She'd ask if he was Frank, tell him her name, and ask if he remembered Susan. If he didn't make the connection, she'd tell him he was her father. After all, what else was there to say? She could do this. She needed to do this. She didn't come all the way across the country to turn tail now.

The fish and chips lived up to their deluxe label, and she realized she enjoyed them. She placed her fork on the plate and wiped her mouth on her napkin. *No more procrastinating.* Gathering her resolve, she exited the booth and headed for the washroom. At least she could reconnoiter.

Every step whittled a sliver off her resolve. By the time she reached the arch, she was shaking. She took another deep breath. Halfway along the hall, a server backed out of swinging doors. Obviously the kitchen. So close. Only steps away. Fear tightened her throat. Thank goodness the door sign said "Staff Only."

The waiter glanced at her. "Washrooms," she managed.

He tipped his head toward another hall. "Over there."

Kelsey turned and looked. Escaping on hyperventilation, she made it to the women's washroom. *That did not go well*. And she'd only been reconnoitering. Kelsey ran water, splashed some on her face and tucked a stray hair strand into place. How would she handle a face to face meet?

She exited the washroom and marched forward until she faced that Staff Only door. Her feet refused to go further and her arms crossed around her body. *Ignore that Staff Only sign. Push it, stick your head in and ask if Frank is around. That's all you have to do. Then he'll come out here, you can say your piece and that's it.*

But what if he's not there? What if he won't come out? What if he's angry you came here? *Oh, go on, just do it.* Did she really want her first meeting with him to be in a kitchen witnessed by his co-workers? Damn. She was getting a headache.

"Can I help you?" The deep voice jolted her out of her funk. She looked behind her. His size suited the big voice. The shorn hair and earring threw her off. She didn't know many men with earrings. They weren't exactly cowboy accessories.

He smiled encouragingly. "Need the washroom?"

She shook her head.

"Looking for a job?"

She managed another head-shake. How could she explain? It was too complicated.

"Want to talk to someone in the kitchen?"

"No." The word burst out. No, she'd changed her mind. No talking to anyone in the kitchen.

He put his hands out in a what-then gesture.

She blinked, kick-starting her brain. *White shirt and black pants.* "You work here."

"Guilty," he said and shot her another smile. "Bartender and bouncer. Double threat."

This time his smile resonated to her toes. *Toes*. She glanced at his feet. He wore cowboy boots. Just like the guys back home.

"You're not from around here," she said. The heat in the narrow hall intensified, and she shifted.

He frowned. "Why would you say that?"

She pointed to the boots. "No one here wears cowboy boots, at least not worn-in, scuffed, heeled boots." She pointed to pictures along the wall. T-shirts, raincoats, boats, fish but not horses, Stetsons or cowboy boots.

"Guilty again."

A door opened and music, loud voices and clatter blasted into the hall. "Hey, Sam, we need you babe." A redhead in a tight top gestured for him to come on down.

"Gotta go," the man called Sam said. He eased past, almost nose to nose. Heat brushed her.

"Next time," he said and touched the edge of her shoulder. "We'll talk about cowboys."

The touch zapped her and the previous zing from his smile paled in comparison. Kelsey watched him for the few steps it took him to reach the bar door. *Cute buns. Muscles. This guy is seriously in shape*. The door swung shut behind him and she looked back, faced the Staff Only sign again. At least he'd taken her mind off Frank for a minute.

"Not bad, eh?" Vi stepped in beside Kelsey.

"Pardon?"

"Sam," Vi said, gesturing with her head toward the now closed bar door. "Oh, to be thirty years younger." Her throaty laugh followed her into the kitchen.

Kelsey fixed her gaze on the slice of revealed kitchen. Counters and hanging pots and a dishwashing unit but only one man visible and he was way younger than Vi. That also made him way younger than Frank. Kelsey sighed and turned away.

Legs shaking, Kelsey returned to the booth. She wiped her palms on her napkin and picked up the wine, considered it and set it aside. She needed real courage, not bottled. That was a nerve-wracking episode although the encounter with the bartender was a pleasant interlude. She sighed, draped her napkin over her lap and picked up her fork. Might as well finish the meal. She didn't think her legs would carry her as far as her car. She needed recovery time.

Her vision field widened to once again take in the room. The music penetrated her consciousness and for the moment all returned to relative normalcy. Full-on-normal had vanished when she opened The Box.

A man circulated in the dining area, catching her attention. Dressed in suit jacket but without a tie, he stopped here and there, talking to diners. The owner checking on his venue? He moved closer until he approached her table. Looked like she was about to find out.

"Was your meal satisfactory?" he asked. "And are you comfortable?" He waved a hand at the room. He must have picked up on her puzzled look. "We renovated and have a new menu."

"Yes, thanks," she said, "It looks great, the atmosphere works and the food is excellent. Is Frank still cooking here?" The question came unbidden.

"Yes," the man replied. "He designed the menu. But tonight, Second Cook is working. Frank has a night off."

Oh for heaven's sake. That whole fiasco in the back hall was for nothing. Frank wasn't even here to be met.

"So, you've been here before?" he asked.

"Actually no. This is my first time."

"But you know Frank?"

"Sure, from back in the day as they say."

His smile widened. "You don't look old enough to have a back in the day."

She shrugged. "University. Waitressing. The usual."

"Of course." He put out his hand. "Please to meet any friend of Frank's. I'm Eric." His glance swept the room. "The owner."

She looked at the hand, not sure where he was headed, but good manners overrode her hesitation. She put her hand in his. "Kelsey."

He held her hand a moment too long. "And do you have a last name Kelsey from back in the day?"

Last name? Maxwell? Binks? Take your pick.

"Yes, I do," she said. "Do you have a last name?"

He laughed. "Touché. Looks like you're ready for dessert." He picked up her empty plate. Not averse to helping out then. "I'll have them bring you one on the house. Cheesecake okay?"

"Thank you." She inclined her head. "Generous of you." She watched him walk away.

She shivered. His tones lacked the generosity suggested by his action. They reminded her of a certain two-timing bull rider. She hadn't thought about Casey in years. At nineteen she'd not seen his false flash-and-honey coated lies. But maybe now she was just overreacting.

Vi arrived with the promised cheesecake. "You get around, honey. First our hunky bartender and then the owner. What have you got that I haven't?" She laughed, her good nature evident in her tones. "Oh, right. I think it's called Youth."

Kelsey sighed. The owner and Vi, and even Sam the Bartender would remember her. She dug out her wallet and deposited a tip. Reluctant to have the owner learn her full name and ask Frank about her, she decided on cash not a credit card. She sighed again. Complications. And all she'd wanted was an unobtrusive meal and a meeting with her father.

· · · · ·

Sam poured the final drink for Jen's tray, flipped the bottle and holstered it in the rack. It wasn't the first time he'd masqueraded as a bartender thanks to skills picked up while working his way through university. He pulled the rag from his waistband and swiped the bar.

"Nice work." The words fell close to his ear, easily heard over the room's cacophony.

Sam turned to face his boss. "Thanks, Eric."

"I gave you the chance since Frank recommended you." Eric's gaze shifted to the room but Sam sensed he was being tested. "I'm happy to see you can do the job."

Eric never stopped to chat. What was he after? Sam maintained his stance. "Drink?"

Eric shook his head. "Say, did you see that gal in the dining area, the one with the bun in her hair?" So he did have a reason for chatting with the hired help.

The woman from the hall. "Got a glimpse when I was over," he said. The one with the mysterious, gray-green eyes. What was her connection to Eric?

"She says she knows Frank."

Sam's muscles tensed. His nephew-cover should be bullet proof since Frank, a loner, didn't have any family. No one should question Sam's relationship to Frank. But there shouldn't be anyone looking for Frank either. "Really," Sam said. "Interesting." And possibly dangerous.

Eric continued to watch the action in the bar. "Apparently she worked with him at some point when she was at university."

Two waitresses arrived with orders and Sam turned to his job, happy for the interruption. "Huh," he said. "Too bad Frank wasn't in tonight. They could have had a reunion." He lined up a row of shot glasses. "She want a job do you think?"

"No," Eric said. "She's too well-dressed. Obviously whatever she took at university paid off." He put one hand on the bar. "Just seems odd that Frank has no one for years and then suddenly both a nephew and an old co-worker show up."

Sam caught the look Eric slanted his way and ignored it. "Life's full of surprises," he said, maintaining a disinterested tone. He reached into the rack for another bottle and when he looked back, Eric was gone.

That was too close. For different reasons, he agreed with Eric's questions. What were the odds that two people from Frank's past would surface at the same time? Of course, he wasn't really from Frank's past but he couldn't say that. He needed to get another look at that woman and ask Frank about her.

Vi materialized. At least she appeared to.

"Quit doing that, would you?" he said.

She laughed. "Little gal with the bun in her hair gets around."

"Who?"

"Pshaw - don't give me that. She might dress fancy, all demure and such, but she's enough to make your head, and Eric's, swing for a second look." She laughed. "He sent her a free dessert. What's your encore?"

"Oh, Vi. You never give up, do you?" Sam's teasing tones took up the two-week long banter between them. The minute she'd learned Sam didn't have a girlfriend, she'd decided to find him one. "He said she knows Frank."

That got her attention. "Frank? Huh." Vi looked toward the door separating the two areas. "Really."

"Since she knows Frank, I might get to meet her again," Sam said. He winked at Vi. "Do you think she's girlfriend material?"

Vi dragged her attention back from some abstract place Sam couldn't see. "What?" She blinked and nudged Sam with her shoulder. "You gonna try and find out?"

Sam shrugged. "Eric was here," he said. He reached for glasses behind her, getting close and lowering his voice to a can't-be-overheard level. "Chatting about her. About Frank." He straightened and watched her face. "Wonder what that was about."

Her smile faded, aging her face. "Don't wonder. Leave it alone if you want to keep the job." She adjusted her blouse. "That's what we do, me and Frank. It's the reason we're still here." And then the smile was back. "Of course, maybe it's because we're damn good at our jobs. You never know." And with a kiss blown in Sam's direction, she was gone.

Frank said little and Vi said less. But Frank had put his job, and possibly his life, on the line when he gave Sam a cover story. Directly or indirectly, the organization under investigation was responsible for numerous murders. If they thought Frank helped set up surveillance on them, they would not be happy.

"Here you go, Jen," he said and placed her drink order on her tray.

Frank and Vi probably saw more than either realized. In her job as hostess, waitress and wait-staff supervisor, Vi roamed restaurant, bar and back rooms. She saw more even if she didn't understand what she saw. But would she share? She might be Frank's 'main squeeze' as she said, but where did her final loyalties lie?

A lull hit the bar, and he grabbed a moment to escape and check the other section. Was that woman still there? *She noticed your boots*. He probably should have shifted to shoes, but the boots gave him a taste of home. That gal was too observant. People with observation skills were often in law enforcement. Was another agency following the leads he'd dug up? He was good at uncovering hidden information. But there were others out there equally good. If they ended up tripping over each other, the bad guys might win.

He reached the arch in the dining area in time to see Miss Hair Bun leave her booth and head for the door. Long strides on long legs. No hesitation, no trolling. She wasn't there for the mingle suggested by the restaurant's name.

"Are you two-timing me with your eyes?" Vi asked. Darn her silent arrivals.

Sam laughed, but only looked at Vi after Miss Hair-Bun disappeared into the front lobby.

"Not at all," he answered Vi's question and kissed her cheek.

"But if she comes back, you might be in trouble."

Vi laughed and left.

Sam headed back to the bar. If the woman came back, he might be in trouble, just not the kind Vi implied. He needed to speak to Frank about her as soon as possible. In the meantime, he'd cross reference with others in the task force to see who was nosing around. And if she paid with a credit card, he'd find her name and check on her.

CHAPTER THREE

Kelsey reached the parking lot before her nerves stampeded. Her hand shook as she tried to insert the key into the door lock. What was she thinking? WAS she even thinking? Laughter bubbled in her throat. Those two questions in tandem were her Dad's favorites whenever she or her brothers screwed up. *Dad. The man who raised me. But my Father is the man on the birth certificate.* Dad, Father—big difference.

In the car she closed her eyes and sat replaying the events in her head. She could have asked the hostess up front if Frank was working. Then she'd have enjoyed her dinner and left. But if he was there, would Vi have brought him to the table? That could have been a disaster. After the fiasco in the back hall she knew didn't want her first meeting with Frank to be public.

What should she do next? She needed a more concrete plan. She opened her eyes and started the car. How DID she want the meeting to go? If she could figure that out, she would find the right words. Meanwhile she should find out a bit more about Frank. Heck, she didn't even know what he looked like. She pulled out of the parking lot. All the digging, all the phone calls she'd made in Ottawa produced minimal information. After calling every Binks in the book, she found one distant cousin. The woman told her Frank lived in Halifax and worked in a restaurant.

Was it only that morning she'd called and learned he worked at *The Mingle*? A car horn snapped her attention back to driving. Streets with names not numbers and patterns zigzagging across the landscape made navigating tricky. The hill led up from the harbor, the Citadel perched on top, and staggered buildings diverted streets. A cow path was straighter than Halifax streets.

Leaving the harbor, she headed up Spring Garden Road, swung the car onto a quieter street and reached her motel. A bit out of the way, quiet and with a housekeeping unit, it worked for her.

Inside her unit, she plugged in the kettle and laid out a mug and tea bag. Tea was everywhere in this province but getting a decent cup of coffee was difficult. She rested her head on the cabinets waiting for the kettle. Maybe she'd acquire a taste for tea if she was around long enough.

Her mind slid to Frank. A private meeting with an exit strategy sounded good. There were key questions she wanted to ask in case he wouldn't see her again. *Do I have his eyes?* The old picture in the box didn't show eye color.

She closed her eyes and visualized that photo. She'd been a toddler held on Frank's left arm, her tiny arms wrapped around his neck and her head close to his. His right arm circled her mother, holding her close. They were laughing, and the first sight of the photo sent that elusive shot of acceptance through her. *Do I remember? Or is it wishful thinking?*

Why was Frank Binks so elusive? She should be able to get a handle on him. PIs were impersonal and they cost money. Besides she never farmed out a job she could do herself. She'd bought a book, *"How to find Anyone, Anywhere,"* but in spite of its good information, she'd found nothing on Frank.

Was he fat or skinny, bald or white-haired? Until today Frank Binks was only a name on her birth certificate. A flat, paper cut-out that didn't trigger connection or caring. Meeting his co-workers and seeing his workplace changed the dynamic. Technology hadn't helped. Stalking might work. The kettle bubbled, and she made the tea. Stalking probably wasn't a smart idea.

She took the tea and settled on the lone armchair. Teacup in one hand, she picked up the frog pencil holder she'd put out for a touch of home. *Friends in Low Places* rang through the room, and she scrambled to answer Brock's call.

"Kel." Brock's voice boomed from the phone. "How's it going?"

Man, she missed him, missed home more than she'd ever expected. She laughed. "Two steps forward and one back," she said. "I've found where he works, but I haven't seen him yet." She sank back into the chair. "I suddenly have so many questions."

"Like what?"

"What if he's married with a family? How will half-brothers or sisters deal with a long lost sibling?" She paused. "More to the point, how will I deal with them? Heavens, Brock, what if he has a wife who hasn't been told about me?"

"Hey, Sis, relax already. Don't put that wagon in front of the horse."

"I know, I know. But Brock, what if he never married Mom?" She'd found neither a marriage certificate nor divorce papers in The Box. Her parents' possible relationship or lack of it raised more questions. She couldn't imagine her demure mother in a one-night stand and certainly the photo told her they'd been together. So what was her mom's relationship to Frank?

"And that has what to do with anything?" Brock's question pointed out how absurd her thoughts were. *Overthink things much?*

"It doesn't matter now but it might have mattered thirty years ago," she argued, unable to let it go. "A single woman with a child still raised eyebrows in some circles back in the eighties. Think about it, do you think all those good folks in Bolton would have looked the other way?"

"Kelsey, give it up. You're fine. We're fine and we're family. Mom lived through whatever happened and she married Dad. We never heard a whisper of anything, did we? It's not your problem, is it?"

He might be right. She laughed. "Brock, when did you get to be so wise?" *But why did Mom leave Frank and marry Will Maxwell?* Brock might not care, but she did.

"When you left me in charge," he said, his voice cocky. "So, when will you talk to this guy?"

"Not sure." She filled him in on Frank's location. "I'm no farther ahead in some ways. Suddenly he's a real person, and I've turned chicken." She sighed. "How are things at home?"

"Okay then. Keep at it. Three things here. Dad wants to know, well, stuff about you." He paused. "Andy glares at me every time he sees me, and David's doing great on the circuit."

Kelsey shivered. David's love affair with the junior rodeo circuit put him at risk from bulls and wild horses. "Tell Dad, Jamie and David that I'm progressing and give them my love," she said. "Ignore Andy. How's Becky?"

Brock cleared his throat. "Great. The daycare spots are all filled, and she's busy. She sure is great with kids." His pride came through in his tone. "When do you think you'll be home?"

Kelsey picked up a hesitation in the question. "Is there something you're not telling me?"

"No, no." Brock's quick answer belied his words. "I have to go. Be careful, Kel. Love ya." Brock ended the call.

Kelsey tossed the phone onto the bed and looked around the room and its ubiquitous motel finishes. Home sounded pretty good. She missed her family and her apartment. Even the green frog failed to cheer her. Tomorrow, she decided and headed for her toothbrush and P.J.s, tomorrow she'd track Frank to a quiet place and confront him.

· · · · ·

Sam shoved his hands in his pockets to slow his pace. The earlier mist had dissipated under bright sun. Traffic flowed as usual along Robie Street. He stopped for the stoplight and took the time to scan the area. Satisfied that he was unobserved, he crossed and doubled back to Greg and Devon's three-story city home.

At the top of the steps he pushed into the old-fashioned, exterior entry. There was a modern electronic doorbell, but he twisted the knob on the old fashioned unit mounted low on the door. The loud clacking echoed in the small space, and in moments the door opened.

"Come on in," Devon said and waddled toward the kitchen. Good thing too. In the narrow space he couldn't have made it past her swollen belly. And if he told her she waddled, she'd hit him. He chuckled silently.

"When are you due?" He should know, but kept forgetting.

"Any day now," she said and placed a hand on her back. "And the sooner the better."

In the kitchen, Greg turned from the coffee pot and extended a mug toward Sam. "Here you go," he said. "Just the way you like it." He patted his wife's belly. "There's herbal tea in the pot for you, love."

"Thanks." Devon's intimate smile for her husband caused Sam to look away. "I'll take mine up to the baby's room and leave you two to business." She poured her tea. "I'm going to pack the suitcase," she said. "It's almost time."

Greg paled, and his gaze stayed on her as she headed back up the hall. When she disappeared from sight, he joined Sam at the table. "This baby thing scares the crap out of me. I'd rather face a crook with a gun."

"You'll be fine," Sam reassured him. Although what he knew about babies and births would fill the head of a screw.

"Like you'd know."

Sam laughed.

"Easy for you to laugh," Greg said, his voice sour. "You don't have to watch your wife go through this. Man, they showed us a movie at the classes." He shuddered. "Brutal."

"That's why I don't have a wife," Sam said.

Greg snorted. "You don't have one because no one will take you."

"You found one," Sam replied, "so there's hope for me yet."

Greg's frown faded. "Now that's something to look forward to." A gleeful grin accompanied his waggling eyebrows. "But enough social niceties." He squared his shoulders and his face sobered. "How's the surveillance?"

"Access to both top floors at the restaurant is strictly controlled," Sam said, "but Frank goes up once a week to fax the grocery orders. When possible, he'll be busy and send me up with it. He's been helpful, but I'm reluctant to put him in danger. I can't ask any more of him." Frank cooperated by choice, but that didn't mean Sam should get him killed.

He sipped his coffee. "If I can get in the office, I'll plant a bug and, if possible, I'll get a picture of the lock on the third floor access. Frank says it's been there since the renovation." He grinned at Greg. "Technology has come a long way since we started in this business."

"No kidding. Cell phones are a wonderful thing."

Sam continued his report. "Once we have the make of the lock, I can figure out how to pick it. My gut says the third floor holds the key to a search warrant. How are you making out with the floor plans?"

Greg pointed to a file on the table between them. "Those are the permits from the renovations. The top floors were done five years ago when they opened. The latest ones are from the main floor renovations this year."

Sam pulled the file closer and looked. "Not much on the actual layout." He read silently and whistled. "They certainly upgraded their electronics."

Greg grunted assent. "There's been another attempt on Zinck's life," he said, taking the conversation in another direction.

Sam's head jerked up. "When? Where?"

"Early yesterday," Greg said. "A poor attempt to knife him in the showers. The bad guys aren't getting any more creative on some levels. I think there's a contract on him and anyone who gets access may give killing him a try." He frowned. "It's not good. Very few know where he is, and after the last attempt, they change his schedule every day."

Sam closed the file and drummed his fingers. "Do you think there's an inside connection feeding them information?"

Greg tipped his head. "With all signs pointing to the longevity of this organization, you have to wonder how they managed to stay under the radar. On the other hand, that long streak without getting caught may leave them complacent." He grinned. "And with us on their trail, their luck may have run out."

Sam hoped Greg was right. Back when they were detectives, the two of them regularly solved difficult cases. "I don't understand why Zinck won't talk to us," he said. "They're out to get him whether he does or not. He might not have anything else."

"Possible," Greg said. "Our best lead, that gambling organization, disappeared."

"You're sure it's gone?" Sam asked. "They didn't just go deeper under?"

"Again, possible," Greg said. "Our best high roller is trolling for a link but no luck."

"How are the others making out?" Sam asked.

"The other two locations look clean," Greg said. "No hint of anything hidden, or illegal. You are the last hope! No pressure buddy." He gave Sam a thumbs-up and took their mugs to the sink. Turning, he leaned against the counter, one ankle crossed over the other.

"Is there another agency investigating this?" Sam asked.

"The Mounties and the HRP work with us, same as before."

"And there are no new operatives snooping around?"

"I don't think so. Why?"

"A woman came in to work last night. She said she knows Frank." Sam filled Greg in on the few details he had. "Frank says he worked with a lot of students over the years and that he couldn't possibly remember one from a decade ago. Since we used Frank to get access, I just wondered if anyone is piggy-backing on our investigation."

"I'll check," Greg said. "I hope no one else is digging. We don't want to spook them."

"No kidding." Sam stood. "I'm off to work." He rolled his shoulders, stretching stiff muscles. "We need to nail these bastards." He shoved his chair into place. "It never changes, does it? The good guys get better tools, like facial recognition, and the bad guys figure out a way around it." Sam didn't expect an answer and didn't get one. "We're back to good old leg-work and surveillance."

This time Greg nodded. "Good luck with that," he said. Sam headed for the front door and Greg followed.

"I almost forgot," Greg said. "If you can't reach me, I might be at the hospital. I'll have the phone off." He paled again obviously thinking about the birth. "You call Lem if you need me. He'll come and tell me. Other than that your alternate contact is Natalie Parker."

"Nat the Gnat?" Sam shook his head. "Travis's little sister. She did do a good job over at Caleb's Cove last year. Glad to see she's moving up."

Greg nodded. "She's turned into a fine investigator and a top-notch case coordinator. The Agency wants to recruit her away from the Mounties." He handed Sam a slip of paper. "Here's her number."

Sam took it. At the last moment he shook Greg's hand and gave him the one-hand-across-the shoulders guy hug. "Good luck with the baby, buddy. And if it's a boy, name it after me."

"Not bloody likely," Greg said and laughed. "Keep your head down." His smile faded. "These guys play for keeps."

Sam didn't doubt it. The body count was mounting across the country. Men with newly minted IDs were found with cut throats. Two had met untimely deaths in car explosions. And anyone local that might have connected the organization to Zinck was also dead.

He'd be safe if he could, otherwise, he'd do what he had to. He chucked Greg on the shoulder. "I'll be in touch." Sam retraced his steps and headed for *The Mingle and Touchdown.*

· · · · ·

Try number two. This time Kelsey was ready with a Plan A and a Plan B. She'd get Frank alone or follow him home and knock on his door. She scored a curbside parking spot that gave her a clear view of the staff door. The building's exterior lighting, a lamp in the parking area and a streetlight provided ample light. It shouldn't be too hard to identify Frank. She could rule out Vi, the bartender and the younger wait-staff. The previous glimpse into the kitchen had shown younger cooking staff. Frank at fifty-something should stand out.

She tapped her fingers to the Celtic music playing on the radio. The restaurant closed at eleven mid-week, and it was almost midnight. A group of younger people left just after she first arrived. Frank should show up soon. Kelsey shifted in her seat and punched off the radio. *What was she doing stalking a man?*

The staff door opened. The bartender and another man stepped out and stood directly under the light. The tall, lean man was the right age. *Frank Binks – has to be.* The bartender slapped the older man on the shoulder and headed for his car. The man zipped his jacket and waited while the car pulled forward and out of the lot.

Kelsey took a deep breath, pulled out her car keys and prepared to meet Frank. Her feet were on the ground when Frank hunched his shoulders and headed down the street in the opposite direction. Darn. Short of yelling after him, she'd never catch up on foot.

She tucked her feet back into the car, and started the engine. By the time she'd made a U-turn, he'd reached the far corner. She sped up. She needed to reach him, pull over to the curb and get out and talk to him. Either he wasn't Frank or he was, and it was time to find out. She passed him, pulled to the curb a half block ahead and unfastened her seatbelt. She was going to do this.

Her feet hit the concrete and she stood. She turned just as another car pulled in beside him. Frank got in the car. NO. Not again. Did the universe not want her to talk to the man? Kelsey sat and watched them pass. Vi was driving. She slapped the steering wheel. *Get moving or you'll lose them.* Right, Plan B, follow him home.

The trip took about five minutes. Vi parked across from an apartment building, and both she and Frank got out of the car. Together they headed toward the apartments. Vi stayed with Frank? Did she live in the same building? What if they lived together? Kelsey cruised past, went around the block and came back. They were gone. Now what?

Forget the privacy thing. She'd find Frank. If Vi was there, so be it. An audience of one wasn't that bad. Kelsey parked, crossed to the building and stepped into a narrow lobby with a row of mailboxes. She counted twenty-four boxes looking for Frank's name.

No luck. Several blank tags. No help. The interior door was locked. She couldn't start ringing buzzers. Not in the middle of the night. And what if Vi lived there and Frank lived somewhere else? Kelsey tucked her hands into her windbreaker pockets and pushed the exterior door open with her shoulder. She stepped out and raised her shoulders against the harbor breeze. Disappointment added to the wind's chill. If she came early enough in the morning, she could catch Frank when he left for work. Plan C? Better than no plan at all. *And if that doesn't work I'll make a Plan D. I'm not giving up.*

· · · · ·

A large pot clattered into the dish drainer as Frank plated the last meal of the night. He twitched, checked over his shoulder and saw the dishwasher wiping the pan sink. The new man was a fast learner and a good worker. Now if he could get him to lay off the aftershave, he'd be just fine. Good thing. Frank was fed up with incompetency in his dishwashers. Getting a good one was difficult. It wasn't a job many folks aspired to.

"You want your knives done?" the man asked.

"No," Frank said, "I'll do my knives." The set cost him a few months' wages, and he let no one touch them. He handed the server the plate and started his own cleanup. By the time the last diner finished and the dishes returned to the kitchen, he was checking his food supplies for the next day. He finished and locked his knife stand in the lower cabinet.

"Night, Frank." The other staff filed out. Frank took off his white jacket and dropped it in the laundry. He stood for a moment and rolled his shoulders. After a hectic night he felt the work in his bones. It was Sam's night off, but Vi might still be around. He walked through the dining area and found it deserted. Drat. Tonight he could really use a drive.

He listened to the silence. Eric had run off as well. It wasn't often he left Frank to lock up. Ah well, walking home wouldn't be that bad. The night air cleared his head after the cooking heat. He'd sleep better for having a walk.

He stopped in the kitchen to turn off the lights and a white flash on the counter caught his eye. He'd forgotten to get the grocery order up to the office. If he wanted his delivery for the morning, it needed to be faxed.

Frank grabbed the page, pushed through to the back hall and

made his way to the stairwell. On the second floor the office door opened easily, and he fitted the order in the fax and dialed the number. While he waited, he surveyed the office.

He'd seen it before, but since Sam came on the scene, he'd started looking at things with new vision. Nothing new, nothing out of place and nothing incriminating. At least not to his eyes. Getting in there wouldn't help Sam. *Unless he wants to plant a bug.* The fax finished and Frank left, closing the office door behind him.

Dim night light lit the hall, the office, a storage area, a bathroom and the locked door to the third floor. *Well, looky there. That door isn't latched.* He froze. The building creaked. Should he go for it? He pulled open the door. *No one's watching.* Prickles played up his neck. *It's okay. Just go.* He stepped in, let the door settle behind him and stopped it from latching.

The stairs spilled into a smaller hall similar to the one on the second floor. A door to the right and one straight ahead were closed. The left one stood ajar, inviting him in. He peered around the door frame and checked the open room that ran the entire side of the building. Equipment lined the room's center. Frank frowned. Copying machines he recognized - the other ones were new to him. He stepped in and looked left. A row of shelves staggered up the wall and paper bins stood shoulder to shoulder along a counter. At the far end, under a smoked glass window, a large desk sported numerous phones. Seemed to him like overkill for running a restaurant.

Frank picked up a blank page and when he felt its weight, rubbed it between thumb and forefinger. Specialty stuff. What did they need it for? It wasn't the color of the menu paper.

A row of two-drawer filing cabinets was tucked under the counter. He tugged one drawer. Locked. He tried the one to the right, and it opened easily revealing drop folders and files. He bent. The labels weren't accounting terms or supplier names. They were individuals, more like personnel files. Frank only recognized one name. Must be old employees.

He pulled open the file he recognized and found credit cards, a library card, bank statements and a resume. Even he understood that other than the resume, those documents weren't kept in a personnel file. The title on the resume caught his attention. Head Chef? At *The Mingle and Touchdown?* He scanned the rest. Uneasiness skittered across his shoulders. *What the heck, this could be me.* He pulled out the file and laid it open on the counter. Even the dates matched. And that wasn't possible.

He flipped through other files. They were all similar. *Sam needs to see this stuff.* A phone rang, and he jerked, gaining a paper cut in the process. He hunched his shoulders against a flash of goose bumps and skittered a look around. Time to go. He scooped up the first file and a sheet of the specialty paper and tucked them into his waist band under his jacket. He adjusted the drop files, leaving no gaps. With a final glance at counter and cabinets, he turned to go. A notebook lay open on the far end. He took two steps and scooped it up. Maybe there'd be something in it Sam could use.

Now a few steps inside the room, he saw the wall previously hidden by the open door. Monitors - five - no six - showed all areas of the building. His gaze focused on a view of the second floor and the stairwell door. Were the views recorded?

Stuffing the notebook into his pocket, Frank swung into the hall and hit the stairs running. Too late to worry about stealth. As if in slow motion, the door at the bottom started to move. His stomach lurched, and he threw his weight against the door ramming it open. The thud triggered cursing. Frank kept moving. He grabbed the rail on the lower stairs and glanced back.

A man sat propped against the wall beside the slowly closing door. His fingers covered his lower face and blood leaked through them. *Looks like he led with his nose.* The man glanced up, rolled to his knees and attempted to stand. Frank took the stairs two at a time, raced through the kitchen and reached the back door. Footsteps pounded behind him. Frank pushed out the door, cast hurried glances around the area and raced to the sidewalk.

"Frank, wait a minute."

A woman's voice? He glanced, saw the woman and kept moving. *Not the time for a chit chat, lady.* He turned in the opposite direction to home and poured on the speed. It might be his paranoia kicking in, but he needed to get out of there. He was already huffing. He couldn't keep the pace for long.

CHAPTER FOUR

Kelsey couldn't believe she'd hit Plan D and once again sat in her car watching the restaurant. Her morning attempt was sidetracked when Frank came out of the apartment building with the bartender. In with Vi at night and out with the bartender in the morning. Did half the bloody staff live in that apartment building?

She slid down in her seat and resumed watch on the exit door. The wait-staff left, Vi left and one man went in. Eric who'd introduced himself as the owner, ran out, jumped in his car and tore out of the parking lot. His spot was the closest to the door, and he was gone. Kelsey backed into Eric's spot. This time, when Frank came out, she'd speak to him no matter what.

The door opened and there he was. Kelsey launched out of her car and realized he was running. "Frank, wait a minute."

He glanced over, responding to his name but instead of stopping, he ran faster, reached the sidewalk and turned left.

No way would she let him leave her behind again. Kelsey headed after him but three steps from the car she stepped on a rock and turned her ankle. She squatted, rubbing the offending joint.

The restaurant door slammed opened again, and she looked up. A second man stood there. He shoved on a pair of glasses and peered around. He too headed for the sidewalk, passing close to her but not looking. He reached the street and stared after Frank. Dark streaks marred his nose and chin. He turned, and the light slashed his face. *That looks like blood*. Kelsey duck-walked backwards, reached the driver's door and stood. She had a bad feeling about this.

The man turned, caught sight of her and changed direction, headed toward her. She got a good look as he swiped one last time under his nose. He wasn't friendly.

Kelsey jerked open her car door, scrambled in and started the engine. She needed to get out of there. She tromped on the gas and gravel spurted from under her wheels. The man jumped to the side, slapped her trunk as she went past and shook his fist. Kelsey turned in the direction Frank had taken, and with one last glance in her rear view mirror, left *The Mingle* behind.

Adrenalin pumped through her. Her heart beat raced. She scanned both sides of the street. If she could find him, she'd offer him a lift. He'd run as if afraid. And there was no doubt that the other man was chasing him. Did Frank hit the man? Make his nose bleed? Why would he do that?

She peered into side streets and finally gave up. Foiled again. This was past annoying. She clamped her mouth closed. The man would go home sometime. She changed direction and headed for his apartment. She'd spend the night in her car if that's what it took.

· · · · ·

Sam yawned and turned onto Frank's street. He'd spent the night at his home office searching and compiling information. Sleep wasn't on the agenda. Thank goodness it was his day off. He'd take Vi and Frank out for breakfast and quiz them. It was time. A night spent scanning accounting files and browsing the web, snooping into systems left him with a new list of questions and leads. First he needed coffee, lots of it. Sleep would have to wait.

He squinted against the early sun that was a bonus for the second day in row. He certainly didn't miss the fog banks and all too frequent winter rain. Cars lined the curbs. In another hour spaces would open up, but at the moment he couldn't see a spot. His peripheral vision alerted him to two men reading papers in a car. His neck hairs prickled. Who read a paper anymore? Most people wouldn't notice, but he wasn't most people. A suspicious nature came high on the list of his qualifications.

One man looked up, appeared to check the apartment building and returned to his paper. And then he was past them. He'd have to double back and try for their plate number.

He rubbed his eyes and resumed searching for a parking spot. What the heck? The rental sedan from the day before was back and occupied. He'd hacked the rental system and found out it was rented to Kelsey Maxwell from Alberta. She'd rented it four days ago. She was the same woman looking for Frank. Her continued interest was excessive if all she wanted was to say hello to an old co-worker.

Who had called the surveillance party without telling him? His unease escalated. There were way too many people watching the building. What did the men want? Was his cover blown somehow? Where they looking for him? Or for Frank?

He spied a parking spot two cars behind the woman but he was on the wrong side of the street. He turned a corner, reversed into a driveway and headed back. What was his next move? Should he confront the men, the woman or should he leave and see who followed him? First things first. Ladies before gentlemen.

Sam parked and exited his car. Passing the sedan, he glanced in. The woman was sitting behind the wheel, asleep. How long had she been there? He knocked on the driver's window. "Hey, sweetie," he announced, "let me in." The woman jerked awake and stared at him.

He knocked again. *Diversion. Just in case.* He'd fake a lover's quarrel. That'd fool the men if they were watching. "Hey, come on. I wasn't that much of a jerk."

The woman lowered her window an inch. "Go away," she said. "I don't want to talk to you." Strands escaped her hair bun, and she looked younger, more vulnerable. Way too soft to be an agent. Sam gave himself a mental slap. That line of thinking had got him into trouble before.

He placed his hands on the car roof and leaned down, bringing his face to window level. "Yes, you do," he said and lowered his voice. "There are two men in a car over there and they are either watching the building or you. Which do you think it is?"

Her pupils dilated and her sharp intake of breath punctuated what might be fear. She leaned forward and peered at them. At least that answered one question. They weren't together.

"For Pete's sake, don't look," Sam said. Given her reaction, she wasn't a trained operative either. So who was she? "Let me in and we'll talk." One-way or the other, he'd find out.

· · · · ·

Kelsey snapped her attention back to the man. She focused on the earring, took in the stubble that lent him an up-all-night-look. The bartender. She'd seen him at his work and leaving the building with Frank the morning before. She swept back one hair-strand, and tucked it behind her ear. She must look a mess. Sun and heat registered. It was morning. She'd been there all night. She looked toward the apartments. And she'd fallen asleep. If Frank came home, she'd missed him. Obviously stalking wasn't her strong suit.

"Well?" The bartender, Sam the waitress had called him, glared through the window.

Kelsey put her head back and closed her eyes. What was the prudent thing to do? *Drive away.* That was her dad's voice in her head. A month ago she would have. But she'd left home determined to make her own decisions. She opened her eyes and unlocked the car. After all, it was daylight on a public street.

Sam slapped the roof and hurried around the front of the car. The tree she'd been lucky enough to park under let flickers of light speckle his broad shoulders. He looked harmless. He joined her in the car, his size filling the space, his scent wafting over her. *Not so harmless.* The thought came and went and before she could speak, his hand was on the back of her head and his lips pressed against hers. Shock roared through her body, bounced at her feet and revisited her chest. Wow, now that was a kiss. And she was in major trouble.

He pulled back, a puzzled look on his face. He wiped his lips.

Did she taste bad? Not her problem that she didn't keep a toothbrush in the car. "What was that?" She gave him the look perfected over years of chastising her brothers.

"Relax," he said. "Just a show for our guests to throw them off the track. Nothing personal."

Nothing personal? Felt pretty damn personal to her. "Track? What track? What on earth are you talking about?"

"Look," he said and settled back in the seat. "You're following Frank. Those two goons are watching the apartment. There's nothing else around here that warrants watching. It's all too coincidental, don't you think? I don't know what's up, but my motto is better safe than sorry."

"Why do you label them goons?" Frank had run away and that man was bleeding. Sam might be right.

"Instincts," he said. "They just don't have a cop look. And who the heck sits in a car reading the paper anymore?"

What was a cop look? "How do YOU know the difference?" She probably shouldn't have let this man in the car. Where did he come from anyway? The building?

"Trust me," he said, "I know." His answer didn't explain a thing. "Look, we can talk here, or we can go inside. I promise you'll be safe." He actually waggled his eyebrows like a bad comedy character. "Once I get my morning dose of Java, I'm harmless."

His clichéd humor wasn't endearing. "Who are you?" she asked.

"I'll tell you if you'll tell me."

Another childish cliché. For Pete's sake, he was as bad as her brothers. Her brothers at age ten.

"Kelsey Maxwell," she said and stuck out her hand. Might as well take the direct approach.

"Sam Edwards," he replied and shook her hand. She noticed a slight hesitation on the Edwards that reminded her of Jamie when he was fudging the truth.

He dropped her hand after one strong squeeze. "Pleased to meet you. Now who are you other than your name? And why are you lurking around here and at *The Mingle*?"

The man didn't pull his punches. She squashed a groan. Now she was using clichés. She stared at the world outside. How much did she want to tell this guy? It wasn't any of his business. "You first," she countered. "You accosted me, remember? Least you can do is explain yourself."

"Look, let's take this inside," he said. "If you're not sure you're safe, call someone, call the police and give them my name and the address." He ran a hand over his eyes, his voice now serious. "Those boys up the street might be armed. My gut tells me they're not here for their health."

What does he know that I don't? She slanted a look at him. His grimly set mouth underscored eyes that watched the street. He wasn't kidding. Frank and running and a bloody nose. Was it serious? Or was this man into scare tactics for some reason?

She shivered and jutted her chin toward the apartments. "Who all lives in that building?"

"Beats me," Sam said. "There are twenty-four units."

"But do you? And Frank? And the hostess?"

"Yes," Sam said.

She wanted to ask if they all lived together although that seemed ridiculous. "That's three apartments?"

Sam's gaze fixed on her, she could feel it. *He's not going to answer.*

He took a breath. "Two," he said. "Vi and Frank."

Did that mean they lived together?

"They each have an apartment. I'm bunking with Frank, my

uncle, until I get settled."

Kelsey felt her mouth drop and snapped it shut. This man was her cousin? So much for that dynamite kiss. "I see," she managed. That information changed things.

Wait a minute. If I go in with Sam, I'll be in Frank's apartment. And maybe he did come home last night. Progress. Her neck was stiff, and she realized suddenly, she had to pee. Three good reasons to go inside. "Let's go," she said.

If he agreed to have her report their whereabouts to the police, he couldn't be all bad. "If you have coffee, we can talk." She dragged her purse from behind the seat and opened the car door. She sent a huge wish to the universe. *Don't let me regret this.*

· · · · ·

Wow, she'd agreed. He didn't think she would and was ready to offer a restaurant location. *Don't give her time to change her mind.* He nodded, left the car quickly and watched her press the lock button on her remote. What had prompted her to agree? His relationship to Frank, or the fact that he lived with him? Either way, Frank was the common denominator.

Kelsey stood by the front bumper, waiting. Several chunks of hair had escaped the bun. As if conscious of his scrutiny, she raised a hand and pulled out whatever held the bun in place. Her hair fell around her shoulders, reached mid-back and curled at the bottom. A good undercover officer depended on well-developed observational skills and an ability to define visual evidence, but for the life of him, he couldn't find a name for the color of her hair. Sam gave up the color challenge and led the way up the street and into the building.

"There is an elevator," he said, pointing. "But it's so slow we walk. We're on the fourth floor." He should, his brain told him, walk in front of her because she wore a skirt and a damn short one at that. Where that bit of etiquette came from he couldn't remember. He looked at her wedge-heeled shoes. He pointed. "Can you manage?"

"Yes." Kelsey chewed her lip and looked around the tiny lobby.

Neither of them said a word on the way up the stairs or down the hall. Walking in front should be less distracting for him, but her presence curled around him and left his back seared. Sam opened the apartment door and stood aside for her to enter. She took a deep breath, the type of breath that might precede a leap off a high diving board, and stepped in. Whatever was happening, it was huge for her.

Sam turned left into the galley kitchen and tossed his keys on the counter. He pulled coffee and filters out of the cabinet. "Here," he said and placed the coffee machine on the counter, "start some coffee. If you have no objection that is."

She parked her purse in the hall and joined him. "No problem. Most men don't make decent coffee, do they?" She pulled her lips back in a smile that held no humor.

He rolled his eyes. "Sexist, are we?" He yawned. "I'll be right back." He turned toward the hall to the bathroom. Passing Frank's room he glanced in the open door. Vacant. Frank must be at Vi's. He'd catch them later, once he'd figured out Kelsey Maxwell. Sam stepped into the bathroom and ran a hand over his chin. Ah to heck with it. He'd shave tomorrow.

He headed back to the kitchen. Coffee aroma lingered in the air. Excellent. At least there was hope for his brain. Kelsey stood in the living room, apparently checking things out. She tucked a stray hair behind her ear and turned.

"Oh, hi. Just looking at photos."

Sam didn't need to check. "What photos?"

"Exactly," she said, not making any sense. "There are none."

Gurgles signaled the coffee's almost-ready state. "I'll get the mugs," he said and turned away. The coffee had better work. He needed clearer thinking.

He put mugs on the counter, opened the fridge and bent to look. Bread, eggs and jam. He could make that work.

Kelsey came back from the living room, and he looked over the fridge door at her. "Breakfast?"

"Bathroom?" she countered. "Then breakfast would be lovely, if it's not too much trouble?"

She was worried about too much trouble? Sam pointed. "Last door on the right."

She nodded and, scooping up her purse, left with that long-legged stride still working for her. Several levels of weird swirled around him. He was playing chef in an apartment that wasn't really his and non-entertaining a woman who was in his not-his bathroom cleaning up after sleeping in her rental car. A car possibly watched by men in another car. Oh god, he needed sleep, coffee and a check-in with Greg.

Sam poured his coffee, drank half a mug in one go and gathered his supplies. He cracked eggs and started work on an omelet. He couldn't really cook and his coffee wasn't great, but he made a mean omelet.

He scrambled, doctored with green onions and cheese and was finished by the time she returned. He glanced over. Her hair was scooped back in a ponytail and her lipstick, no, it was more like lip gloss, was freshened. No woman should look that good after a night in her car.

She inhaled. "Mm mm, smells great. Anything I can do?"

"What, you don't want to take over?" He managed to keep his tone mild, deliberately void of sarcasm. What was it about this woman that prompted such retorts?

She stepped closer, crossed her arms and cocked her head to one side, inspecting his work. "No, you seem to be doing fine although the proof is in the eating." She poured coffee into the mug he'd set out for her and cradled it between her hands.

She is laughing at me. He groaned. Clichés. His own fault for starting it. He nodded to the dining area. "Have a seat, it's almost ready." He slid the food onto the plates and added the toast. And there they were, face to face over the food with questions hanging between them.

"Eat up," Sam said and followed his own advice. Kelsey matched him, eating without hesitation and washing it down with coffee. She wasn't shy about her appetite.

Sam finished and sat back, coffee in hand. "Now," he said, "let's get to business. Why are you following Frank? And don't give me the I-worked-with-him line."

Kelsey aligned her knife and fork on her plate, licked her lips and looked at him.

Damn, she's going to lie.

"It's personal. I need to talk to him first. He's family."

"Try again. Frank says he has no family."

"He has you."

Sam shifted in his chair, caught in his own lie. "No family OTHER than me and my mother."

"That may be what you think, but here I am to prove otherwise."

Sam watched her, and she met his gaze. *Well, I'll be damned. She believes what she is saying.* "Huh," he replied.

"My turn," she said. "Where is Frank?"

"Probably at Vi's," Sam replied and watched her expression change. That threw her. "He's there a few nights a week."

"But he does live here?" She looked toward the living room.

The lime green sofa and chair, the coffee table and end tables with screw-in legs transported viewers into the seventies. She was right in her earlier assessment. Frank lived without pictures, family or otherwise.

"No family to have pictures of," he said, half to himself. This was getting them nowhere. He remembered the men in the car. "Are you sure you don't have any idea why those men downstairs are here?"

She looked at her mug, placed it carefully beside her plate. "Not really." She leaned forward with one arm on the table edge. She hunched her shoulders and fiddled with the mug.

Big lie. One of omission if nothing else. Sam straightened and leaned forward, getting close enough to command her attention. "What does *not really* mean?"

She looked up. "I saw something." She hesitated. "Last night when I was waiting for Frank."

"Here?" Sam asked. Just how long was she in the car?

She shook her head. "At the restaurant. I'd wanted to catch him alone and talk to him." She didn't go on.

"And," Sam prompted. "Why didn't you?"

· · · · ·

Kelsey lowered her head and ran a finger over the flowers on the edge of the placemat. Why hadn't she talked to Frank? Asleep in the car, she'd dreamed versions of the event. A face-wash and coffee didn't entirely dispel her brain's fuzziness. She took a deep breath and focused on the reality, not the dreams.

"He left in a hurry, and I couldn't catch him." Keep it simple.

"What do you mean by in a hurry?" Sam sighed. "He's a fifty-something man who doesn't drive. How could you not catch him?"

"He WAS running and when I went after him, I twisted my ankle." She shrugged and got up to get the coffee pot.

"Look, just tell me everything. This piece by piece is painful." He sounded exasperated.

"If you wouldn't jump in so fast, it might help." She poured them both refills. "Besides, there isn't much to tell, and I don't see why you care. When he shows up, ask him." She switched off the coffee machine and stood behind her chair. Narrowing her eyes, she let her internal radar work. Raising three brothers had given her useful skills.

"I'm missing something," Sam muttered. "Look, this doesn't make sense. Why were you there and why stay in your car overnight? You'd have easily arrived here before he did. Why didn't you catch him before he came into the building? Why didn't you catch up with him and, I don't know, give the man a drive home?"

"You think that didn't occur to me? I tried. I couldn't find him and as of two this morning he hadn't showed." She sat and folded her hands around her coffee cup. She'd slipped into what her dad would call obstinate mode, digging in her heels when it was counterproductive. Her habit of fighting the inconsequential wasn't helping. She needed to remember to pick her battles.

Add that to Sam's questions and the men and she had reason to worry. What if Frank was in real trouble? Sam was Frank's nephew. Who better to tell?

"Okay, here's what I saw." She walked Sam through the details of Frank's taking off and the man with the bloody nose.

Sam's tension escalated visibly as she talked. "Why didn't you tell me this in the beginning?"

Kelsey sighed. "I didn't know you, I'm exhausted and not thinking clearly, I didn't think it was serious and it didn't occur to me you cared one-way or the other. Pick a reason. I figured he came in after I fell asleep. No biggie." There must be a simple answer. "Can't you just call and ask?"

Sam pushed back and headed for the phone. He punched in a number. "Vi," he said, "is Frank with you?" Apparently he got a no. "When did you see him last?" Sam waited. "And not since then? So he closed up?"

Sam paced as far as the curly-cord allowed. "Oh, nothing. I was out all night and wondered where he is this morning."

Kelsey covered her mouth to hide a smile. Where was he all night? Frank went to Vi's. Where did Sam go? *None of your business.*

"Probably went to Tim's for coffee." Sam laughed. "Right, I hope he brings one for me too. Thanks Vi." He hung up.

Sam replaced the handset and stood there, staring at the phone with all hint of laughter gone. Apprehension skated over her skin.

Sam believed this was serious.

"Try his cell," Kelsey said.

Sam shook his head and walked back to the table. "He doesn't have one."

"Seriously? Even my ninety-two-year old landlord has one."

"Frank doesn't believe in them," Sam said. "Describe the guy who chased Frank."

"You sure ask a lot of questions," she said. *Stop being so grumpy. Sam doesn't deserve it.*

Sam glared. "Tell me. If I can figure out who it was, I might understand if it is serious or not."

"Sorry," she said, "lack of sleep." She closed her eyes. "There was a lot of head space when he came through the door. So I'd say short and slight. He wore a button-up shirt and trousers, not jeans." She opened her eyes. "He had a pair of glasses in his hand." She mimicked the action. "That's what he did when he stopped, he put them on. And he peered through them."

She shivered. How clearly had he seen her? "Do you think he sent those men?" Did they want her as well as Frank? She frowned. "I think it's time you tell me what this is about. Late night chases and bloody noses and two goons, as you call them, sitting out there in that car. That's not normal stuff." *At least not normal in my life.*

Sam leaned back, hooked his arms over the chair. His gaze never left her face. He never blinked, as far as she could see. Was he weighing things up in his head?

"Well?" she asked and threw out both hands in a tell-me-what's-up non-verbal question.

"Where did you come from?" Sam asked, "And why?"

"Now that's a conversation changer." She tucked her legs to one side, set both elbows on the table and crossed her forearms. "What does it matter and what business is it of yours?" Although as Frank's nephew, maybe it was his business. Frank didn't have a wife, at least not a current one. Thank goodness for that. The nephew was enough of a pain.

"Before I tell anyone things, I like to have a handle on who I'm dealing with. How do I know you didn't do something to trigger the goon squad? Are they connected to you?"

He had a point. He didn't know she was harmless. *And I don't know if he is.* But working with goons? This man's background was way different than hers. Is HE dangerous?

"For Pete's sake. I'm from Bolton, Alberta. I have a personal matter I need to talk to Frank about. It's not criminal. Just personal." She lifted her chin. "How about you?"

Sam frowned. "Red Deer," he said and stopped as if he'd been ready to say more and thought better of it. Disinclined to elaborate, was he? At least Red Deer explained the cowboy boots.

"And?" She mimicked his earlier question. "Why are you here?"

Sam stiffened and that jaw muscle twitched. Added to the scruffy chin and the earring, the jaw twitch sent a shiver through her. He didn't want to answer. She wasn't sure why, but whatever was happening, Sam was in the middle of it. It was more likely they were connected to him, not her. "Those guys might be looking for you?"

He didn't respond. He pulled out his cell phone and punched in one number. Who did he have on speed dial? He got no answer and flipped off the phone.

"Come on," he said. "Let's go look for Frank." He grabbed his keys and stood by the door. "And see if those goons want to play."

Kelsey sighed. She'd seen that look often enough, the one that said the male of the species was done talking. A father and three brothers had taught her that much. She added her dishes to his in the sink and, picking up her purse as she went by, followed him out. At least if she stuck with him, she increased her options for contacting Frank.

CHAPTER FIVE

Out on the street, the two goons still sat lounging in their car. They'd given up the papers, lowered the windows and rolled up their sleeves. Eventually the heat might drive them away, but for now they were managing.

"It's not polite to stare," Sam said and stepped up blocking her view. "We'll take my car."

Kelsey bit back her first retort and nodded. She'd let him win this one. At the car, he opened the passenger door first. He did have manners. Before he joined her in the car, her phone played Brock's distinctive ring.

She dug in her purse and pulled out a tissue, a comb, a whistle Brock had given her for safety and, finally, her phone.. "Brock," she said. "What's up?"

Sam slipped into the driver's seat, turned the key and lowered the windows but didn't start the car. The better to eavesdrop? He'd be disappointed with this conversation.

"Not much," Brock answered. "How's it going there? You talk to him yet?"

"No," Kelsey hesitated, "but I did talk to another family member although he isn't much help." She turned a fake smile in Sam's direction.

"He's there?" Brock said.

"You always were perceptive," she replied.

"Who is he? Do you have another brother?" He didn't sound all that pleased with the concept.

"No. I'll fill you in later." She planted her elbow on the door and leaned toward the open air, welcoming the wispy breeze. Her move didn't completely leave Sam out. "I should find out more by this evening."

Sam's polite attempt at disinterest evaporated, and he turned to watch her. He leaned partially against the driver's door but kept his gaze on her.

"So what's the holdup?" Brock said. "We want you to come home, Kel. We're your family."

Translation, HE wanted her home. "Brock, what's up?" It wasn't like him to be grumpy.

Sam raised an eyebrow and came to attention, and she regretted her sharp tone. Kelsey eyed the buildings across the street. Decades old wood-siding, mixed paint colors and varying heights reminded her just how far from home she was.

"It's Becky," Brock said, sounding odd.

"You two fight?" Kelsey asked.

"Not exactly." Brock drew the words out. "We might get married." He paused, "Um," he said, "like soon."

Kelsey's brain went into overdrive. *Becky's pregnant.* "Didn't we have that conversation?" she asked. "The one about…." She turned straight in the seat and flung out a hand. Three fingers curled and one pointed as if he were in front of her. She shook it once. *Like he can see you?* She pressed her hand into her lap.

"Yeah, yeah of course. I'm not stupid." Brock sighed. "Just unlucky. One broke."

At least he'd tried. Nice that he'd listened to her occasionally. Time for damage control. "Has she been to a doctor? Bought a home test?"

Sam grinned. *Easy for him to laugh.* She ignored his pointed look. *This is not his business.*

"Ah," Brock said, drawing her back. "No."

"So you're panicking before you have the details? How along ago did this happen?"

"Ah," Brock repeated. "Two nights ago."

"Now who's putting the cart before the horse?" She teased him. "And you raise cattle? There are some things you should understand here." There was only a throat clearing on the other end. "So," she continued. "Give it some time, get to a drugstore and or the doctor and then we'll talk."

"Thanks, Kel." Brock sounded relieved. "I figured you could help. You're the best."

"I love you too," Kelsey said. "Now go and behave yourself." She disconnected and blew out, stirring a lone strand of hair across her forehead. She'd assumed the job of mothering siblings would be over when the youngest hit eighteen. Showed what she understood about parenthood, surrogate or otherwise.

"Not a boyfriend," Sam said, "or your father. At least that's my guess. And if you have kids, they are way too young for that conversation. Friend?"

"Brother," Kelsey said her mind still on the conversation. "Oldest one." What parents must go through. And girls might be worse. At least her brothers understood responsibility. Her dad had given the boys good advice, even if it wasn't specific. *Don't sleep with a girl if you can't see her as your wife and the mother of your children. Anything less, keep it in your pants.* For him to say that much was a stretch. Not that she'd actually heard him. Brock had filled her in.

She dropped the phone in her purse and ran her fingers over her face. Oh dear, if Brock and Becky rushed into marriage, she couldn't contemplate the fallout never mind the logistics. She'd have to go home.

"Earth to Kelsey." Sam's voice poked her.

"What?" She snapped her head around and stared.

"How many brothers?"

"What?"

"You said that was the oldest one. How many?"

"Three total," she answered before her brain fully realigned with the situation. "Now, weren't we leaving?"

"Ah, a conversation changer," Sam said, using her words. "Fair enough." He reached for the ignition, edged away from the curb and headed toward the harbor. "We'll start at *The Mingle*," he said. "Maybe someone knows what's happening." He checked his rearview mirror as they approached the first corner. "The goons have decided to play," he said. "We have a tail."

Goons and tails. Brothers and pregnancy. A Dad and a Father. It was beginning to sound like she should leave well enough alone and go home. Around the corner the street fell away toward the harbor, and Kelsey looked along the unfamiliar canyon created by irregularly sized office buildings. A blue patch at the bottom of the street marked the water and as many curves as actual corners marked their route.

They topped a hill and headed closer to the waterfront. One of the bridges loomed on the horizon. The entire city of Dartmouth spread out on the other end of that bridge. Thank goodness she'd located Frank before she'd had to call every restaurant on the Dartmouth side of the bridge. She sighed. Not that finding him was working well. It was as if everyone and everything was conspiring to prevent her from meeting him. *And now he's missing.*

She pulled her attention back to the car and Sam. She couldn't go home. Too much time invested, too close to her goal. Besides as her Dad was fond of saying, he hadn't raised any quitters. She'd better pay attention to the situation.

Sam drove with one hand on top of the wheel and the other arm resting on the open window. No white shirt and black pants. "Aren't you working today?" She lifted her gaze to his face. Of course with that scruffy look, he wouldn't be working. Her spirits lifted. With her own personal guide, she'd find Frank. One more try.

. . . . .

Sam shot an inquiring glance in Kelsey's direction. "Pardon?"

"No white shirt and black pants," she said.

"What are you, a detective?" He turned onto the final street. When she didn't answer, he shot her another look. "It's my day off," he added. She nodded. Whatever her thoughts, she kept them to herself. That phone call had shifted her mood, but he understood siblings. His younger sister wasn't above reeling him in for help. *Sounds like she's pretty tight with her brothers.*

A few staff cars squatted in the restaurant parking lot. He made a loop and parked with the car headed toward the exit.

"Wait here?" He made it a question. "I'll just be a minute."

She looked ready to object but shot a glance at the building and nodded. "No problem. But if you find Frank, give me a shout. I really need to talk to him."

"Yes, I got that part," he said. "You NEED to talk to him? Why, did he inherit money or something?"

"Or something." Her voice lacked her earlier snap. She looked away and Sam let it go. He'd find out soon enough what she wanted with Frank. *Right now I need to find Frank.* If he didn't, he'd have to ramp up his search.

"Watch the street," he said. "See if there's any sight of our tail."

He left Kelsey scanning the street and went inside. Vi was already there, folding napkins around cutlery.

"Did Frank come in?" he asked.

"No." She frowned, looked around and lowered her voice. "He didn't show up at home?"

Sam shook his head. "He wouldn't have," he hesitated, "fallen off the wagon?"

"God no," Vi said. "After thirteen years, I can't see it." Her gaze turned fierce. "No," she repeated. Why Frank didn't marry this woman, or at least live with her, was a mystery to Sam. She was darn good for him.

Sam raised both hands, palms out. "Sorry. Do you have any idea," he asked, "where he might be?"

"He should be here," she said. "If he isn't coming in, I need to tell the kitchen so they get organized without him." She took two steps and stopped. "When I find him, I'll pummel the man for not showing up. Eric is already cranky enough."

Sam's attention perked. In the two weeks he'd been there, Eric had displayed an even temperament. "Does he get cranky often?" he asked. Vi shook her head.

Did last night's events trigger Eric's irritability? "What's he on about this morning?"

She shrugged. "He didn't say. Just stormed through, spit out a few orders and raced up the stairs. And he went right to the top floor. Grumpy old goat." She tossed her head and shot a look upward. When she looked back, worry replaced irritation. "Man, Frank needs to be careful or he'll be out the door. Eric's been known to sack staff for less than a missed shift."

Sam's unease escalated. If his investigation went sideways, Frank could be in danger of more than a firing. His head pounded. He needed to find out what had happened between Frank and the other man.

"Have you seen a short, slight man with glasses who might be on staff?"

"Why?"

"Saw him talking to Frank yesterday." Sam lied.

"Might be the accountant," Vi said. "He's sometimes holed up in the offices." She pointed up. "We see him occasionally. He's a quiet man, horned rim glasses and all. Talk about your stereotypes. Can't think he'd have anything to say to Frank though."

"Thanks. Give me a shout if he turns up, would you?"

"Frank or the accountant?" Her tone was teasing. Vi always bounced back.

"Either or both," Sam answered.

She did a quick look back. "Okay then," she said. "Return the favor if you find Frank?" Sam nodded and she left.

His gut served up that the-shit-is-hitting-the-fan feel. He didn't like it, not one bit. Lem and Frank went back decades. That was how he'd got the introduction to Frank. Lem might suggest where Frank would go for help. The guys from the weekly league at the pool hall might have an idea as well. He'd call Lem first, and without a better suggestion, he'd visit the pool hall. *But what do I do with Kelsey?*

He couldn't risk leaving her alone. Too many dead already. She might not have any idea what was happening, but she may have seen too much. Until he figured it out, he'd err on the side of caution. Sam stopped with his hand on the door. *That woman is a complication I don't need.*

· · · · ·

Frank sat with his back against a tree his butt barely protected from the damp ground by a newspaper he'd plucked out of the garbage. He'd forgotten how hard the ground was, how damp the night air and how expensive bad coffee in a cardboard cup could be.

His arms rested on his pulled up knees and he shifted, causing the package to crinkle against his chest. At least now the file and paper were in a large manila envelope. Henry gave it to him when he offered the bed in the back room. But as much as he trusted Henry, he didn't want to put the man in danger. They went back years, to sailing days and good jobs and wives. To the days before the rum had flushed him into a different life.

One toss sent the empty coffee cup into the green, wire garbage can. He'd have liked to wipe it with a sanitized wipe to remove DNA. Some days, the sensation that someone was watching him was overwhelming. Other days, life was normal. He comprehended the difference, but couldn't always choose how he felt. The forced surveillance in jail started it, but the paranoia, as the doctors labeled it, never fully left.

But there was no one he could blame. Getting drunk, fighting with his boss and then stabbing him was his own doing. Drunk enough not to remember if he'd done it accidentally or on purpose was way too drunk. It hadn't mattered. He'd ended up doing time. By the time he'd got out, Susan and Katya were gone.

He tipped his head against the tree and closed his eyes, tuning in to the sounds. Two birds nattered above him. A slight breeze brushed the tree, the sound not soft enough to be a rustle, not sharp enough to be a clatter. He'd spent years drunk, sleeping in parks and culverts in good weather and heading to the homeless shelters in bad. Back then he wouldn't have noticed the birds or the breeze. He'd have been too consumed with locating the next drink.

A cough echoed around him, and he jerked up. He checked the open area, the rock pile off to the right and the bush on the left. There was a second cough. Tension drained away. Some poor slob was behind the bushes. A drunk who couldn't or wouldn't get sober. He snorted. He couldn't judge. If he hadn't been scared sober, he might not be where he was. He laughed. Where he was, was back sleeping in a park. Ironic?

He rarely looked back. Besides, he'd obscured information with rum and, when he'd sobered up, it was lost forever. Life was easier if he didn't think about Susan and Katya. His heart seized. That little girl was his life, but even for her he wasn't able to leave the bottle alone. Susan did the right thing and it was better forgotten. He had a job, an apartment and hidden stashes of cash. He even had a girlfriend. At least until last night.

Frank pushed against the tree and struggled to his feet. Now he wasn't so sure. He'd stolen from his boss, who was also his landlord, his girlfriend's employer and landlord and the only person to give them both a break when they'd first been sober. If he couldn't fix this, he was screwed. He'd helped Sam out of guilt over A.J. He should have left well enough alone.

Frank picked up the paper, folded it and tucked it under his arm. He might need a seat again. Head down, he shuffled out of the park onto a path. Best to look the part. Without the shelter of rocks and trees, the breeze became wind and cut through his clothes. He faced it and hurried forward. *Toward what? What do I really have to lose?*

The question came unbidden, and jarred his life into focus. He lived one day at a time, with no bank account, no car, no driver's license, and no belongings past the basic necessities. No bloody record he was even alive. They paid him in cash, took his rent out of his pay, and didn't report him to the tax man. They'd never balked at his history, so he'd never asked for more.

He kept Vi on the periphery of his life. He'd never told her about Susan and Katya, never talked about his time inside. She knew about his drinking because they'd met at an AA meeting. At least once a week they both still attended. He laughed without mirth. Now wasn't that a heck of a date night? *You're not technically homeless, but you are one sorry sod.*

Frank reached the street, watched the cars pass until he was sure he was unnoticed. One thing about homelessness, even a faked one, was that folks overlooked you. He checked his watch. Almost time to go to the culvert. With any luck, Sam would figure things out and get the message to meet him there. In the meantime he'd rustle up some food. At least this time, he had money for McDonald's. No garbage-can breakfast for him. Be thankful for small mercies.

· · · · ·

Frank was officially missing, and guilt tinged Sam's uneasiness. He tromped across the parking lot to the car. Kelsey slumped in the seat, her head propped against the car window. The goons, her late night sighting and his over-the-top experience with crime kicked in and for one eternal second he thought she'd been murdered. *My fault.*

He reached for her door handle, and she shifted her shoulders and adjusted her head. Asleep. Of course she was. She'd been in her car all night watching for Frank. Sam planted both hands on the car roof and let the adrenalin slide away. His current overreaction was premature, but given what he knew, not totally unfounded.

He pushed off the car and looked again. Her lips fluttered, and he grinned. Did she snore? At least her exhaustion gave him a good reason to deposit her at her motel. He headed around the car, stopped at the front fender and resting his butt against it, reached for his phone. First he needed to call Greg.

One-button dialing put them in touch. "Hey, there are developments," he said and rapidly ran through the relevant events.

"Crap," Greg said when he finished. "You need to find Frank, ASAP." He sighed. "And who is this Maxwell woman and why was she in the parking lot last night?"

"I have some info," Sam said and yawned. "She's here from Alberta to talk to Frank about family, that's all she'll say. She's an accountant according to LinkedIn, but I'm not sure if she's the messenger or the family." Sam considered. "She seems innocent enough."

Greg snorted. "All women you meet undercover are innocent. She must be hot."

"That's harsh. I didn't think they were ALL innocent." *Just the really hot ones and then only the first few times I was undercover.* "I haven't been that way in years." He had learned a hard lesson or two along the way. "And what makes you think Kelsey Maxwell is hot?"

Greg laughed. "Because you think she's innocent."

"Go to hell," Sam said.

Greg's reply sounded suspiciously like a grunt. "Do you think Frank saw something he shouldn't have?" he said, getting back to business.

"That's my guess," Sam said, "and Kelsey may be an innocent bystander, but she may have seen too much, even if she doesn't realize it. I need to find Frank and figure out who that man was."

"I hear you. I'll run through Eric Chappell's list of employees and associates again. We have photo ID on most of the regulars. With luck, I'll find a match. What's your next move?"

"I'll check the pool hall," Sam said. "Can you ask Lem for a list of other places and people? Get him to give me a call?"

"Will do," Greg said. "Do you still have Natalie's phone number?"

"Of course," Sam said. "Programmed in the phone and in my trap-like brain."

"You may need it soon," Greg said. "Devon had a backache all morning and apparently that's a type of labor or a sign of labor or something." His voice escalated, betraying his tension.

"Good luck, man," Sam said. "Go do your husband and father bit. We'll be fine without you." He hit the off button and stood for a moment. Greg Cunningham a father. It was a stretch. Lone wolf, chameleon, king of long-term undercover gigs. Greg the marrying kind? *I guess anyone can change.*

A knocking broke through his reverie. He looked over and saw Kelsey leaning forward in her seat. Nap-time over. Sam joined her in the car.

"So," she said, "what did you find out?"

"Not a heck of a lot," Sam replied. "Where are you staying? I'll drop you off."

"No. I'll stay with you." She buckled her seatbelt. "Where do we look first?"

"WE are not looking anywhere," Sam said. "You're going back to your room so you can get a real nap."

"If you leave me behind," she said, her tone annoyingly reasonable, "I'll follow you."

Sam looked at her sideways. "Without your car?" Parked in front of Frank's it wouldn't do her much good. The two men on his tail he could shake without trouble. Kelsey would be too easy to follow. They would have her description and plate number even if they weren't physically watching the car. He couldn't let her use that car.

"Doesn't matter," Kelsey said. "I'm not telling you where I'm staying and I'm NOT getting out of this car."

Sam tipped his head against the headrest and stared at the car's ceiling. *Save me from stubborn women.*

"Look," she said, "I agree it's not smart to pick up my car. I get it that the guy saw me last night. I realize you didn't find Frank. And I haven't forgotten those goons following us. I have no idea what you think this is about, but you think it's serious. You plan to look for Frank and at the moment, my guess is that I am probably safest WITH you. Just in case."

Sam lowered his head and gripped the steering wheel with both hands. The only thing worse than a stubborn woman, was a stubborn woman making sense. She was right and, since he didn't want to take the time to find a safe house, he might as well take her along.

"Fine," he said, "for now. Just don't get in my way." He started the car and pulled onto the street headed for *Henry's Bar and Pool Hall.*

. . . . .

Henry's Bar and Pool Hall was just two blocks off an industrial section along the docks. Chain link fence bordered the parking lot. Gray metal buildings stretched away on the far sides of the fence. The two-story wood frame building squatted in the middle of a pothole-riddled parking lot. With its upstairs apartment, the red and blue neon sign and the barred windows, it outdated the metal buildings and fences. *Looks like there should be bikers.*

Sam cruised past, pulled a U-y in an access road and stopped. He could see back along the street but wouldn't be immediately visible if anyone had followed them. The mid-morning work bustle hummed around them. A forklift made forays into stacks of pallets in one yard, but no traffic moved along the street.

"Did we lose them?" Kelsey asked. She'd been quiet during the convoluted drive. Was it her lack of sleep or the realization of serious trouble?

"Yup," Sam said. He'd better be right. Putting Frank's friends in unnecessary danger wasn't an option. He'd learned that Frank was careful, secretive. No one at work knew about his pool night or Henry, or Lem for that matter. At least, neither Frank nor Vi would have told them. Sam certainly didn't want to be the one to lead those goons to Henry.

Ten minutes ticked by. Finally, Sam put the car in gear and moved to within half a block of the pool hall. He pulled to the curb and shut off the car. Avoiding the parking lot was a small precaution, but he couldn't be too careful. Better safe than sorry. Another adage he'd learned to obey over the years.

"Wait here. There may be no one here anyway," he said although he knew he'd find Henry. He wanted to talk to him without Kelsey.

Her chin came up. Objection on its way. He pointed to the street. "Watch for our buddies," he said. "I'll leave the key. If they show, get the hell out of here. Meet me later at the *Tim Horton's* on the far side of the Macdonald Bridge, Wyse Road."

"Which bridge is that?" she asked.

"Use your cell phone and maps. You'll figure it out. The locals call it the old bridge."

She closed her mouth and crossed her arms but stayed in her seat. For now. He wouldn't put money on her staying there long. He'd better make this a quick trip.

Sam picked his way around the pot-holes to the back of the building and knocked on the door. He stepped back from the door, balanced on the edge of the small landing and waited with his gaze on the handle. Sure enough, the handle turned and the door opened a crack. "Henry," he said. "It's Sam." Which last name had Lem given Henry? "Sam Edwards," he added.

The door opened full width. Henry stood with one hand on his broom and gave Sam his characteristic head-to-toe once-over. He dragged his stubby fingers through thick, silver hair, scratched the back of his stocky neck and stood back. "So it is. Well, come on in then, since you're here. Not open yet, ya know?"

He parked his broom and gave Sam a guy-hug and slap on the back. "I likes the new look," he said and pointed. "You need a job as a bouncer, boyo, I'll hire youse."

"Most of your clients are too old to fight." Sam laughed. "Actually, they're so old they'd call it a rumble."

"Maybe so," Henry said. "Maybe so." He nodded toward the bar. "Want a draft?" Sam shook his head, and Henry gestured. "Grab a seat." He turned, hitched his trousers tighter under his belly and moved off to the bar. "A coffee?"

"I'm good," Sam said. "I need to find Frank."

Henry stopped, his back still toward Sam, his bull-width shoulders tight. "That so. What? Aren't you rooming with him? Didn't the old dog come home last night?"

"That he didn't and his number one squeeze," Sam said, slipping into Henry's lingo, "hasn't seen him. Didn't show for work either."

Henry's shoulders slumped. "Damn." He turned to face Sam, his face no longer smiling. "I thought he'd make it home, that he was exaggerating." He turned over a chair and wrapped his hands on the back of it, steadying himself.

"Okay, Henry, what's up?" Sam asked. His mood darkened. Henry's grim face didn't suggest good news.

A knock echoed in the back hall. Henry looked toward the door and shifted to walk away.

"Ignore it," Sam said. *It has to be Kelsey.* "You're closed, right?" He wanted to finish this conversation without Kelsey present.

"I let you in, didn't I?" Henry said. "Maybe it's Frank." He let go of the chair.

Before Sam could stop him, he was at the back door. Sam moved to where he could see the door. What if it isn't Kelsey? He tensed, ready to act if the knock at the door heralded goons not girl. "Be careful," he admonished.

Henry shot a look over his shoulder and nodded. He opened the door enough to peer out and kept one foot firmly wedged against the bottom edge.

"We're closed," he said and pushed the door.

"Just a minute." Kelsey's voice. Sam relaxed.

"I'm looking for Sam or Frank," Kelsey said.

"Not here," Henry said.

"Didn't your mother teach you it's not nice to lie? I know Sam is in there."

Mother-mode. She'd done it with him a couple of times. She'd done it in the call with her brother. *It's her coping mechanism.*

"Let her in." Sam slapped a hand on his leg and flipped his fingers. "She's with me."

Henry looked back at Sam. "You let a lady wait alone outside? In this neighborhood? Shame on you." He opened the door. "Come in my dear," he said.

Kelsey obeyed and once inside shot Sam a challenging tilt of her chin. "Thank you," she said, turning her gaze to Henry.

"Henry." Sam gestured between the two of them. "Meet Kelsey Maxwell. She says she's part of Frank's family."

He met Kelsey's gaze. "Henry and Frank go way back."

Drat. He should have remembered that earlier. Henry might be able to tell him how Kelsey was connected. He sighed. "Henry, we need to finish." He raised an eyebrow.

Henry was busy shaking Kelsey's hand. "A minute, Sam, a minute." He sandwiched her hand in his and gave her his obvious head-to-toe once-over. "No disrespect," he said to her, "but you can't blame an old man for looking." He turned to Sam. "She's easy to look at." He let Kelsey have her hand back.

Sam shook his head. Always a flirt. The Newfie in Henry surfaced when a good-looking woman arrived. It might be his shock of silver hair, rotund belly and twinkling eyes, but even the younger women never took offense. And Henry couldn't seem to help himself, no matter the occasion.

"You'll have to excuse us, missy. Me and Sam got business," Henry said.

Kelsey stepped from the shadowy hall into the fully lit bar.

Henry stared at her face in the light, blinked once and froze. His breath whistled in, hissed out, and he put a hand on each of her shoulders peering at her.

"Well, I'll be a skinned fish." Wonder tinged his tones. "I never believed I'd see you ever again." He pulled Kelsey into a hug.

CHAPTER SIX

Kelsey stood frozen in the man's embrace. Skinned fish? What was he talking about?

Henry let her go and stepped back. "Sorry, Katya. Too much too soon. You probably don't remember me." A grin lit his face. "Oh, my, little Katya."

Kelsey stared and her gut rolled over. *He called me Katya, like on the birth certificate.*

"You know me?" Her knees quivered and the room shifted around her. She inhaled beer and chips odor and straightened her spine. Henry nodded. The hall stabilized and her knees held. *He knows me.*

Henry grinned from ear to ear. "Know you? Lord thunderin' girl, I used to bounce you on my knee." His gaze slid to a history she couldn't see. "You loved *I'se the B'y That Built the Boat.*" He blinked and looked back. "Little Katya all grown up - and you grew up good. Have you seen Frank? He never said."

His words echoed in her skull. *A real person knows me as Katya Binks. All true – the birth certificate, the pictures – all true.* Her mouth dried, anchoring her tongue to the roof of her mouth. "Oh" was all she could say, and again, "Oh."

It was real. No more doubts, no more maybes. Her gut contracted and she pressed a fist against her middle to quiet the gut-flutters. Her gaze shifted from Henry to Sam. *Help me.*

Sam's gaze connected with hers and with a sharp nod he jumped into the conversation. "What the heck are you talking about?" he said to Henry. He reached for her, drew her against him. She went without protest. If she didn't she might collapse.

His heat touched her, offsetting the chill radiating from her middle. Support. It might be from an almost-stranger, but she'd take it. Steadied, she faced Henry, ready to accept her reality.

Henry frowned at Sam. "How come you called her Kelsey?"

"That's what she calls herself," Sam said. "Why did you call her Katya?"

Henry's gaze turned fierce. "Humph." He spoke to Kelsey. "She changed your first name too." His lips tight, he shook his head. "Shouldn't erase someone like that. It's not right."

Erased? She'd focused on the details of searching for Frank and escaping smothering at home. She'd never thought about who she'd been in the past. *But I'm still me. It's only a name.*

She hugged her middle. *Mom, what did you do?*

Blood pounded in her ears. *She took me away and Frank let me go.*

Her jaw clamped, her hands fisted. *They lied to me.*

Am I Kelsey Maxwell or Katya Binks? *Damn it, either way I'm still me.*

Henry's indignation was on her behalf, or Frank's. Didn't matter. Henry was part of her history, and he obviously cared. She stepped away from Sam and put a hand on Henry's shoulder. "It's just a name."

Sam shifted behind her. "Humph. I'll be damned. You're related to Frank."

"Related?" Henry said. "She's his daughter." He put a hand on Kelsey's cheek and, when he hugged her, she leaned into him.

"Wait till Frank sees you," Henry whispered. "He's going to split wide open with joy."

My father will be happy to see me. His best friend said so and best friends knew things like that. She pulled out of Henry's embrace. Dizziness washed over her. She'd started her quest out of curiosity. Had she sublimated her emotions because she feared her father's reception? Or had she been afraid of what she'd find out about her mother? No more blinders.

Behind her, Sam cleared his throat.

She pulled out of Henry's embrace and a quiver shook her. She understood the phenomenon of quaking after a crisis. When Jamie fell off a horse and split his scalp, she'd handled the blood, the drive to the doctor, the holding Jamie's hand for the stitches. And THEN she'd fallen apart. Rubber knees, tears and all. A second quiver shook her. She should sit. She looked at Henry. "Could I get a glass of water, please?"

"Sure, sure," he said and patted her shoulder before turning away. "Coming right up."

Kelsey's knees trembled. She turned to Sam. "I need to sit."

His gaze raked her face, his questions and accusation evident in the look. But he nodded and, grabbing a chair off the nearest table, turned it over. "Here you go."

Henry returned with the water. Sam took it and handed it to Kelsey. She tipped her head back and drained the glass. She lowered the glass, smiled at Henry. "Thanks. I needed that."

"So Frank is your father," Sam said. He stood in front of her, his arms crossed.

"Yes." Her voice came out low and husky. She stared at his khaki-covered knees.

"Did you know that?" he said.

"I have paper work that says so, but. . ." Her voice trailed off, and she held the glass in both hands running her thumbs over the surface. "But it never felt real until I heard Henry say it."

"It's real, sweetie," Henry said and patted her on the shoulder. "Your mom is Susan?"

She nodded. "Was, she died about ten years ago." Ten years during which Kelsey filled the gap and attended to everyone else in her family.

"Sorry for that, sweetie." Henry sighed. "Sorry for that. She was a real looker, a nice girl." He frowned. "But she never told you about Frank?"

Kelsey stared at the glass. Her mother never talked about her past. Kelsey had no idea how her parents met, where her mom went to school, what she'd done as a kid. *I know nothing. Nothing about my biological father, and not even about my mother.*

"Now that's something," Henry said, "not telling a little girl about her father. Had something to do with her marrying again, I suppose."

Kelsey looked up. "You know that?" Her birth parents were in contact? For years?

Henry shifted from foot to foot. "Frank used to get into the sauce, ya know, and blabber on about stuff. He always kept your picture in his wallet. Susan sent him one each year on your birthday. For a few years anyway. Then they stopped. He told me she got married. Man, the day he signed those release forms for your adoption, he tied on a bender to end all benders. Poured him into the cot in the back room that night, I did."

Frank had photos? Knew things about her? "This is all too much," Kelsey said and handed Henry the glass. The water didn't forestall the headache behind her eyes. "I need to talk to Frank."

· · · · ·

Sam's voice floated above her. "We all need to talk to him," he said. "Henry, before we were interrupted you were about to tell me what you know." She found the hand he kept on her shoulder reassuring as the conversation flowed around her.

This is Your Life. An old, old TV show she'd seen on reruns. She'd never imagined her life might be show worthy. She swallowed a laugh. Laughter might lead to tears. *Besides, this isn't funny.* She stretched her back and lifted her head. She needed to listen to the men.

"He was here before dawn," Henry said. "I haven't seen him that shook up in years."

Sam paced. "Did he say where he was headed? Did he tell you anything?"

"Yup." Henry walked behind the bar. "He needs to see you but said he doesn't want to call you because you have a cell. You know what he thinks about cell phones." He shook his head. "Him and his paranoia." He snorted. "He bought us each one of those bug detector things last year. Probably paid way too much for them off some Spy Store site."

Paranoia? What was her father afraid of? Kelsey removed her hair elastic, reassembled her hair and refastened the ponytail.

Henry was continuing. "But he figured you'd show up here sooner or later. Said he'd be where he used to live - when things were really bad for him."

What does Henry mean by really bad?

"Do you know where that is?" Henry asked.

Sam slapped his hand against his leg. "No idea. I assume you can tell me?"

Henry pulled out a napkin. "It's under a bridge in a culvert."

Her father had lived in a culvert?

Here." He drew some lines, labeled the streets, marked an X and handed it to Sam. "That's where he'll be in the morning for the next couple of days. He was certain you'd show up." He capped his pen, and his gaze honed in on Sam's face. "Why was he so sure you'd find him?"

Kelsey shifted her gaze to Sam. That was a question she'd like to hear him answer.

Sam turned his immobile, unreadable face away from them. "Nothing I can share."

That was an admission of something to hide. She could feel it.

"Humph." Henry said. "Whatever you say." He came out from behind the bar. "Frank has a folder but said he could only give it to you in person. And he has information you need. What's up anyway?" Henry persisted.

Reality check. You have not ended up in Oz. The surreal atmosphere in her head suggested otherwise. Kelsey held her breath, eased it out on a long exhale. Time to get back in the action.

Sam shook his head. "You're better off not knowing." He flicked his fingers against his thigh. "In the meantime, if anyone asks. . ."

Henry nodded. "Don't worry. See nothing. Hear nothing. Say nothing." He pointed to a shelf behind him where the three monkeys sat in their age-old row. "Bartender's creed."

· · · · ·

The final wisp of fog lifted from Kelsey's brain. Her search for Frank had morphed into something dangerous. Not that she'd back off. "What next?" she asked Sam. She'd decided what SHE was going to do, but since they only had one car, she needed Sam's help. If he wouldn't help, she'd find another way.

Sam ignored her. "Henry, can you get her to her hotel?"

"No," she said. "That's not an option."

"My car's in the shop," Henry said.

Sam pulled out his phone. "Greg can send someone to take her to a safe house."

"No," she said. "I won't go." They weren't hearing her. Had her voice disappeared?

"Lem would come for her," Henry said.

Kelsey stepped between them and held a hand in front of each of their faces. "STOP RIGHT THERE." She was sick of men deciding what was best for her.

They gaped as if she'd suddenly appeared in front of them. Sam opened his mouth, and she glared. Henry had the audacity to chuckle. "You," she said to him, "need to realize I am not a toddler anymore."

"Um," he said, his facial expression validating her guess.

"And you," she said pointing at Sam. "You are not going anywhere without ME."

"But. . ." Sam's head started shaking side-to-side in a big fat no.

She slapped his shoulder. "Stop right there. I won't buy the 'keep-me-safe card' or the 'you'll-be-in-my-way card' or. . ." She sputtered, dropped her hand and squared her shoulders. "Or any other lame excuse. You plan to look for Frank, right?"

Sam's sheepish look betrayed the truth.

She whirled around and grabbed the napkin off the bar. "I have the directions." She raised her chin challenging him. "With or without you, I'll find the place."

Henry waved a hand. "Folks, you're overlooking one thing here. It's afternoon. Frank will have already left."

Kelsey tucked the napkin into her shirt front. Sam wouldn't dare go after it there. "You are welcome to do what you want," she said to Sam. There was no way he was cutting her out of the search. "I'm sure Henry will draw you another map." She turned to Henry. "Can you recommend a cab company? I need to get back to my car."

"You are one annoying woman," Sam muttered, but she could tell his heart wasn't in the insult. "You don't need a cab. I'll take you."

"And tomorrow?" she asked.

"I'll take you with me." He shook his head. "You'll only go on your own if I don't."

She grinned. "Such a gentleman." She turned away, scooped up her bag from the floor by the chair and reached the door before she heard him behind her.

At the door Sam paused. "Henry, have you got that bug detector thing here?"

"Sure," Henry said, "I keep it behind the bar and check the place to make Frank happy. He might stop coming in if I didn't."

"Can I borrow it?"

Kelsey tipped her head, listening as Henry passed Sam the device. A shiver slithered down her back. For a fraction of time, the concept of staying safe while Sam looked for Frank appealed to her. Sam returned, and she shook off her doubt.

She pushed the wide bar, opened the door fully and stepped into the parking area.

"Lock up." Sam called over his shoulder. He stood on the step until the lock clunked into place behind them.

She let the smile bubbling inside her rise to her face. All the complications aside, she was going to meet her father. She wasn't stupid. She understood that the off-beat events meant danger. Adrenalin zinged through her. Just like in barrel racing.

She shot a glance at Sam. His walk, his attitude, his questions and the fact that Frank assumed Sam would come looking for him spoke to his identity. Was he police? She narrowed her eyes as the idea took hold. That would explain things.

· · · · ·

Sam scanned the road in both directions, counted off the access gates to various industrial properties. No suspicious vehicles and no sign of the tail-car from earlier. Kelsey buckled in and crossed her arms. Her tight lips and slight frown warned that a storm was coming. She had questions. In her place, he'd have them too. How much should he tell her?

They turned the first corner, and she shifted in her seat. He heard her intake of breath and braced for a tirade. From the corner of his eye he saw her rub her eyes with thumb and forefinger of one hand. One arm still hugged her middle. She brought the other hand down and covered her mouth.

Finally, she clasped both hands in her lap and stretched tall in the seat. "What is the problem?" she asked. "And why is Frank in the middle of it?"

Sam scratched his cheek with one finger. "I'm not sure why Frank is hiding." That much was the truth. "We'll find out when we meet with him."

Her muffled response carried a world of disbelief. "But you suspect things. You have details, tidbits that are pointing you somewhere."

Sam navigated one corner, changed lanes and made a left hand turn onto Frank's street. "Not enough to speculate," Sam said. "And if what I guess at turns out to be true, knowledge could put you in danger."

"Ha." She snorted. "You have already convinced me I'm in trouble, even if I'm not sure why. How much worse could it be?"

Sam didn't answer. Silence thickened. Tension escalated. Crime scene photos flashed in his memory, scenes of slashed necks and copious amounts of blood. He swiped his eyes, shucking off the images. He didn't want her to end up like that. He needed to talk to Frank before he said more.

"Later," he said and parallel parked across from the apartment building. He yawned. "I'm approaching thirty-six hours without sleep. Let's meet for supper and I'll tell you the story."

Kelsey opened her door and feet already out looked back at him. "I don't want the story," she said. "I want the truth."

He inclined his head. He'd figure out how much to tell her once he'd talked to Greg. "Fair enough." He locked his car and followed her. "Hang on," he said and produced the bug detector he'd retrieved from Henry. Compact, rectangular, it could have been a cell phone except for its larger size. Her vehicle was free of unwanted devices.

"I'll pick you up," he said as he closed the driver's door behind her. "Where are you staying?" She raised an eyebrow, plucked a business card off the console and handed it to him. He took it and stood staring after her as she drove away and never looked back.

Sam waited until she turned the corner before crossing to the building. He stepped into the lobby, and backing against the wall, watched the street for several minutes. Satisfied no one followed her, he headed for Frank's apartment.

He unlocked the door and stopped a step inside. The faint odor of a cheap, popular aftershave lingered. *Frank doesn't wear aftershave. Someone's been here.* Sam checked the apartment. The intruder was gone, the aftershave the only evidence of his visit. If he searched, he knew what he was doing. Sam retrieved the bug detector and started a sweep.

The gadget beeped. Sam inspected the receiver on the old phone. Screwing off the cap, he found the device. Not very original. But then they probably didn't expect anyone to search. Showed how little they understood about Frank, never mind Sam. He found other devices in both bedside lamps and in the kitchen. They were meticulous. And they wanted Frank.

Sam's phone vibrated, and he checked the caller ID. Vi. "Hi," he said.

"Did you find Frank?"

"No," he answered. "Where are you?"

"On my way home," she said.

"I'll meet you," Sam said. "I'm leaving now." Diversionary tactics. He didn't need the listeners to show up. The range on the devices wasn't great. A listener would be close. He exited and let the door close behind him with a resounding click. They'd be watching for him out front, of that he was sure. He could hang out in the stairwell and call Greg while he waited for Vi to arrive.

"Greg." Sam sat on the top step. "Things are escalating. I think Frank took something. And these boys want it back."

"What can I do?" Greg asked.

Sam filled Greg in on the devices and the intruder. "Can you do a full, low-key forensics on Frank's place?"

"Consider it done," Greg said. "I'll send 'the gas company guys' and then make sure Natalie has the results, in case I'm not around."

"Thanks," Sam said. The air pressure shifted and steps echoed on the stairs. "Gotta go," he said. "I'll stay in touch. I think Vi's home."

Sam clattered down the stairs and pushed through the door onto Vi's floor in time to see her approach her apartment. Vi dug out her key and reached for the lock. Hand inches from the dead bolt, she froze. She looked both ways, saw Sam and indicated her apartment with a tilt of her head and a raise of her eyebrows. With one finger she pushed the door. No key necessary. Sam broke into a run.

Vi charged out of sight, hollering, "What the hell are you doing?"

Seconds later she stumbled back and landed against the door frame. A man burst into the hall and, keeping his face averted, ran for the other stairwell. No wonder the aftershave odor lingered. Sam must have arrived at Frank's right after the man left. He sped up and raced after the man whose generic jacket and baseball cap made identification impossible.

One after another they slammed through the door and down the stairs. The man jumped the last few stairs to the landing, used the rail for leverage and swung against the exit door. Sam was only moments behind him. He hit sunlight, scanned the area and cursed as a car accelerated away from the curb. The plate was obscured, the windows tinted, but it was the same car that had been there in the morning.

Sam headed back to Vi's. She stood in the middle of her living room.

"Damn thieves." She said, "but at least I interrupted before he took anything." Her laugh was shaky. "Did you get a look at him?"

Sam shook his head, but said, "I saw him." He spoke loud enough to be heard if there were listening devices. He put his finger on his lips. "Whisper."

Vi slumped against the wall and stared at Sam. "They're looking for Frank, aren't they?"

Sam nodded.

"What the hell did that man do?"

"Look, they bugged Frank's place and probably yours as well. And they know enough to look for Frank here." He let the implications sink in. "You need to go somewhere."

Vi nodded. "I have a sister in Dartmouth," she said. "Can I get a few things?"

"Quietly," Sam said, "we don't want them to pick up on your leaving." He led the way inside and searched while Vi packed. He found three bugs, showed her and ushered her to the door. He winked. "Okay then," he said in a normal tone, "I'll call the police for you."

He dialed Greg's phone. "I'd like to report an intruder," he said, and fed the details to Greg. That task out of the way, he walked Vi to her car and watched her drive away.

He turned back to the building. Now what? He needed sleep, but would staying at Frank's be prudent? His phone rang and he answered.

"Sam." It was Kelsey. She swallowed audibly. "Someone's been in my room."

So much for sleep. "On my way," he said. "Go to the hotel office and wait where there are people." He shoved the phone in his pocket and headed for his car. The intruders, whoever they were, were busy boys.

· · · · ·

Kelsey shifted on the large lobby chair, turned a page on the magazine she wasn't reading and looked for the umpteenth time at the parking lot. *Finally. Sam.* Her shoulders relaxed. She raised a hand as he entered.

"What happened?" he said, not wasting time on pleasantries.

"I parked," she said, "and walked to the deli." She pointed up the street. "I needed a coffee." She sighed. Man had she needed a coffee.

"And," Sam prompted.

"My unit is on the ground floor," she said, "all the housekeeping units are, and I went in." She shivered. "I got goose bumps. At first I considered I was overreacting, but then there was this smell, sort of like perfume but..." she waved her hand unable to describe the scent.

"Bad aftershave?" Sam asked.

"That's it." She tucked her hands under her thighs and leaned forward. "It spooked me." She laughed. It wasn't funny. "So I called you." She shrugged. "I guessed it might not be an ordinary thief."

"Did you check to see if anything is missing?"

She shook her head. "I backed out and went to the car. There's nothing to take. I keep all the important things in here." She patted the large shoulder bag she'd purchased for travelling.

She looked up as the desk clerk came into the lobby with a cup of coffee. He stopped in front of them. "Miss Maxwell, did your brother find you?"

"Pardon?"

My brothers are in Alberta. Has something terrible happened? Wake up, girl, it wasn't a real brother.

"Ah," she licked her lips. "What did he look like?"

The clerk looked at her oddly.

"I have three brothers," she said, "they all look different."

The clerk nodded. "This one was tall," he said, gesturing with the coffee cup, "stocky, like he works out."

"Okay then, that sorts it out." She smiled at him.

The clerk started away and paused. "No disrespect," he said, "but you might want to suggest he lay off the aftershave."

"I've tried," Kelsey said and forced a laugh. "But guys don't listen to their sisters." The man chuckled on his way back to his counter.

"What next?" she asked Sam, her gaze now fixed on the carpet. Her stomach gurgled and burped harsh caffeine. She should have skipped the coffee.

"First I need to make a phone call." Sam stood and held out a hand. "After that, we'll go to a safe place and get some sleep." He yawned. "I've been up for over thirty-six hours."

She took his hand and let him help her out of the deep sofa. "Do you think those men are following me in case I can lead them to Frank?" Her heart lurched. "Or do they want me because of what I saw the other night?" She turned to Sam. "I didn't see anything," she said. "I saw one guy chasing the other. Oh and the blood. And the guys watching the apartment."

Of course they are after me.

"Never mind," she said before Sam could answer. "Let's get out of here."

CHAPTER SEVEN

Frank leaned against the metal wall, his shoulders urged forward by the culvert's curve. The isolated corner had little traffic, and he would hear if anyone approached. Morning number two. *Hope Sam shows today.* He didn't like returning to the same place too often. Breakfast from the golden arches filled his stomach. Eating there offended his culinary senses, but it was fast, easy and anonymous. He shifted position again. *Come on, Sam, show up.*

He watched the shadows at the sunny end of the culvert and knew without checking his watch that he'd been there well over an hour. He glanced to the far end, the dark side in more ways than lighting. A.J. had liked to sleep there. Frank shuddered. *And A.J. died there.* He looked away and touched the paperwork still inside his jacket.

A car slowed on the road above him. He pushed away, prepared to move fast if he needed to run. A car door slammed followed by another. Two people? Sam would come alone. Frank edged to the mouth of the culvert and peered out, watching the slope the led to the road. He bent his knees and readied his body. Sam appeared at the road's edge and Frank relaxed. All clear. He stepped into the open and raised a hand.

Another person came into view and Frank flicked his gaze from Sam to the woman behind him. Sam turned and held out a hand as if to assist her. She shook her head and Sam shrugged and led the way. Frank's gaze dropped to her feet. Given her shoes she should have taken the help.

Frank looked again as the pair slipped and slid down the graveled slope. He scrunched his eyes and looked again. *Susan?* He must be losing it. Susan would be way older. He looked again. Susan's hair and long legs. Katya? His pulse raced and his throat clogged. Blinking rapidly, he tried to see through threatening tears.

Sam reached the bottom of the slope. Frank ignored him, his attention consumed by the young woman. He drew a breath but couldn't breathe. So much like her mother. She looked up and he saw her eyes. Eyes like his own, a peculiar green-gray color that changed with weather and clothing choices. His knees buckled and he sank to the ground. *My daughter.*

"Katya," he said, his voice a raspy whisper.

She stopped in front of him, knelt and settled back on her heels. Her gaze met his. Matching tears welled in her eyes.

Frank raised a hand to touch her, closed his fingers and let his fist fall to his knee. *Is she real?* So many times he'd dreamed of her walking back into his life but awakened to reality and no Katya. He raised his hand again. *If I touch her will she disappear?*

The vision raised her hand and grasped his. *Flesh and blood. She's real.* His tears spilled down his face. "You came back," he said. "You came home from away."

"Yes," she said, her voice husky with unshed tears.

Frank leaned forward and she met him, wrapping her arms around him, hiding her face against his shoulder. Solid, warm, real. His baby girl felt so right in his embrace. *Finally.* A sob escaped, and he wasn't sure if it was his or hers.

He pulled back, put a hand on her face and whispered her name. She smiled around her tears. "Daddy?" The one word nearly undid him. He bowed his head thanking the universe for her return. The struggle to stand and find tissues gave him time to gain control. He touched her shoulder, and she gripped his hand and held on. Just like when she was little.

· · · · ·

Sam paced. He'd retreated to give Frank and Kelsey a modicum of privacy. He scanned the hillside and road. He swept his inspection into the tunnel and brought it to rest on father and daughter. Reunions aside, there were issues to deal with. If they didn't, Frank could end up on the run and any further father-daughter stuff would be improbable.

"Frank," Sam said, "we need to talk."

Frank didn't take his gaze off Kelsey. "In a minute," he said, and cleared his throat.

Sam understood and again tried to pull Frank into the current problem. "Frank," he said, "what about *The Mingle*? Why did you take off? Are you okay?"

"I'm fine, now," Frank said, his gaze on Kelsey. "Quite fine."

"Frank," Sam injected urgency into his tone.

Frank blinked and looked at Sam. "Oh, right. That." But his mind obviously wasn't on the running and hiding issue. "Where did you find her?" he asked. He turned to Kelsey. "Katya, how did you find me?"

Kelsey answered with a smile. "It wasn't easy. You're a hard man to track." She didn't correct him on the name issue.

Frank nodded. "Good, I mean, good it's hard." He looked at their joined hands. "But you did find me."

The wonder in his voice touched Sam. He was happy for them. But time was passing and they were exposed.

Above them a car approached and slowed. Reflexively, Sam looked up but couldn't see anything. *Sounds like they stopped behind my car*. Car doors slammed just enough out of sync to tell him there were at least two people.

Frank's gaze snapped to Sam's, his eyes focused and his attention visibly returned to the moment. "Oh, oh," he said, "we need to move. Follow me. I can get us out of here."

On the roadside above, two men stepped into view. They stood on the shoulder and looked around. Sam recognized the instant they focused on him, Kelsey and Frank.

"Let's go," Frank said.

"They look like the men who've been tailing us," Sam said, already moving. He glanced up again. The breeze flipped back the jacket on the taller man. "The big one has a gun. Let's move it."

Frank tugged on Kelsey's hand. "Run," he said and headed into the culvert. Kelsey tucked her purse strap over her head and anchored her purse against her body and ran. Sam shot one last look at the men slipping down the slope and took up the rear.

At the far end of the culvert they splashed through water, broke into the open and hit a concrete-lined ditch. A few feet along the ditch Frank turned up the hill. They scrambled up the graveled slope. Ahead of Sam, Kelsey slid back, her high platform heels twisting her feet. No time for propriety. Sam placed a hand on either side of her hips and pushed. She didn't even look back.

Frank led them onto the road and again took Kelsey's hand. Sam moved into the spot beside her. He glanced back as they raced away from the cars. Motion at the road edge drew his attention. A head appeared above the location of the culvert. "More speed," Sam said.

Frank nodded and pointed right. He dropped Kelsey's hand, jumped the embankment and turned to help her. Sam slid down to join them and followed Frank around the metal fence. He ducked behind bushes.

"Good," Frank said puffing, "it's still here."

The IT was a cut in the chain link. Frank pulled back the section and urged Kelsey through. She didn't say a word, didn't look at Sam or Frank. She just did what was required.

Frank bent and stepped through the opening. He looked as Sam followed. "Pull it closed," he said and turned away.

Sam bent and edged into the opening. His shoulder caught and he backed up and ducked lower. The hole wasn't intended for a six foot man. He struggled through, tugged the section into place and followed Frank and Kelsey. Ahead of them storage units lined a compound. Frank cut between two buildings and hesitated. Leaning a shoulder on one wall, he poked his head out. Kelsey stood behind Frank, one hand on his shoulder.

Sam stood against the other building and took his own look. A paved area divided the first buildings from a matching row across the way. Cracks dissected the pavement, and weeds grew bravely in the gaps. Sam checked both directions. Was the compound deserted?

"Come on," Frank said, and crossed the open space to the alley on the far side. From there he ducked around the back of the buildings and stopped. "We'll be okay here," he said and backed his butt against the wall. His chest heaved and he leaned forward, hands on his knees. "I'm too old for this."

Sam faced Frank, his feet planted in a wide stance. "Frank," he said. "What did you do that they want you so badly. Those boys have guns."

Beside him, Kelsey jerked. She hugged her body and worried her bottom lip with her teeth. But she said nothing. Sam zeroed in on her face. Her pupils were dilated, her skin shiny with moisture. Shock? He tucked an arm around her and felt her lean into him.

"I got up to the third floor," Frank said, diverting Sam's attention. "Just like you thought, it's got a lot going on."

Yes. He'd thought the third floor held answers. Maybe now they'd get a warrant to search the place. If he could get Frank to the right authorities and convince a judge. "Explain."

"High tech stuff," Frank said and described the equipment, phones and files. "And surveillance cameras," he added, "at least five of them. They sure wanted to keep tabs on what was going on downstairs."

Cameras? It sounded like the operation could create identification documents and then some. "Given the surveillance cameras, we can assume they have your visit on file?"

Frank nodded. "At the very least, they saw me going into the stairwell." He ran a hand over his chin. "Then there's the guy I knocked on his ass." He flipped a look at Kelsey. "Sorry for the language. He got a good look at me for sure even though he was bleeding like a stuck pig."

"He followed you out," Kelsey said, her voice thin. It was the first thing she'd said since meeting Frank.

Frank stared at her. "How the hell do you know?"

A shudder shook her. "I was there," she said, and pulling out of Sam's support, ran both hands over her face. "In the parking lot. I called to you." She tightened her lips and squared her shoulders. "I tried to follow you in my car, but you disappeared too quickly."

"That was you?" Frank ran both hands over his head. "That means they saw you. Cameras," he added, "at least two were trained on the parking lot. They'll have your car plates."

What a mess. That explained how they'd found her. At this point she was just a witness but if they found out she was Frank's daughter? It wouldn't take them long to figure out that having her would give them leverage against Frank.

"Go on," Sam said to Frank. He looked at Kelsey, but her gaze was fixed on her father. She stood with her arms crossed although not hugging her body like before. Her stance wasn't much different than Sam's. She hadn't panicked, or fainted or wailed. Way easier to protect a level-headed person than a panicking one. Damn, but he was beginning to like this woman.

"I took one file," Frank said and unzipped his jacket. "Here, have a look." He held out a large manila envelope. "Henry gave me the envelope, but the original file and contents are inside. And a notebook. Not sure what's in it. I'm thinking that's what they're after."

"What's in the file?" Sam flipped up the flap and peered in.

"Employee records," Frank said, "personal documents, a passport. Stuff like that. Only problem is, it's current information and the guy on the documents has been dead for years."

Sam's gaze shot from the envelope to Frank's face. "How do you know he's dead?"

"He was my drinking buddy." Frank worried the knuckles on his left hand. "We often slept in the culvert." He shifted. "I woke up one morning, went to get A.J. and he was dead. I was so hung over I booted it out of there. Left him." He hung his head.

"You are sure he was REALLY dead?" Sam asked. The observation skills of a hung-over drunk could be questionable.

"Oh yeah - no pulse, no breath, cold and turning stiff." He shook his head. "But the funny thing is there was never any notice of anyone finding his body. But the body disappeared. I went back and looked later. I never heard a word since until I saw his name in that file." He nodded at the envelope in Sam's hands.

"Sure you didn't miss the news about him?" Sam read the name, noted the documents and looked at Kelsey. How was she taking all this? He couldn't tell.

"You were drinking pretty heavy back then." Sam said to Frank.

Frank shook his head. "Nope, A.J.'s death was it for me. I went to an AA meeting that afternoon and haven't had a drink since. I watched the news, picked up the papers. No mention of A.J. or an unknown dead derelict anywhere."

A full ID built around an unreported dead man. "Did you tell anyone?"

Frank nodded. "I called it in. Told the police where he'd died." He shook his head, his lips pressed tight. "Nothing happened."

"Which way did they go?" The words floated on the wind, coming from the fence. Sam tensed and held up his hand. Frank and Kelsey looked in the direction of the sounds.

"Here," came an answering shout. "There's a hole in the fence behind this bush."

"They found it." Frank took both of Kelsey's hands in his. "I always loved you little one." He looked at Sam. "Take care of her."

He grabbed the envelope from Sam's hands, and stuck it under his arm. Before Sam figured out what he was up to, Frank disappeared around the building headed for the paved central area. "I'll be in touch," he called back. "Don't worry."

The damn idiot is playing decoy.

"No," Kelsey took a step toward Frank's retreating form.

Sam grabbed her.

She lurched forward, trying to follow Frank.

He wasn't any happier about Frank's decoy tactics than she was."
Stay put," he said. "He'll be fine. He knows his way around. He's
done it to keep you safe." He listened to the footsteps disappear in
the distance, and as she gave up the struggle, he tugged her along
behind the buildings in the opposite direction. "Give him that
opportunity and bloody well stay safe." He uttered the words
through clenched teeth.

· · · · ·

Sam stopped at the end of the buildings. Kelsey peered around
him at an overgrown field.

"Do you think he got away?" she asked.

Sam looked behind and shook his head. "We can only hope he
knew what he was doing." A half-smile tugged at his mouth. "I
didn't hear any gunshots. That's a good sign."

"Sure, right," Kelsey said. "They could have silencers." Damn,
she'd watched too many CSI shows.

She focused on the building behind Sam. *He escaped, he
escaped.* She needed to believe it. She needed to believe she'd see
him again. So many unasked questions. She blinked. *Don't go there
now.* She adjusted the purse strap across her body, gripped it and
drew in a ragged breath. The tension and grief shrank. *I can do this.*

"We need to get out of here," she said. "We should report all this
and get the police looking for Frank and those men."

"Do you think," Sam said, his tone wry. "Come on." He took her
hand and started away from the buildings. "First we need to figure
out how to get out of this compound."

Sympathy might have unleashed tears. Humor she could handle.
Kelsey followed Sam.

· · · · ·

Sam pulled Kelsey up a small rise toward the fence and stopped
beside three scrawny trees. He didn't have a plan to get out of the
yard, at least not yet. He shot a glance at Kelsey. She didn't look
happy, but the set of her jaw and the square of her shoulders told him
she was in control. He couldn't imagine what she was thinking, but
at least she wasn't dissolving into tears.

Beside him, Kelsey looked up. "It's a bit high." She leaned back and looked again. "And it has razor wire."

There was no mistaking the curled stretches of wire. He nodded. "It's a problem." Her height and slim build belied her strength. He'd felt it when he held her back. She was tiny but certainly no bit of fluff.

"I suppose I could boost you over the top."

"I'd rather not," she said, "I've seen what that wire can do to flesh."

"I hear you." He ran a thumb over the back of her hand and cocked his head. He'd heard no footsteps or voices since they'd left the buildings. "Do you hear anything?" he asked.

Kelsey stood with her eyes closed. After long moments she said, "Only distant traffic and some kind of horn." She opened her eyes. "What are you thinking?"

"If they're gone, we can follow the fence around and get out the way we came in." He paused. "Or we can follow it the other way and see if there's a way out at the front." This was a plan in the making. "Inside this fence we're fish in a barrel. Whatever we do, we need to get out and find somewhere else to hide until we're sure they're gone."

"You're assuming they are still chasing Frank?" Kelsey asked. He heard the subtext and like her, hoped they hadn't caught him.

"We can hope," he said. "Sorry, don't mean to sound cold, but at this point we need them distracted." When he'd started this operation, he'd never dreamed it would be Frank's life complicating issues. Or Frank's life on the line.

"With any luck," he added, "we might be able to get to my car."

"What other options are there?" She adjusted her purse, pushing it behind her.

"If we go any other way, we'd need to be sure we were safe and then call for a taxi."

"Let's check the car option," she said and started along the fence. "I don't think I could stand announcing my location and then waiting, even if it is for a cab."

She had a point. Sam took one last look behind them at the shabby buildings, scruffy grass and chain link fence. Abandoned. He stepped in behind Kelsey. Looked like they were headed for the hole they'd come in through.

CHAPTER EIGHT

Sam put a hand against the concrete pillar and balanced on his feet. They'd escaped the yard through the original hole and made their way to the culvert and ramp near his car. He rocked on his heels once and paced the width of the pillar. He ran a hand over his head. How had those men found them? Henry and Greg were the only people who knew where they would meet Frank.

First they needed to get out of there. He needed to check his car and contact Greg and get Kelsey to safety. *And if something happens to you?* As much as he'd like to think it wouldn't, he couldn't be stupid and ignore the possibility. Kelsey needed an alternate plan.

He kept his voice low. "Give me your phone," he said and held out his hand.

She abandoned massaging her feet and looked up. "Why?"

"Just give me the phone," he said. "If anything happens to me, you need someone you can trust, right?"

For a moment she looked like she might argue. "Right," she said and opened a flap on her purse and pulled out the phone.

He programmed in a number. "Lady on the other end is Natalie Parker," he said and handed back the phone. "She'll help you if need be. Just tell her Travis's friend, Sam, sent you."

"Who are they?" Kelsey asked as she thumbed the phone and read the number.

"A longtime friend and his little sister," Sam said. "People I can trust. Nat is law enforcement. She can protect you."

"Trust," she said. "Do you have trouble trusting people?" She looked up at him. He didn't answer, and she looked at her phone.

And if there's a leak in the department? Damn. She needed more than Natalie's number.

"Phone," he said again.

She frowned but complied.

He punched in Jackson's number and returned her phone. "Back up plan," he said. "Jackson Ritcey is one of my partners. He'll help if Natalie can't."

She gave a nod and put the phone away. "Got it," she said.

One more safeguard in place. A knot in Sam's back eased. Phones on vibrate were the first safeguard. He turned his public phone off completely to avoid GPS tracking as a second precaution. The burner phone was back at home or he'd have ditched the other one already.

After Frank's description of the electronics on the third floor, Sam didn't doubt Eric and his boys could track anything. His phone number was on his employment record at *The Mingle*. They could find him.

Kelsey rested her wrists on pulled-up knees. "You're a cop," she said.

Sam considered denying it, but there was no longer any reason to do so. "Sort of."

"Humph. Is your name really Sam Edwards?"

"Sam Edward Logan," he said and stuck his hands in his pockets. "Edwards is what I use for undercover."

"I see," she said and lapsed into silence, resting her head in her hands.

Sam sighed. She probably blamed him for all this running and hiding and chasing. And that by association, it was also his fault she was in danger. She'd come looking for her father and found way more than she'd bargained for. Too late now.

Muffled slams echoed against concrete. Kelsey lifted her head and looked at him, her eyebrows raised in an unspoken question. He nodded and held out a hand to help her up.

A car engine started and in moments, the goons' car came around the curve into sight. He could see two people in the front. Were there only two door slams? He couldn't be sure. He checked the windows but the tinting made it impossible to see in. If Frank was there, he couldn't tell.

Kelsey shifted and he looked over. Her gaze met his, the question in her eyes obvious.

Sam shrugged and shook his head.

Her shoulders slumped, and she leaned toward him. He put an arm around her and they watched until the car disappeared. Damn, but he was weary. Too many bursts of adrenalin in one day left him drained. And he still needed to get them out of there safely.

"Hang back," he said, "I'll get my car. If they are watching and return, get out of here."

"But," she said.

"No buts. If you have to run, call that number programmed into your phone. Natalie will tell you what to do. Trust her. Tell her everything."

She glowered at him. "Fine. But you staying safe is a better option."

He grinned. "Didn't know you cared." The climb up was tricky and sent gravel rattling. He stopped near his car. If he was in their place, what would he do? A car bomb seemed extreme, and they probably didn't carry explosives around with them. He gave himself a mental slap. What was he thinking? Car bombs were a ridiculous overkill scenario.

But they did put listening devices in the apartments. No good in a car though, unless they were close by. He planted one hand on his hip and ran the other over his head. They might have GPS devices. *Get real. Maybe they just sliced your tires.* Sam's gaze snapped to the front tires. They looked intact. He went closer, checked all four. They were fine. So much for the obvious.

They didn't find Frank. The concept reassured him. *If anything, they've planted a tracking device hoping I'll lead them to Frank.* Since he didn't know Frank's location, that wasn't a current risk. For now, it was safe to use the car.

The late afternoon air hung heavy with sea moisture and a sea gull circled above. No other answers there. He flipped out the key and reached for the door. He needed to get them away from there and the car was the fastest way. He did a quick check. Damn, the buggers got Frank's bug detector. He shouldn't have left it in the car.

Sam put the key in the ignition, paused and wiped his sweating palms on his pant legs. *What if they did put in an explosive?* In one swift motion he turned the key and nudged the gas pedal. *Don't be a dumb-ass. You didn't really think it would blow up?* The car started. Sam's breath whooshed out, and he slammed the car door. He pulled forward and picked up Kelsey.

"Where are we going?" She asked. She gripped her purse strap and held her body stiffly forward on the seat.

Sam couldn't help it. Assume the worst. The might have left a listening device, they might be parked close by. He shook his head and put a finger to his lips.

She frowned.

Sam pointed to his ear and circled his finger in the air, taking in the car's interior.

She pinched her lips together and narrowed her eyes, giving him a look.

She isn't stupid, she'll figure it out.

"Ah," she said. She'd got it.

He pointed across the harbor. Her gaze followed his point, and she stared across the water at Dartmouth. She gave an exaggerated sigh and nodded.

Sam concentrated on driving. He should get rid of the car. Even if they didn't put in a tracking device, they had the description and plate number. Without Frank's bug detector he couldn't check. No, he'd have to dump the car.

My phone. They might have tracked it to the culvert. If he'd known about their equipment, he'd have left it off. He'd keep it turned off until he could get the burner phone he had in his place for backup.

A joint in the bridge clunked under the wheels. Sam dug out a token. Excellent misdirection though, if he turned on his phone and left it behind. That was an option. The only thing left was to decide whether to call Greg for a pick-up or use public transit to get to safety.

· · · · ·

The metal bridge deck created a low hum punctuated by the thump of crossing the odd seam. Kelsey surveyed the harbor through the guardrail. Georges Island hunkered between rolling waves, and a single-sailed boat cut through the waters beside it. The sail boat wasn't the famous Bluenose Schooner. It would be much larger. The square blue and white vessel cutting across the harbor would be a ferry. Sun sparkled on the water. Perfect tourist layout.

Now that she was free from focusing on running and pushing her legs to take one more step, her thoughts spiraled into a maelstrom. *He left me.* Kelsey gripped her purse, digging her fingers into the fabric. A replay of her mother's death exploded into the present. *She left me.*

Past and present overlapped. An echo of an even deeper history resonated through her. Her attention evaporated. *How could they?* She bent forward, resting her forehead on her hands.

Anguish and tears overflowed. Sorrow poured into the car's interior. *Not fair. Not fair. Why did they have to go?* She clenched her fists and struck the dash. Pain stabbed her hand and punctured her sorrow bubble. Grief hissed out like steam from a kettle.

She sighed. *There's a hand on my back.* The hand circled, and a deep voice uttered nonsense. Sam. Kelsey cleared her throat and released her tension. *Enough.*

Swiping her face dry, she sat up. She stared at the windshield. That had been some meltdown. What must Sam think? What did she think? She'd never experienced pain like that, not even when her mother died. She hiccupped and dug in her purse for a tissue. If she used her sleeve, it would be the final embarrassment.

"Sorry." She muttered, blew her nose and shoved the tissue into the depths of her purse.

She sniffed and met the gaze Sam shot at her. "Sorry," she said again, "don't know what came over me."

Sam rubbed the back of his head and flicked his gaze from road to her and back. "Nothing to be sorry for," he said. "You've processed a lot in a short period of time."

"Thanks," she said and cleared her throat again. She hadn't felt this awkward since she'd found Casey naked in a loft with her primary barrel racing competitor. That time anger got her through. But finding her father, looking into eyes so like her own and feeling his touch on her cheek was no comparison. *I called him Daddy.*

She struggled to stuff her emotions into a mental box. She needed to get back to details. *Frank. Sam. Running. Storage yard. Bad guys. Driving. Escape.* The litany helped. *Find Frank.* Kelsey lifted her chin. The expectation of finding Frank would get her through this.

Sam slowed the car, lowered the window, and without stopping flipped a coin into the basket on the toll booth. He veered right off the bridge exit, followed a street that looped back toward the harbor and the ferry terminal.

They stopped at a streetlight, and she watched the ferry dock. Sam turned the corner. She read the sign, Portland Street. It wound narrowly away from the harbor, gaining elevation the further inland they went. Wood-frame houses like the ones on the Halifax Peninsula gave way to rows of brick apartments.

On the other side of the street, a subdivision of square houses sprawled along treed streets. Sam hung a right onto a residential street and parallel- parked between two vehicles.

She looked up the street. "There's more room up there."

"This is fine," Sam said. "It won't be as noticeable." He opened his door. "Let's go."

She got out. "What are we doing?"

"Creating a diversion," he said. "If they track the car, they'll think we're here in Dartmouth."

Kelsey balanced on the edge of the curb, weariness permeating her body. "Okay. The car stays here. What about us?"

Sam dug in the trunk and pulled out a duffle bag. "We walk," he said, and pointed over his shoulder. "Penhorn Mall is up there." He examined the duffle bag, dumped out the contents. He stood for long moments, one hand on the raised trunk lid, the other on his hip. Finally he sorted the items, checked each carefully and added a few to the bag. The rest he left in the trunk.

"I have no idea what they might have tampered with, if anything," he said and slammed the trunk.

Kelsey hitched her purse into its cross-body position, looked at the now-offensive high heels. "Let's do it." She only hoped it wasn't far to the mall. What she wouldn't give for a pair of running shoes. Wearing heels to look taller had lost its appeal.

Back at the main drag, Sam led her across the street and once again uphill. "At the mall," he said, "we can get some food."

Her stomach rumbled. Good idea. She squinted at the sun, now low in the sky. It must be suppertime. She stumbled, partly because of a sidewalk crack, partly because of the shoes.

He looked at her feet. "We'll get you some flat shoes. That is if you'd like some."

"Like some? I'd kill for some." She lapsed into silence and trudged beside him.

Sam was as good as his word. Pizza and shoes. Kelsey walked the store aisles and picked out a pair of laced flats. She tried them "These will work," she said.

"Can you pay with a credit card?" Sam asked as they headed to the front.

"Why?" That question again. She was always asking it. She wanted to laugh. Was it any wonder? She'd never learned the protocol for being on the run and evading goons. "Not arguing," she said. "I just figure you have a reason for everything we're doing right now."

Sam laughed. "Smart girl. If we leave a trail, I'd like it to be on this side of the bridge. Save cash for when we're back in Halifax."

She stopped and confronted him. "If you really think they are tracking me," she asked, "shouldn't we just go to the police?"

"Ah hell, be damned if I know what's best here," Sam said and stroked her upper arm. "But they've been in business for decades, and we suspect they have a contact in the police department."

"What? A crooked cop? A snitch?"

He shrugged. "Might be an officer, or support staff. We haven't been able to figure it out, but they manage to stay one step ahead. At least, as far as we know, they still think I'm Sam Edwards, bartender."

"As far as you know?"

He shifted his shoulders and looked over her head. "But since they saw me with Frank today, it doesn't matter who or what I am. They'll be looking for me."

She sighed and handed him the shoes. They weren't going to the police and they were not going to get protection. She pulled the band off her ponytail, finger-combed her hair and replaced the tail.

Sam handed back the shoes. "If we go to the police, I might end up answering so many questions they'll keep me for days. And they'd lock us up for safety. Then who will look for Frank? If the wrong person finds him first…" He stopped, letting her fill in the blank.

The heavy knot in Kelsey's middle tightened. Her phone vibrated. She jumped. Raising her gaze to Sam's, she pulled out the cell. Brock. Twice in one day? Or was it another day already? *I'm in serious overload.*

"So," Brock said in answer to her hello, "did you meet him?"

"Yes."

"And?"

"It's complicated and," she looked around, "right at the moment I'm buying shoes."

"So if you're shopping, you're okay?" Brock sounded relieved.

Okay? She'd probably never be okay again. But she couldn't begin to get into it with Brock. An urge to laugh swept over her. "Sure," she lied, "I'm fine." A vague recollection of his earlier conversation played in her head. "And you? Are you fine?" Scintillating conversation. If anyone was listening, it wouldn't help them. *Now she was paranoid.*

"I think so," he said. "I told Becky what you said, and we're checking things out. I'll keep you posted."

"Okay," she said, and her brain stalled. "Okay."

Brock didn't seem to notice. "Right," he said, "I'll call tomorrow." And he was gone.

Kelsey stared at the phone in one hand, the shoes in the other. She looked up to see Sam watching her and a mom with two kids hurrying along the aisle. Surreal.

"Shoes," she said to Sam. "Let's go pay for them." Would she even be able to answer Brock's call tomorrow?

· · · · ·

Sam leaned against the ferry railing, in the lee of a support beam and checked the decks behind and below. At the moment he saw no one suspicious. Kelsey stood beside him facing forward, watching the Halifax shorefront and dock getting closer.

The brisk breeze on the upper deck tugged at her hair and every few minutes she swiped a stray strand away from her face. She'd wound the ponytail into a loose bun on the back of her head and stuck in some pins. The wind seemed to be trying to undo it all. He reached over and pulled out the pins. She shot him a look, reached back and dragged her hand over the ponytail.

"It was all coming undone anyway," he said.

"Lot of undoing going around," she said and faced the wind again. "This seems so familiar. In spite of all the craziness. . ." She glanced around. "I'm excited or buoyed. Not sure how to explain it, but riding the ferry is a feel-good happening."

"Maybe you're an ocean girl at heart." Sam said. She inclined her head. "Did Frank take you on the ferry when you were a kid?"

"I thought of that. Another question to ask him," she said and rested her forearms on the railing, worrying one hand with the other in a gesture he'd seen Frank use.

Sam pulled out his phone. He'd decided not to leave it as a decoy. There was an answering device to record calls, and he'd double rigged the system to record his outgoing calls as well. He could access the recordings from any phone or computer. He hit the power button. A final message check and he'd send the phone to Davy Jones' Locker.

He glanced at the waves parting in front of the ferry. Murky and dark, the water covered years of sludge and grime. Once the phone sank to harbor bottom, no one would find it.

The phone activated and vibrated in his hand. Two texts. The first from Greg was succinct. *In labor. Going to the hospital.* So contact with Greg was out for the time being. The second text was equally short but far more disturbing. *Visitors*, it said, *need help. Henry.* On a Sunday night, the bar was closed. There should be no visitors.

"Trouble," Sam said and looked at the distance to the pier. "We need to get off this boat."

"I don't think we should swim," Kelsey said and turned to him. She met his gaze, sobered. "What's wrong?" Her face paled under the breeze-induced ruddiness. "Is it Frank?"

"Henry," Sam said. "He's got trouble." Greg was out of touch, Nat Parker wasn't familiar with Henry and Sam didn't have time to explain. He pushed the button connecting him to Lem's phone and got voice mail. "Henry needs help," he said and turned off the phone.

The ferry nudged the buffers and clanged solid in the moorings. "You still have your phone," he said and Kelsey nodded. He removed the battery and dropped his phone into the harbor. Scooping up his kit bag, he turned from the railing. Her phone would have to be enough.

"Time to go," he said, and headed for the interior staircase. He ignored the sign telling them to stay off the stairs during docking. Kelsey followed him and the clang of feet on the metal treads resonated in his pulse.

He flicked his gaze over the faces of departing and incoming passengers. Vigilance always. His mentor's mandate. He guided Kelsey through the crowd. One hand on her back, he directed her to the right along the boardwalk behind the law courts. Ducking through the Historic Properties he stayed out of the thick of passengers who headed left toward the buses.

"Come on," he said and breaking into a run, ducked through a narrow passage between banks of boutiques. His instincts screamed for speed. The *Marriott Hotel* and *The Delta* with high traffic levels were just along the waterfront. There should be a taxi. This wasn't the time to wait for a bus. He needed to get to Henry's place NOW.

• • • • •

"Stop here," Sam told the taxi driver. He shoved money at him and followed Kelsey out of the cab. The driver pulled a U-turn and disappeared up the hill. "Come on." Sam slung his kit over his shoulder, grabbed Kelsey's hand and ran. There were still three blocks to go.

The parking lot was empty and the bar lights off. He left the road and raced through shadows. *Big yard light out.* Sam stopped by the wall and watched the back step. *No light over the door.* A line of light sliced the landing. *Door's not closed, inside night light?* He eased his kit to the ground.

Kelsey stood close in the fuzzy dark, and he could feel her heat and hear her breathing. He put a finger on her lips and the flat of his hand against her upper chest. He breathed against her ear. "Wait." She shook her head. "Please," he whispered. She nodded and shivered.

Sam crept forward, swung around the rail and onto the step. *No sounds.* He opened the door, welcomed an adrenalin rush. Once inside he glanced up. The exit sign provided the dim light. Sam eased forward until he could see the bar.

A clock ticked. A tap dripped. A click and whir echoed. His heart jumped. *It's the fridge.* He relaxed and peered into the large barroom.

Although his eyes were adjusted to the darkness, he could barely make out the tables. He pressed his eyes closed. Odors of stale beer and cleaning agents permeated the air. A groan broke the stillness. Sam turned and felt for a light switch. Eyes at half-mast to avoid light-shock, he flicked the switch. Light flooded the bar and he tensed, ready to respond.

His eyes adjusted and he inspected the room. A second groan pulled his attention behind him. He swung around and took the three steps to Henry's office door. Henry lay on his side, blood pooling in front of his face. *He groaned. He's alive.*

Sam leaned into the hall. "Kelsey," he yelled. "I need help."

The door slammed and her footsteps echoed in the hall. She must have moved to the step before he called. "What?" she asked and stepped into the room. She gasped. Her face paled, and she knelt on the other side of Henry.

"He's alive," Sam said. "See if you can find a blanket." He looked up and pointed. "There's a bedroom next door. He keeps it for the over-intoxicated to sleep it off. Should be a blanket in there."

Kelsey sucked air, pinched her lips tight and hurried away.

Sam inventoried Henry's injuries. *Broken nose. Explains the blood.* He ran his hand over each limb. *Right arm might be broken.* He checked Henry's right fingers and winced. More than one of them was obviously broken. *They tortured him.*

Sam handled Henry's hand as gently as possible, but Henry moaned. He opened swollen and rapidly discoloring eyes.

"Wanted Frank." Henry licked his split lip. "Knew he'd been here. Knew you'd been here. Didn't tell." He raised his left hand. "Here," he said. His eyes closed.

Sam checked Henry's left hand, pried open the fingers and saw a button. The old coot managed to get evidence. *Take it or leave for the cops?* He left it. He ran a quick hand over Henry's legs. They seemed to be intact. The one thing he couldn't check was the abdomen.

Kelsey returned and spread a blanket over Henry and tucked it in along his back.

Henry groaned again. "Desk," he muttered. "Photos." And he drifted into unconsciousness. Small mercies. A little time out of it was a good thing. Henry would be in a world of hurt when he came to. *If he lives. If there are no internal injuries.*

"Call 911," Sam said. "Use the bar phone." He did not want her cell number on record. "Pull your sleeve over your hand. Disguise your voice." Diversionary tactics. "And I need your phone."

She handed it over and headed for the bar.

Sam dialed Lem's number and Lem answered. Thank goodness.

"Where are you?" Lem asked. "What's going on?"

"I'm at the bar," Sam said. "It's not good. We've called 911, but I can't stick around to answer questions. Where are you?"

"Almost there," Lem said. "I'll take over. What should I know?"

"Henry called for help. The lights were out in the lot and over the door when you arrived. There was no one here. You found him in his office. He's bleeding from his nose and face, his right arm and several fingers appear broken. There might be internal bleeding. They worked him over pretty good. You checked, called 911 on the bar phone and then got a blanket out of the back room."

"They're on their way," Kelsey said and knelt beside Sam, placing a hand on Henry's shoulder. Her forehead puckered and her lips were compressed. She looked up, her eyes dark. "The men looking for Frank did this, didn't they?"

Sam nodded and held up a finger. "And Lem," he continued, alluding to his undercover work, "you have no idea why someone would do this."

"That's not a stretch," Lem said. "I never understand why people resort to violence. Besides, the man runs a bar in one of the roughest parts of town. What is there to say? Okay, I'm on the street now. You can go." He hung up before Sam could thank him. He wondered briefly what Lem did in his former life that left him so competent in such situations.

Sam held the phone over Henry's hand and, making sure the phone's date stamp was engaged, snapped pictures. He got a close-up of the fabric and threads clinging to the button. Police forensics might find evidence. Greg would get him the info later.

Sam emailed the photos to Greg and to his own secured email and handed Kelsey her phone. He twitched the blanket under Henry's chin. He hated to leave him, but Lem would arrive momentarily. He'd done all he could for Henry, but the men might go after Vi. Staying with her sister, she would be traceable.

Cooling his heels in a police station and answering questions would waste precious time. These guys had just ramped up their game, and Sam needed to stop them. A chill coated his spine. How did they find Henry? And how had they learned Sam had been there? The only person privy to his visit was Greg. *Greg was at the police station when you talked to him. The informant again?*

"What did he mean about the desk and photos?" Kelsey asked.

Sam stood and scanned the desk top. He shook his head. "There are none here," he said, "at least not now." He stepped over Henry and held out a hand. "Let's go." He needed to get one step ahead of these guys. Playing catch up was not the way to win.

· · · · ·

Kelsey exited the bar, the sensation of slow motion wrapped around her. The moments it took Sam to retrieve his bag and her purse played out. She accepted her purse and followed Sam.

Let's go, he'd said. Going was all they'd done.

Leave in a hurry. Leave to escape.

An internal click snapped her from slow-motion to full speed. A dash took them across the parking lot to a stand of bushes. *I want to go home.*

But they'd find me. Home didn't guarantee safety. And it would put her family in danger. Branches scraped her, and she raised her arm shielding her face. Ahead of her Sam ploughed a trail through the bushy patch. Headlights raked the area briefly and a car engine died in the night. Lem. Kelsey's stomach flutters quieted. Henry was no longer alone.

Smacked by a wayward branch, she jerked back and paid more attention. She didn't need a good smacking. Or did she? Eric Chappell had seen her. That man chasing Frank had seen her. Heck, they probably printed still-photos from the surveillance tapes. They'd found her hotel and her rental car. She'd wandered Willy-Nilly through their world. Oh yes, they'd find her.

She ducked lower, hugged the purse tighter and followed Sam into a warehouse lot. *My purse holds the proof Frank is my father.* Those documents had upturned HER life. And the documents Frank took? What did they do? Why did he think Sam needed them? And why did the bad guys want them back badly enough to kill? *I'm freaking myself out here.*

She ran full tilt into Sam's back. He'd led them behind a large building and stopped. He lowered his head and listened. Kelsey stood and breathed. At the moment, she was happy to do only that. The ambulance siren wailed closer, died in the parking lot at Henry's. Night stillness magnified the slam of doors, the raised voices and the clatter of gurney wheels.

Sam backed against the wall and, wrapping an arm around her shoulders, drew her to him. His strong one-arm hug absorbed worry, questions and all. His face rested against her hair, and his breath huffed warmly against her ear. "He'll be fine." His ragged whisper reassured her. "Just fine."

Kelsey shoved the purse aside, tucked an arm around his middle and leaned on him. Lean on me. Good song. Good idea. Sam shifted, settling her against him and locking his hands behind her waist. She let her face rest on his shoulder, snuggled her cheek against his neck.

He smells good. Heck, he did more than smell good. Not only his physical support held her, but also the most amazing sense of security wrapped around her.

How long?

How long what?

How long since someone hugged me, really hugged as if they cared, as if they supported me, would keep me safe?

Her throat tightened. Her eyes itched. Every fiber in her body ached with sorrow. *Not since Mom died.* She drew a ragged breath, fighting threatening sobs. *Way too long. I've stood on my own way too long. And I just figured this out now?* But why now? Why here? She sniffed. *It's Sam.* He projected caring, security and competency. Three excellent attributes to have on your side if you are fleeing bad guys. She almost laughed. Even if it was only temporary, she'd take it.

"They'll be searching," Sam whispered. "Looking for clues." But he didn't move. "We should probably put distance between us and them." Was that reluctance she heard in his voice? Did he feel the connection? She snuggled. He hugged harder. Oh yes, he felt it too. Go figure.

Sam cleared his throat.

Time's up. She pulled back.

His hands unlocked, letting her go. *I don't want to go away from Sam.* Kelsey squared her shoulders and banished the childish plea. It was time to go and, she took a good look at Sam, there were questions she needed answered. Questions that had nothing to do with her father and their shared history. Those would have to wait until someone wasn't trying to kill her. Right now, she and Sam needed to get to safety.

CHAPTER NINE

"Where are we going?" Kelsey asked. It was the first thing she'd said in almost three hours. And in those three hours she'd followed him through bushes, climbed over fences and snuck from shadow to shadow as they fled the dock area.

Sam shook off his weariness and peered into the late night fog cloaking Brunswick Street. He pulled Kelsey into one more shaded spot and surveyed the way ahead. A car passed on a close-by street, a barking and distant dog stopped its ruckus on a yelp. No lights shone from the windows in the building. No people hurried along the street. Safe.

The light in the main entry to his condo building cut a swath on the sidewalk. Without his remote control, he couldn't turn it off. But the control was back in the car. They'd use the dimly lit side door.

He took Kelsey's hand in his, curling his fingers around her cold ones. She hadn't complained or hesitated ever since they'd listened to the medics take Henry away. He'd been aroused by her closeness and prompted to protect her.

He couldn't explain it, but somehow the connection between them had shifted in those quiet moments. He knew it as surely as he knew she was tired and confused and that she would soon demand answers. He sighed. How many could he give her?

"Come on." He led the way to the side door, along the back hall and up the narrow fire stairs. They zigzagged up the back of the old church converted to condos. Kelsey stayed close, and his awareness of her drummed through him.

At the top floor, he opened the door to his unit. Kelsey watched but said nothing. Inside, no lights flashed a warning and no beeps sounded an alert. Sam punched buttons on the security system.

Kelsey shivered in the entry. Her arms once again trapped her purse against her middle. A fuzzy halo of fine hair capped her head.

Dark circles accented her eyes. "Where are we?"

Sam dropped his bag. "My place."

"Your place?" She stepped further into the main room. "Nice," she said. "Does it have a HOT shower?"

Sam laughed. After all they'd been through, her first priority was a shower? More likely it was the heat she wanted. "Yes." He pointed to the circular staircase at the back of the apartment. "Up there. Look for towels in the cabinet. Go ahead if you like." While she showered he'd figure out exactly what he could tell her. For the life of him, in spite of the long walk, he hadn't reached any decisions.

Without a word she crossed the hardwood floor and climbed toward the loft bedroom and bath. Sam eyed her short skirt and dropped his gaze to her legs. For a tiny woman, she sure had long ones. "I'll lay out a T-shirt and sweats for you," he said and licked his lips. *Just like Little Red Riding Hood's wolf.*

She looked over the rail, framed by the old beams in the vaulted ceiling. "Thanks," she said her smile fleeting. And she was gone.

Sam went to his den and tapped his keyboards. Leaving them to wake, he went and provided the promised clothing. At the top of the loft stairs he paused and let the sound of running water soothe him. *That shower is washing over her and she's naked.* Desire flashed through him, taking him by surprise. He squashed it and ran down the stairs. Inappropriate.

In the den he accessed his voice mails and watched the sequences running on multiple screens. The Trojan program he and Jeff had managed to install on *The Mingle's* business computers tracked all their activity.

Clicking through his codes, Sam accessed his voice mail. Greg's voice boomed off the machine. "It's a girl." Sam smiled, trying to picture his taciturn buddy with a baby girl. "Call me later," Greg added and the message was done. Sam glanced at the clock. Congratulatory calls could wait until morning. He was happy for Greg, but the timing sucked. With a new baby, Greg didn't need to be drawn into the investigation. Sam would have to call Parker. Later.

He sat back in his chair, sighed and watched the screen through hooded eyes. Staying awake was getting harder. He yawned. Frank's theft ramped up the odds. The men he was chasing were every bit as ruthless as he'd feared, and they were way too technically savvy for his liking. He crossed his arms and tucked in his fingers. And there was that little issue of a mole. Whatever he told Parker might be overheard, passed on, compromising everything.

Henry hadn't given up any information on Frank, but that meant the goons didn't get what they wanted. What would they do next? Oh crap. They'd be looking for Vi. And he'd sent Vi off to her sister's place in Dartmouth.

Sam groaned. Not safe for her or the sister. He needed to get both women into hiding. Sam yawned and his brain stalled. *Lem, Kelsey, Eric, the little man with the glasses.* How did he handle it all? The heat dissipated the damp cold he'd dragged in with him and he dozed.

"Hey."

Sam jerked upright, swinging the chair around. Kelsey stood there in sweats with rolled up cuffs and a T-shirt reaching her knees. A towel wrapped her head like a turban. The effect should have been comical. For Sam it was anything but. An urge to tuck her in somewhere and keep her safe washed over him. Oh brother. He was slipping into a danger area, falling for a woman while on the case. At least this time the woman was on the right side of the law. It was an improvement over his old habits.

"Do you have a hair dryer?"

Sam ran a hand over his clipped hair. "No."

She looked.

He looked.

Neither moved.

"You could turn on the oven and let the heat dry your hair." He'd seen his mother do that once years ago.

Her smile lit her face and laughter danced in her eyes. "Are you suggesting I should put my head in the oven?" The hot shower must have restored her good humor. "That's not very nice."

"I suppose not," he said and crossed the room. He pulled the towel off. "But let's try it anyway. I can fluff it or comb it or something." He combed the air with one hand. "My sister used to do this thing with her fingers."

You're going to run your fingers through her hair? It was both the best and the worst idea he'd had all day.

· · · · ·

Kelsey looked at Sam's fingers and licked her lips. Her scalp tingled and the sensation slid deep into her belly. She wanted him to touch her, to caress her head, her skin. She'd felt like that with that cowboy back in her rodeo days. *And look how that turned out.* Not a good plan.

She wrapped both hands around the towel to keep them off his face. "I can handle it," she said, "but thanks for the offer." She tugged the towel, extracting it from his grip.

He let it go and his hand fell to his side. He flipped his fingers against his jeans in a way she'd seen him do earlier.

"Any time," he said and his husky voice caused her tingle to escalate. "I'd love to run my hands through your hair," his gaze caressed her body, "among other things." He stepped back and headed across the great room. "Come on," he said. "I'll turn the oven on."

It was like he'd turned off the heat. Kelsey chewed her upper lip. Was he flirting or serious? She shook her head, loosening her wet hair. Holding it off her face, she strolled after him. Probably just flirting. They were in the middle of. ... What were they in the middle of? She sighed and sat on the stool Sam provided in front of the oven.

"I think now is a good time for you to tell me what is going on," she said, shifting so her back was to Sam.

"We're being chased by bad guys."

She blew out, moving a strand of hair out of her vision line. "Do you think? That's the worst non-answer I've ever heard. And raising three younger brothers, I heard a lot." She bent at the waist and flipped her hair over. "Expand please," she said from under the curtain of hair. "Add details, reasons, names, purposes. Anything to help make sense of the running." It was a tactic that worked with her brothers.

The silence lasted so long she wasn't sure he would answer. She flipped her hair back, letting it cascade over her shoulders, and swiveled on the stool. "Well," she said, "I'm waiting."

"Are you sure you're not a school teacher?" he asked.

She raised an eyebrow and skewered him with a look. "Stop evading."

Sam grinned. "You do the interrogation thing pretty good." He held up his hands in surrender as she rose off the stool.

"Short version. I was a police officer with a cross border task force. Currently I work with a special security firm under contract to that task force. There are people of interest connected to *The Mingle and Touchdown.* I was there observing. Bartending is a useful cover."

"Undercover?"

"More or less. Mostly just watching rather than infiltrating."

"How does," she hesitated, "Frank fit?"

"It's a someone-who-knows-someone-who-knows-someone situation. Once we'd isolated Eric Chappell as a person of interest, we needed a closer look. I got a roundabout introduction to Frank. At the same time, the police cooperated by picking up the bartender on some minor warrants. An introduction and a fake connection to Frank, and I stepped into the job."

"So you're not Frank's nephew?"

"No," he said and grinned. "Will you let me help dry your hair now?"

There he went again with the innuendos. She shook her head. "What does the little man with the bloody nose have to do with Frank? And that file Frank stole, what is it? It seems to me they want the file AND Frank."

Sam looked away, his face scrunched. "Damn, I can't believe I forgot that file. It's proof that the operation I'm tracking exists and is tied to *The Mingle and Touchdown.*"

Kelsey pulled her hair back and held it with one hand. She shut the oven door, turned off the heat and joined Sam. "What operation and what was in the file?"

"It's a group giving new identifications to criminals. That file holds an entire life," Sam said. "Every document and record a person needs to prove who they are and what they've done. And since Frank says the man in there has been dead for over a decade, the current history is fiction, believable fiction, but fiction."

"What does it mean?" she asked.

"It means that someone was about to buy a new identity. Given the airline reservations to Winnipeg, he was relocating." He paced the small space between sofa and coffee table. "It takes time and money to create a file like that. And the airline ticket suggests it's already been assigned to someone. No wonder they are upset with the theft."

"And the little man?" she asked again.

Sam shook his head. "We'll have to figure that one out. Vi, said he was the accountant. But since it's not bookkeeping they're doing on the third floor, I'll go with forger, graphic wiz or some other type that can create authentic-looking documents."

"Those men saw us with Frank," she said. "They probably have me on tape from that night. They nearly killed Henry." Any warmth she'd garnered from the shower and her time in front of the oven fled and cold swept over her skin. "They want me too, don't they?"

Sam faced her. "Yes." His voice was low but this time not husky. There was no mistaking how serious he was. "And if they find out you are Frank's daughter, if they realize how much you mean to him, they'll want you even more."

Kelsey's knees buckled. Sam caught her and helped her to the sofa. She sat, looked up at him. "What do we do?" Her brained stalled.

Sam sat and pulled her against him, finally running his fingers through her hair. Reassuring. Caring. She put her head on his shoulder.

"First thing in the morning," Sam said and brushed his lips over her hair, "we call my contact and get you to a safe house."

Safe sounded good. Leaving Sam, not so good. "What will you do?"

His humph rumbled in his chest. "I'll go catch the bad guys."

Silly as it was, safety wrapped around her. Sam would get the bad guys and she'd be safe. Frank would be safe. It might or might not be true but, after running and hiding, she was tired and she wanted to believe the best. She held on to the concept that the truth would look more manageable in daylight.

"But right now," Sam said. "We both need sleep. You can take the bed."

She edged back from the security of Sam's support. That bed upstairs was huge. "You come too," she said. "I won't sleep a wink if I'm alone. I'll worry." She attempted a laugh. "Worrying in the middle of the night is something I'm good at." She put her elbows on her knees. "I became an expert when my brothers started going out at night."

Oh god, will I ever see them again?

"I won't end up in some witness protection program, will I?" she asked. "I'll get to go home to my family, back to my life?"

"No problem," Sam said. Standing, he extended a hand. She took it and allowed him to pull her to her feet. "I'll get you home again."

She wished she could believe him.

. . . . .

Sam tugged. Kelsey took the step needed to be body to body with him. He ran his thumb over her hand. Soft feminine skin. The contact ricocheted up his arm, across his chest and ended in his groin. "I'm not so sure that's a good idea," he said and grinned. Heat played in the minuscule space between them. "You are one hot lady and I can't help my reactions."

She gave his hand a shake. "Thanks for the compliment," she said, "but I think you'll be a gentleman about it." She looked at the loft. "That's a king sized bed, right."

He nodded.

"Back in the day," she said, "when there were not enough beds, and it was a family's turn to keep the school teacher, she slept with the hired man."

Sam raised his eyebrows. "I'll bet that was an education for one of them."

She swatted him. "The bed would have a rolled blanket in the middle to prevent contact and often a curtain was hung dividing the bed visually as well."

"A wet blanket effect."

She tipped her head. "I suppose it was." She dropped his hand and squared her shoulders. "If those folks could do it in a double bed and behave, we can manage in a king sized one."

A logical argument. And he certainly enjoyed having her close even if the resulting reactions left him slightly uncomfortable. "I can handle it," he said, "if you can. No changing your mind in the middle of the night."

"No chance," she said, "and it's already the middle of the night." She plucked at the sweatshirt. "Thanks for the clothes," she said, "they're warm." A grin crossed her face. "Not so attractive, but warm."

Sam's blood rose. "You look just fine," he said, his voice gruff. With her hair tumbled around her face and that trusting look in her eyes, she'd look great in anything, or nothing. "We'll find you new clothes tomorrow," he said making a promise he could keep.

"Thanks." Kelsey turned away. "Let's get some sleep. Tomorrow will be here too soon."

The night, the quiet in the apartment and camaraderie blended, forming a cloak-like barrier against the outside world. Sam glanced toward his office. Outside were bad guys and danger, problems to be solved. In here there were only the two of them. Morning would be soon enough to chase the information in that file. A few hours wouldn't make any difference. "I'll shut down the office," he said, "and be right up."

He scanned the screens and saw that all his planted tracking programs were keeping tabs on computers he shouldn't be able to access. He picked up his secure phone and started texting.

Are you getting all this?

Yes. Hit pay dirt. Warrant tomorrow?

Will do what I can.

A thumbs-up symbol popped onto the screen.

Jeff Brown—a man of few words but unlimited technical skills—a man who made a good business contact. Sam switched on the security system, turned out the light and headed upstairs.

He found Kelsey folding the bedding, arranging the comforter and the blanket each in half lengthwise making pseudo sleeping bags. One opened on her side, the other on his. The folded edges met in the middle. Effective contact prevention.

She raised her eyes, acknowledging Sam's arrival, and removed her earrings. The casual personal gestured socked his gut. She turned away and put them on the bedside table and added her phone. *Like we did this every night.* He adjusted his slacks to accommodate his body's reaction. It might be a very long night.

Weird familiarity permeated the room. In tandem, they sat on the bed, turned and slid into the half-cocoons made by the folded bedding.

He lay on his back, hands behind his head. Now what? *Turn out the lights.* "Are you ready," he said and glanced over to see her mimicking his position.

There was a slight hitch in her breath as she answered. "Ready for what?"

He chuckled, happy that she was feeling the moment too. "For the lights to go out."

"Oh, sure, of course."

He reached up and hit the switch on the wall over the bed,

turning off both side lamps. Darkness settled around them. Moonlight slanted in the transom window above the bed and disappeared into the vaulted room below. Her body created fascinating hills and valleys beneath the covers. His imagination tried to go under there with her and he reeled it in.

He felt her yawn and couldn't suppress his responding one. He tucked the blanket against his chest with his arms on top. "Have you heard from your brother?" he asked, remembering the pregnancy conversation.

"Brock," she said. "He sent a text. They're not pregnant."

"You sound close to Brock," he said. "How about the others?"

"Not like Brock," she said. "I raised them after Mom died and the younger two still see me more as a parent." Silence hung in the darkness punctuated with her breathing.

His eyes closed, heavy with sleep but his brain kept working. "Big job, raising three boys. What about your dad?"

Her sigh whispered over him. "He was there," she said, "but never quite sure how to handle us." She yawned again. "Somebody had to look after them," she said. "I didn't mind."

The covers shifted, and she rolled toward him. He matched her roll, could barely see her face but felt her warmth.

"How about you?" she asked. "Do you have siblings?"

"Jade," he said, "she's younger by three years.

"Nice," Kelsey said, "I always wanted a sister." She laughed. "And here I am with three very rowdy brothers who create laundry by the basketful." Another yawn overtook her. "But they can all cook, do laundry and sew on a button," she said. "My job is done."

And yet Brock called her with problems. Her job wasn't as finished as she might think. "I love my little sister but I'd have liked the brothers," he said. "Little sisters can be a real pain."

She sniffed. "You should hear what my brothers say about older sisters." She yawned, snuggled in her blanket and closed her eyes. "Sorry," she whispered. "I'm so tired."

"No problem," he said. "Sleep well." Sam waited while her body relaxed and her breathing slowed. She seemed to carry that "someone has to do it" attitude into everything. She'd run, helped, followed and never complained. He could spend time with a woman like her.

Convinced she was asleep he extended his hand and rested it on her arm. And as resilient as she appeared to be, she didn't hesitate to ask when she needed him close. He closed his eyes. She deserved to be safe and headed home to her brothers. He'd make sure it happened and keep his own reactions out of the mix. Heat and exhaustion combined in a potent cocktail. He slid into sleep in the middle of his to-do list.

· · · · ·

Frank shuffled around the corner onto Brunswick Street, scrutinizing the sidewalks and cars without lifting his head. Hope Cottage and a hot brunch were his next stop. Years ago, his only meals often came from the Hope Kitchen and in later years he regularly donated pots of stew. This time he had cash but it would only go so far. More importantly, he held no intention of frequenting only one place. Staying on the move meant safety.

He grabbed the front of the oversized raincoat he'd picked up at the secondhand store and pulled in and out, creating a cooling breeze to dispel the heat building inside it. He would have liked a toque. But in the warm weather, it would mark him rather than hide him. The men looking for him could be anywhere. Thank goodness he had years of practice in hiding. He kept his head lowered but his senses on the alert. At least these days he was sober.

He stopped at the door. "Hey, Bernie, what's up?"

"Frank, are you cooking today?" Bernie frowned. "What's with the get-up?"

Frank shrugged. "Little problem," he said. "Appreciate you not mentioning I've been here."

"No problem. But there was someone here already. Two fellows, big guys. Said they worked with you at *The Mingle*?"

Frank skittered a look around. "What did you tell them?"

Bernie grinned. "What do you think? Not a damn thing."

"Good. Okay, I'm gonna grab a bite, if that's okay?"

"Sure, go on in." He opened the door, and Frank headed inside to the food counter.

He found a seat in a far corner and kept his back to the wall. Half his stew was gone when she walked into the line of one of his visual sweeps. He stilled his spoon and lifted his chin. The turban and earth-toned poncho didn't disguise her walk. He'd recognize her anywhere. "Vi," he said softly, and studied his sandwich as she took the seat across from him. He tilted his head asking an unspoken question.

She nodded, started on her stew. "Knew I'd find you if I looked in all the right places."

Vi was probably the only person that did know his haunts. Back when they both started on the sobriety route, they'd hung out together visiting places in a jumbled rotation. Back then, he'd been excessively suspicious of just about everything. Time to resurrect that vigilance. If Vi was here, something had gone wrong.

He froze with his sandwich in front of his mouth. Katya? Sam? Had they been caught? His gut rebelled, and he gave up his room inspections and really looked at her. He'd never told her anything about Katya past or present. "Is Sam safe?"

She looked up, surprised. "Of course, and that gal Kelsey, she's with him. Lem said so."

Frank's shoulders eased and he swallowed hard. His little girl was safe. She was with Sam, and Sam could keep her safe. *Trust it.* But that brief encounter with her was not enough. He wanted more. *Her safety comes first.*

Why else would Vi be here?

"Several things happened," she said. "Someone put a listening device in both our apartments. Sam found them and we moved out. But most important, Henry's in the hospital."

A shiver skittered over Frank. Shoving his hands under the table, he rubbed at the knuckles on his left hand. *Get a grip. Stay calm. Don't attract attention.* Frank's stew sat heavy in his stomach, and the sweat built up under the coat, turned clammy.

"What happened?"

"Two men beat the crap out of him. Rotten cowards." She clenched her fist. "Sam found him and Lem went and took care of him. He'll live."

Frank closed his eyes and braced his forearms on the table. His chest seized, and it was all he could do to force in a breath. They'd found his oldest friend. *My fault. Should never have gone there.* He'd gotten slack. He'd believed the doctors. *No one is watching you, Mr. Binks.* He shouldn't have listened to them.

"It's not anyone's fault," Vi said and touched his hand.

What if she's next? Frank lifted his gaze. He met hers, looked past her and nodded. Damn, he couldn't lose her either. He gave his head a shake. *You took that file. That's what's wrong. They are ordinary bad guys. You can outwit ordinary bad guys.*

But who could he trust? Sam? Lem? Urgency snaked up his spine. He and Vi needed to go immediately. Keep moving. First dictate of evasion.

"The oak tree," he said and pushed back his chair. She nodded. She'd meet him there. In the past, they never left a place together. Good time to start that again.

Frank shuffled away, placed his dishes in the bins and without looking around, headed for the street. As much as he wanted to run, staying incognito required stealth and care. Frank looked right and shuffled off to the left, his back curled and his heart heavy. Ordinary or not, those guys wouldn't give up.

· · · · ·

Sam jerked awake. His heart pounded in rhythm with an ungodly noise resonating through the condo. He pushed to sit and got caught on the covers. What the heck? The alarm insisted he attend to it. He tore at the blanket, managed a sitting position and glanced at the clock. He'd slept way too long.

"What's wrong?"

He froze at the female voice and turned to look. *Kelsey*. The day before rushed into his memory.

"What is that?" She rubbed her forehead. "And can you please make it stop."

He stood. "Computer alarms." He used the railing for leverage and swung down the circular stairs three at a time. He should have put in that fireman's pole Greg suggested. At the bottom he broke into a run headed for the office.

What triggered the system? Intruders? Hackers? He slapped on the light, threw himself into the chair and scanned the screens. Codes flashed on the secondary screen. *Damn, someone is hacking me.* He hit keys and punched in codes to block the takeover. A delete program came up. *They're trying to erase my hard drive.* He typed faster, looking from keys to screen and back.

He booted the intruder. Before they could re-establish contact, he signed off and cut the power. He sprawled in the chair and ran a hand over his face. That was too close for comfort. He took a deep breath. He'd stopped them, but how much damage was done? They must have found his planted program and traced it back. Whoever they used for their computers was damn good. No one had ever been able to do that to one of his programs before.

"What happened?"

Sam swiveled. Kelsey stood in the door, her hair in disarray and her eyes sleepy. If he didn't know better, he'd think she'd been kissed hard and left wanting. "Hackers," he said.

"Who would want to hack you?" she asked.

He chuckled. "The people I hacked first," he said. "Guess they didn't want me getting their secrets." Damn, but he wanted their information. He'd downloaded and printed accounting documents, but he needed daily records, transactions and emails. And with Greg busy, he needed somebody to help decipher it all.

Kelsey yawned and stretched. An enticing sight. "Huh," she said and raised an eyebrow. "Probably serves you right."

He sighed and left the chair. "I suppose tit-for-tat exists in some worlds. But remember, I'm the good guy and they're the bad guys and I have to catch them somehow."

"So you have a wiretap order or whatever it's called?"

Damn those TV detective shows. He shrugged. No answer was the best defense.

"I need coffee," he said. "You want some?"

She perked up. "Thank goodness you said coffee and not tea. I am so sick of tea."

It was the first time he'd seen her look petulant and he laughed. "I hear you. One of the big differences between east and west is the tea and coffee choice. Come on, I have just the java for the morning after."

"After what?" She poked him has he passed her. "Escaping from bad guys? Running to avoid the police?"

"You had to bring that up," he said. "Ah well. We still need coffee." He glanced back at the office. "And then I need to boot up without an internet connection and check for damage."

The aroma tickled Kelsey's nose. *Ah, coffee, glorious coffee.* She wrapped her hands around a gigantic mug of the stuff and followed Sam back to his office. She eyed him head to toe. Easy to look at. Taking up residence in a corner chair, she tucked up her feet and sipped.

Sam slugged back a mouthful of coffee and set down the mug, unplugged his router and started the computer. His equipment was impressive, obviously not a typical home set-up. But who ran

hacking programs from home? He'd said he was with law
enforcement, but that shouldn't give him leave to stick his nose into
other computers. Shouldn't that be done at whatever police
department handled that stuff?

Sam muttered and typed, typed and muttered. His concentration
seemed total. She let her gaze drift around the room. The back wall
sported a large prairie scene. Looked like home. The solid wood
desk stretched along one wall. A photo of Sam with two young men
and a girl hung on the wall above a wedding shot of one of those
men.

Piles of books and papers covered the desk top, each set stacked
and aligned. In spite of the volume of material, it was neat. Nice.
Order worked for her. She sighed, realized her coffee cup was empty
and stood. She crossed to the desk and looked in Sam's mug. Also
empty.

"I'll get more coffee," she said and took his mug. A photo in a
standing frame caught her eye. She leaned in. A couple stood with
two children in a typical family grouping. The teenage boy looked
like the dad in stature but his features favored the mother. A quick
glance at Sam confirmed her suspicion. As an adult he looked even
more like his parents. She grinned. He seemed to have kept the best
of them.

Crossing to the kitchen, she stumbled on an unrolling cuff. She
put the mugs on the counter and squatted to roll it back up. The
coffee kick-started her brain and memories assailed her. Goose
bumps pricked her back. Henry? How was he? And where was
Frank?

Last night, when Sam suggested a safe house, it sounded like a
darn good option. This morning she didn't think so. Sitting and
waiting irritated her. She preferred to be kept in the loop and to have
a say in things. She'd stay. She ran her tongue over her teeth. She
needed a clean-up, especially if she needed to convince Sam to let
her hang around.

Upstairs she found her purse where she'd left it in the bathroom,
and managed a make-shift toilette. With hair wrestled into a
ponytail, teeth brushed and a whisk of gloss on her lips she felt
human again. She went downstairs and retrieved two coffees on her
way to the office.

Half way across the living room, she grinned. Sam wouldn't like her decision one little bit. Too bad. Whatever happened, she was staying with him until they found Frank. Frank had been so happy to see her. Her grin faded taking her good mood with it. Obviously, letting her go wasn't his choice. So why had he? And why had her mother taken her? Niggling questions.

Sam's voice rolled over her and she paused in the office doorway. He was on the phone.

"We need to speed things up, Nat. They found me in their computers. They'll go underground. I think I have them believing they deleted my hard drive. That should buy us some time." He stopped to listen.

"Look Nat, yes, you're my contact, but can you decipher accounting documents? Huh. I didn't think so. We don't know who else we can trust, so I'm not handing them over to anyone but Greg." He paused, then lunged forward in his seat. "He what? Took a week off. I thought he was only gone for a couple of days. Okay, okay. Let me think about it." He hung up.

Accounting documents? Kelsey smiled. She had an in. "I can help," she said and crossed the room and handed him his coffee.

He looked up at her and inhaled over the top of his mug. "You already have." He sighed. "But I need more than coffee. I need someone who understands accounting records and has the patience to comb through them looking for obscure connections."

"Seriously," she said and turned to rest her butt against the desk so she could watch his face. "I am an accountant. I've been told I'm pretty darn good at it. I'm the one who gets assigned the snarled messes. And I think by now you can trust me." She leaned toward him, looked directly into his chocolate brown eyes and dropped her voice a tone. "After all, we just spent the night together and I didn't smother you in your sleep."

Sam choked on his coffee. She pounded his back as he coughed. At least she'd got his attention.

CHAPTER TEN

Sam banished the vision of Kelsey, pillows and his bedroom and finished his coughing. He'd done the background check. He knew she was an accountant. He flipped his attention to the stack of documents he'd printed during his overnight marathon a few days ago. Someone had to go through them.

"Well," he said, "I don't think we'd get approval." Who was he kidding? There was no thinking about it. If Natalie found out that Kelsey was there, that she was Frank's daughter, she'd veto having her help. She'd also have a security team on the way right now to take her into protective custody.

Why didn't you tell Natalie about Kelsey? He took in Kelsey's tawny hair, gray-green eyes and her now glossy lips. His innards squirmed. Parker didn't ask. If it was Greg, he'd remind Sam of his old habit of falling for a woman in the case. *And have you?*

Kelsey raised her mug and sipped. Her eyes sparkled above the rim as if she was still laughing. Oh crap. He was in trouble. *Yes, I've fallen for her.* And even though that was all the more reason to put her in protective custody, he was going to let her stay.

He stood almost knocking her off her perch. "Let's see what you can do," he said and scooped up the stack of accounts before he could change his mind. "You can work on the dining room table." He stopped in the doorway and looked back. "Come on, then." She was beside him in a heartbeat, his heartbeat, the rapid one that occurred when she got too close.

"I think they're in date order," he said, tapping a finger on the stack of documents. "We're trying to see where they are laundering money."

She nodded.

"We need transactions that connect the network of visible and shell companies. Also look for any purchases of materials that could be used for documents. Probably need to look at the payroll. That file Frank has tells us they are good at what they do. If the dead guy holds Frank's job, how do they record Frank? Which one is listed on the payroll? Have fun," he added. "I'll go see if anyone has found Frank." He patted her shoulder and left.

His phone rang as he entered the office.

"They got Dr. Zinck." Natalie Parker's tight announcement rocked him.

"WHAT? How, when?"

"We arranged a transfer," she said. "When they opened the van at the other end, Zinck and the guard were dead. The man who'd closed and locked the van is missing. No record of who he is. He wore a uniform and produced proper identification. But he doesn't exist."

"How the hell could that happen?"

Silence.

"Worst fears realized," she said, her voice tight. "They have an inside contact. A damn good one."

They got Zinck, they could get a witness in protection. A vivid visual of Kelsey with her neck slashed flashed across his inner screens. *Thank God I kept her with me.*

"Has anyone found Frank?" he asked.

"Ah-hmm. No."

"I think we should keep it that way. Don't want him to end up like Dr. Zinck. He's safer outside the police department."

"You may be right," Parker said.

She agreed? That was a step forward.

"Can you find him?" she asked.

"Not sure. Do you have security on Henry at the hospital?"

"Not possible," she said, "Lem checked Henry out this morning."

"What the hell is that old coot up to?" *Lem took Henry to Caleb's Cove.*

"A care-giving re-play?" Parker asked. "Caleb's Cove recovery system?"

"No need to advertise that," Sam said. "What about Vi?"

"For her safety, we were watching, but since she left her sister's place, no sign of her. The sister isn't cooperating. Said Vi asked her not to talk to the police." She sighed. "She might talk to you. Meanwhile, I'll try Lem. If I can't reach him, I'll get Jackson. He can always seem to find Lem."

He'd forgotten Parker knew most of the people in Caleb's Cove better than he did. "Right," Sam said. "Keep me in the loop. I'm almost done here. I'll follow up with Vi's sister."

"And if you get me justification to search *The Mingle* ," Parker said, "I'll get a warrant." She rang off.

Kelsey smothered a cheer. She was staying. With Sam. Working to find Frank. She laid out the financial statements, general ledgers and payroll list and started scanning. Cross-referencing entries, she tracked back and forth through the documents. Using *The Mingle and Touchdown* as the key player, she began building a network of suppliers and accounts payable, referencing the total amounts spent against recorded income.

The books balanced. Income came from *The Mingle* and from a place called the *Soup and Sandwich Lunch Bar*. Output included the usual grocery purchases, cleaning costs and bar expenses. Supplies were purchased for the usual items — toilet paper, dish soap, paper towels. In the winter there were snow removal costs and in the summer, parking lot maintenance. Heating, electrical, water and sewer costs made the lists, as did phone services including internet costs.

And payroll? She scanned the list of employees. Frank wasn't there. What was she missing? He rented an apartment and bought food, he must be paid somehow. She counted employees and closed her eyes, revisiting her night at *The Mingle*. Something else was off. The listed employee numbers far exceeded her estimates of necessary staff, even considering that some might work part-time.

Padded. They were working the numbers. What else was out of proportion? She pulled the list of utility payments and counted. Way too many electrical and heating accounts on that list. One extra account might be for the lunch counter on Hollis Street, but the others? She needed the actual bills with location addresses. Shenanigans lurked below the obvious numbers, she was sure of it. And the dead man WAS on the payroll. For a dead man, he was making a nice chunk of change. Time to talk to Sam.

• • • • •

Music on the radio gave way to news as Sam and Jeff, working in their respective locations, connected through secure internet links, finished the retrieval and repair mission. The tracking program was reinstated and extra links established. Sam hit the final key. With a touch of luck, the hacker on the other end would miss the new infiltration. But it was a chess game and it wasn't over yet.

Goose bumps chased awareness up his back. He looked over his shoulder, already knowing that Kelsey was standing behind him. She held a sheaf of papers and displayed a frown.

"Sam, I think you're right about the money laundering. On the surface they balance, but the income on Tuesdays is as high as on Saturdays. That's unusual for a restaurant. And," she paused, "on their payroll documents, Frank Binks does NOT exist."

"What? But he gets money, he pays his bills." Sam swiveled and took the pages she held out. Even without an accounting background, he could have noticed that. He should have looked at those documents sooner. *And when did you have time?*

"Exactly," Kelsey said. "And they have a huge amount of staff for the size of the place." She pointed at the payroll lists in his hands. "You worked there. Can you confirm if all the staff is actually still active?"

Sam scanned the list. Jen and Vi were on the list as were a few others he'd worked with. Some names he didn't recognize at all. "We need to find out who is paying Frank."

Police are investigating after a body was found near Africville Park early this morning.

Sam held up a finger and turned his attention to the announcement.

A woman taking an early morning jog along Africville Road noticed a body in the ditch and called police, said a Halifax Regional Police spokesperson.

Officers went to the scene and found the body of a man in the ditch on Africville Road, halfway between the church and the container terminal.

Police have blocked off Africville Road near Barrington Street to the Windsor Street Exchange. No traffic is allowed through. There's no estimate on when the road will reopen.

In another story in the same area, the owner of Henry's Bar and Pool Hall, was found severely beaten last night. It is not known if the two incidents are related.

Police are asking anyone who may have seen any suspicious

activity in the area of Africville Road last evening or this morning to call them or Crime Stoppers.

Kelsey, her eyes wide, put a hand on Sam's shoulder. Her fingers dug into him. "Frank?"

Sam covered her hand with his. "Could be anyone," he said, even though he'd thought about Frank too. The announcer moved to the weather, and Sam clicked the radio link shut. "But we'll find out."

Natalie's phone shunted him directly to her voicemail. She was on the line. Cursing under his breath, he disconnected and wracked his brain for another contact to call. There was an informant. That much he believed. Calling just anyone wasn't an option.

The burner phone he'd activated earlier rang. He punched in, activating the speaker mode, and signaling Kelsey to be quiet. "Logan here."

"Did you hear the news?"

"Yes. Have they identified the victim?"

"Not Frank," Natalie said.

Kelsey's fingers relaxed the grip on his shoulder.

Thank goodness.

"But the man worked with him. He's been a dishwasher at *The Mingle* for the past few weeks."

"Tell me he was hit by a car."

"Ah-hmm. Don't we wish? Knife," she said succinctly, "slashed throat just like the others." Sam didn't bother keeping his curses silent.

"And," she added, "they found the murder weapon. There are fingerprints, smudged but they are hoping for a match. But we know how long that'll take." She paused and the silence stretched too long.

Sam's gut contracted. "And?" he asked, knowing the rest wasn't good news.

"It's a cook's knife." Again the long pause that signaled unwanted news. "It came from the set Frank keeps locked in the kitchen at *The Mingle*."

Beside him, Kelsey gasped and the rest of the accounting papers hit the floor.

How many days had it been since Frank stole that file? He closed his eyes and sorted day from night. "Frank has not been back to *The Mingle* for three days."

"Can you prove that?" Parker asked. "The manager there says

Frank stopped by two days ago."

"Eric Chappell is lying."

"Ah-hmmm," Parker said. "But here's the thing. Mr. Chappell didn't see Frank. He heard it from the dishwasher, the one who is now dead. Mr. Chappell said he wondered why Frank didn't show up for work. He said Frank's history was no secret, but he'd never believed Frank would actually kill someone. Unless like the last time, he was drunk."

Kelsey's hand still rested on Sam's shoulder. Her fingers bit into his flesh again. Sam covered her fingers with his. She was hearing about Frank's history for the first time. Damn, Frank should be the one to tell her. Too late.

"Chappell is full of it. He knows darn well why Frank didn't show up, and it has him worried. This is a frame-up."

Parker's sigh whooshed through the phone. "YOU may think that, but we have to follow procedures." He noted that she put the knowledge all on him. Didn't she believe Frank was innocent of murder?

Parker launched into her official spiel. "And until we can discredit Eric Chappell, or get Frank to provide an alibi, the homicide investigators will proceed with what they have. They are looking for Frank." Her frustration colored her tones. "Do you have anything you can give me, Sam? Anything that will prove Frank was somewhere else last night. Or information that points to another suspect."

"There is that file, the one with the false documents on a dead man. We have the equipment and security cameras that Frank saw upstairs at *The Mingle*."

"All hearsay at the moment. You don't have Frank or the file, do you?"

Put like that, it sounded weak even to him. Kelsey did see Frank leave that night. She'd seen the man chasing him. But that proved nothing. He was close to having enough data to get the warrants. But not close enough. And he had nothing to suggest that Eric's crew was involved in the attack on Henry, or the death of the dishwasher or in a frame-up of Frank.

"I'll get proof," Sam said. "You get me all the reports from Henry's attack and the murder."

"Ah-hmm. You don't want much, do you? If I go digging

around, homicide is going to want to know why our special task force is interested. They'll want reciprocal information and our efforts to keep our suspicions and leads out of the general stream will fail. Dr. Zink is already dead. What else will happen?" She didn't need to go further.

Sam sighed. He'd have to do this the hard way. "Get what you can," he said. "Attend briefings, eavesdrop – whatever you can do without officially requesting information."

"I can do that." She didn't object to him calling the shots. He was, after all, the co-lead on the investigation. She was just his contact. "What is your next move?"

"Find Frank," Sam said. "Find his alibi. That false ID business has gone on long enough. These bastards are helping criminals and probably terrorists. I'll get us enough proof to get a warrant to search that damn building."

· · · · ·

Kelsey's head reeled. Any sense of normalcy she'd achieved overnight scattered in front of Parker's information. Her father used to drink. Henry said so. *But kill someone? With a knife?* She wanted to puke.

"Sam." She stopped to swallow. "Did Frank kill someone before?"

Sam stood and wrapped her in a hug. "No. The man didn't die."

She pressed her face against Sam's chest and absorbed that statement. Oh crap. "But he did knife someone?"

"Yes." She heard the regret in Sam's voice. She was sure it wasn't for Frank, so it must be for her. *Nice of him to care.*

"Do you know what happened?"

"Only the official report. You need to ask Frank about it."

If we ever find him. "And the official report?"

"Frank was drinking on the job. His boss called him on it. Frank whirled around from carving a roast, and the boss ended up on the floor with the knife in him. No one saw exactly what happened. Between Frank's alcoholic state and the boss's shock, the report was muddled. But Frank did eighteen months for assault."

Frank, my father, was an alcoholic with a temper. And once an alcoholic, always an alcoholic. Or so she'd heard. Was Frank drinking again? Did her appearance in his life push him into an old state of mind? "Do you think Frank. . .?"

Sam slid his hands to her shoulders and held her back far enough to look her in the face. "No. Don't even go there. This is a frame-up, pure and simple." Sam pushed a stray hair off her face and kissed her forehead. His simple gestures restored her equilibrium.

"Now go get ready," he said. "We need to find Frank."

She grasped Sam's wrists, kept them anchored on her shoulders. "What happens if we can't?"

He met her gaze. "There are several possible outcomes," he said. "It's up to us to achieve the best one."

That didn't really answer the question. She put one hand on his cheek, gazed into his eyes. He wasn't going to elaborate. "The best one? Promise?"

He nodded.

She turned away. At the door, she looked back. "How can we find him? You said you didn't know where to look."

Sam held up the phone. "I'll start with Vi's sister. And then see if Henry can suggest places." He gave her a wink. "Don't worry. We'll find him."

Kelsey headed to the loft. He'd better be right.

Five minutes later, she descended the stairs, with her repacked purse and her own clothes. The new flat shoes worked. The short skirt didn't. "I need a pair of jeans," she said and joined Sam by the door.

Sam tilted his head and took a good look. "Shame to cover up those great legs, but I get it. We'll find somewhere to get clothes more suited."

The unreality of it hit her. Nervous laughter bubbled. "What IS considered appropriate attire for tracking suspects? Or finding a missing father?"

Sam's brief smile didn't dispel the serious set to his face. He locked the double-sided deadbolt. "Let's go."

They headed into the narrow stairwell. What did you find out?" she asked Sam's back.

"Lil's not picking up her calls. It makes me nervous. It's a cell and Vi said Lil is obsessive about answering it." He opened the exit door, leaned out and looked in all directions. "All clear."

A cold finger traced down Kelsey's back. Two options for Lil occurred to her. "Do you think the police took her in for questioning, looking for Vi to help them find Frank?"

Sam's hand was warm against her back. He guided her toward the back of the building. "Could be," he answered. He didn't mention any other option.

Diagonally across the parking area behind the building, a black half-ton was backed into a spot under a tree. Double rear wheels and running boards. It looked like home to her. Sam unlocked the passenger door.

"Need a hand?" he asked, standing back.

She eyed the height. Even with the running board, the skirt was going to be a problem. "Just keep your eyes to yourself," she said. "I grew up climbing into these things." She grabbed the doorframe, put one foot on the running board and lifted, swinging her butt into the seat. Settling, she sighed and looked around. There was even a Stetson hanging in the back. "Now this is a vehicle. But whose car did we ditch in Dartmouth?"

Sam slammed his door. "Agency vehicle registered to Sam Edwards for the duration."

The truck's engine roared to life. He adjusted the GPS, punched in an address and shifted gear. Backing out, he navigated the parking lot and nosed into the street.

"First stop. Lil's house in Dartmouth."

Lil's place. Kelsey buckled up. *Will Lil be there? Or is she with the police?* The shiver returned. The other option left her cold.

CHAPTER ELEVEN

Sam followed the GPS directions and turned off Portland Street, made a right at the second corner and drove slowly past house after house, the truck thumping over poorly repaired asphalt. Yard layouts changed, bush types changed and here and there fully mature trees loomed, but the split entry homes with single drive-under garages were all the same.

"There. Number twenty-nine." Kelsey pointed to a house on the right side of the street. A Toyota RAV4 sat nose-to-nose with the garage door. A chestnut tree shaded the picture window, but even with open curtains, there was no sign of activity.

"That's the one," he said. "Looks like she's home." He pulled out his phone and dialed her number. No answer, no machine and no action through the windows. A familiar precognition of trouble crept over his skin. Sam pulled around the curve and stopped by the curb. No residents lingered in the yards, no kids played on the street. Putting the truck back in gear, he made a U-turn and headed back toward Lil's.

A mid-sized school bus perched in the driveway next to Lil's. It blocked the line of vision to Lil's house. *If we can't see in, no one can see us either*. He parked, taking advantage of the school bus, and leaned over, reaching behind the passenger seat. He extracted vinyl gloves and stuffed them in his waist band. "Wait here," he said and, leaving the engine running, exited the vehicle. He strolled face forward and head up. The I-belong-here attitude made for good cover. He ducked around Lil's vehicle, took the three steps to the front walk in a bound, scooted around an overgrown bush and rang the doorbell. He opened the storm door as if anticipating an invitation to enter.

No invitation came. With his hand pulled into his sleeve, he tried the latch and the main door opened easily. "Lil," he called. "I'm here." *Always act as if you have a right to be there.* "Hey, Lil," he called again and waited.

He heard nothing and stepped inside, closing the door behind him. The split entry provided stairs going up and down. He scanned the upper level taking in the railing along the living room and the kitchen visible through a doorway. Below him, a narrow hall gave access to three open doors. Which way to go first?

A glug and the whoosh of water alerted him to a functioning washing machine. He pulled the gloves from his waistband, snapped them on and eased down the steps. No point in leaving fingerprints. If Lil was doing laundry, she might not have heard him.

"Lil," he called again, "Vi sent me." No response. He followed the washing sounds and found a laundry room, but no Lil. A quick inspection through the other doorways and into a bathroom produced no results.

Treading lightly, he took the stairs to the upper level two at a time and stood at the kitchen entrance. Bright sunlight flooded the room, and odors suggestive of stew or soup floated in the air. To his left a large dining table stood between patio doors and the living room arch. He took two steps forward. A pair of feet crossed his line of vision.

"Bloody hell."

His gaze swept the area, wall to wall and from cabinets to patio door. No pantry, no heavy curtains, no hiding spots. He crossed to the feet, sighed and knelt on one knee beside the body. For a long moment he supported his head on one hand. Poor woman. Sighing again, he inspected the body. The woman, although shorter, bore a strong family resemblance to Vi. Lil.

Her left fingers jutted crookedly. Just like Henry's. A fresh cut scored one cheek. At least her throat wasn't slit. Sam reached for her carotid. She was warm, but unlike Henry, she didn't have a pulse. It looked like they'd tortured her for information. Whether they got it or not, he had no way of finding out. And there was nothing he could do for her now.

He raised his head. Not a sound in the house except the now spinning washing machine.

Washer still running, warm body. This is a fresh kill.

He stood and edged away, gooseflesh crawling over his back. He backed into the corner between sink and stove and lifted the lid on a huge pot. Hamburger stew. His stomach growled reminding him they'd skipped breakfast and it was already well after lunch time. He turned off the burner. *A lot of stew for one woman.* Why was she making so much?

He let his gaze drift over the counters. What might give him information? The drawer to the right of the stove drew his attention. He pulled it open and found the ubiquitous address book, take-out food flyers and miscellaneous paper scraps. He closed the drawer and caught sight of a calendar pinned to the wall between upper and lower cabinets.

No notations for today. About to turn away, he saw the note for the next day. "Stew/Hope Cottage." What was Hope Cottage? And where was it? Sam flipped his fingers against his leg.

Notify the police. The idea came and went. He needed to find Frank before the bad guys. Good thing he didn't mind breaking protocols. Crap. Protocols. He reached out and turned the stew burner back on to low. *Can't be changing the crime scene.*

They'd traced Vi's sister and risked killing her in broad daylight. *Their behavior is escalating. They want Frank. Now.* Sam walked the hall and found only neatly made beds, tidy rooms and lace curtains. Back in the center of the house, he paused. Did they want Frank? The file and notebook? Or was this a no-one-messes-with-us-and-lives-to-talk-about scenario.

I should go. Sam stopped and pulled out his cell. He entered Hope Cottage in the search engine. *Leave no lead un-investigated.* He skimmed the information. The cottage served lunch and early supper to the homeless and volunteer groups provided stew. Frank had been homeless for years. On the run, he might go back there.

He sighed and found a bath towel. Protocols went out the window. He turned off the heat and wrapped the stew pot in the towel. Waste not, want not. If he delivered stew, the folks at Hope Cottage might be willing to answer questions. At the door he turned and leaned in.

"See you, Lil. I'll get this delivered," he hollered and closed the door. Whistling for effect, he headed to the truck, regret for Lil's death deep in his gut. *I need to stop those guys before someone else dies. But how?*

· · · · ·

Kelsey tapped her hands on her thighs and scanned the street.

Three days ago, she'd have insisted on accompanying Sam, but the happenings of those three days changed her mind. This time, she was still absorbing her father's history. Was that the reason her mother left and never told Kelsey? But Frank cried when he met her and put himself in danger to keep her safe. It felt disloyal to even suspect he might have killed a man.

Sam headed toward her. He seemed to be whistling. That was a good sign. What was he carrying? He reached the truck. Balancing the bundle in one arm, he swung open the door. The towel fell back revealing a large double-handled pot.

"Here," he said. "Can you grab this?" He leaned and extended the bundle toward her. The aroma washed over her, prodding her appetite.

"What's with the pot?"

Sam looked both ways before swinging into the truck. "Long story." He clicked his seat belt closed. He was no longer whistling. A muscle in his jaw twitched.

Not so good.

Sam closed his eyes and tipped his head back. She waited. For three heart beats he appeared to be breathing deeply.

Give him a moment.

He sat up, reached for the ignition and started the truck. "Did you see anyone, any action or any movement while I was gone?" His terse, staccato words pelted her.

She shivered. "It's deserted." She'd have welcomed a distraction. The heat from the pot soaked through the towel, warming her legs. "Sam, update please?"

Sam grunted, shoulder-checked, and put the truck into gear. Retracing their route, he headed to Portland Street. His silence boosted her apprehension. What was he not telling her?

Sam waited at the main intersection for a break in the traffic, drumming his fingers on the steering wheel. Tension swelled in the cab, pushing on the windows and skittering over her skin.

On the far side of the busy main drag, the access road was bracketed by brick pylons and partial walls. Bastions of the neighborhood? Roofs intersected tree tops and larger buildings climbed the slope at the back and stuck out above the tree line. Evidence that people lived there, worked there. But no cars waited at that side of the intersection No people walked the sidewalk.

Sam pulled into a gap in the flow of impersonal cars on the main road. A block ahead, the light turned red and he stopped. He leaned forward, stretched his shoulders and sat back. "Lil isn't talking. They got to her."

"You mean she's. . ." The words piled into her throat, a traffic jam of ideas.

Sam's sigh finished the sentence for her. Apparently he didn't want to give voice to the words either. "I need to get the police in there." The light changed, releasing the stream of cars. "Bad enough I left a crime scene unattended."

Another attack. Another body. Kelsey closed her eyes. *I'm an accountant from Bolton, Alberta. Small town. Never any murders. I'm not equipped for murders. How did I end up in the middle of this?*

She hugged the pot, leaned forward and all but curled up. *I can't do this. I just can't do this.* Her thoughts veered from death and focused instead on her bare legs pressing against the pot's warmth. She needed a diversion from Lil's death. *I should never have started with the skirts.* She chortled, a cry that transformed to a laugh. As if short skirts had anything to do with the trouble they were in. *But I do need jeans.*

"Are you okay?" Sam asked. "What's funny?"

"Nothing," she said, "everything." He nodded.

She slanted a look at him, his right hand on top of the wheel, his left fingers hooked in the bottom. How did he stay so calm? Her gaze slid to his face, took in the tight cords in his neck, the firmly pressed lips and the furrow between his eyes. *He's not that calm.*

Murder. It rumbled through her. *Don't go there.*

"We need a clothing store," she said. Anything to divert her thoughts.

Sam's head jerked toward her. He glanced at her legs. "Right," he said and flipped on the turn signal. "I saw a Thrift Store at the mall by the bridge. We can stop there."

Kelsey forced her attention to the world around them. *So many trees. Everything crowded and canopied.* She sure could use the familiar vista of open fields that stretched from Calgary toward the foothills. She longed for the open skies at home. Longed to hear Brock tell a silly joke and David brag about his latest bull ride. She sighed. At least wearing denim she'd be more like herself. Jeans were going to feel so good.

· · · · ·

The Dartmouth Shopping Centre sprawled at the junction of busy roads only blocks from the old bridge. Choosing a stall closest to an exit, Sam backed in and shut off the motor. Sun glinted off parked cars and puffs of breeze stirred detritus left by shoppers. The only movement on the view was a single shopper trudging toward the buildings. Traffic hummed along bordering streets. *So freaking normal.*

You're the only one who saw the body.

Me and the killer.

He stretched his neck to the left and then the right, engaging tense muscles. He reached for his phone. It was time someone else found out.

One ring and, "Parker here."

Lil shouldn't be dead. "Didn't you have a team watching Vi's sister?"

"She never went anywhere. They pulled them this morning. Not my choice."

"Great, just bloody great." Sam slumped. "You need to get someone over there," he said. Would Parker pick up on the resignation in his voice? "Make sure they get into the house." He jabbed his thumb on the off button.

Damn don't they get it that these guys are dangerous?

Prickles staggered across his shoulders and into his hair. *Is the mole calling the shots?* If that were true, danger stalked all of them. He sighed. Either way, Lil was dead.

He opened the truck door, propped one foot on the running board and waited, head deceptively tilted against the headrest. No one paid any attention to them. Satisfied they were alone, he sat up. "Let's go."

Kelsey slid out of the truck, turned back and set the stew pot carefully on the floor. Without comment, she retrieved her purse and looped the strap over her shoulder.

She'd been subdued since they left Lil's place. He couldn't blame her. His mood was out-of-body unreal-type low. His gut gave him insistent signals unrelated to hunger. He'd left the scene of two crimes, the second more serious than the first. He was in big trouble. *You're doing what you need to do. You're no good to anyone if you are in custody.* But was it really justified? Were they as out of time as he suspected?

Kelsey stared straight ahead and plodded toward the buildings. He dropped an arm around her shoulders and offered a hug. She leaned into him. *Body contact, comforting for both of us.* He was way past thinking about getting her to safety. He liked having her with him. He could keep her as safe as needed. *Don't tempt fate with that statement.* He ignored his conscience.

The thrift store doors slapped shut behind them, and Sam inspected the racks of clothing, inhaled the mix of stale and antiseptic and absorbed the heavy silence. Kelsey headed for the rack marked JEANS and started riffling through them. Sam stood to one side of the door, his awareness split between the cavernous space inside and the sleepy parking area outside. No cars entered the lot and only two elderly women were shopping in the household goods section. Molecule by molecule his tension dissipated.

MEN'S JACKETS. He should change too. Misdirection worked for appearance as well as location. He strolled across the front, checking the parking area through the large plate glass windows. He turned down an aisle and reached the jackets. He'd found the extra large section when Kelsey arrived beside him with a stack of clothing over her arm.

She lifted her chin toward the dressing rooms near the front entrance. "I'm going to try these on."

He nodded and watched until she was in a cubicle with the door closed. Shifting his attention back to the rack, he spied a sturdy denim jacket. Slipping off his windbreaker and tossing it on top of the rack, he tried on the denim jacket and shifted his shoulders. It would do the trick.

The bell over the front door jangled and Sam froze, turning his full attention to the sound. A middle-aged man in sweatshirt and kakis shuffled toward Men's Jeans. No threat. Sam went back to checking the denim jacket for pockets.

He counted four outer pockets and one inner one. Picking up his windbreaker, he turned toward the till. A scream rose and echoed in the store. Adrenalin flooded him, and he whipped around.

"Get out!" The shout reverberated off the warehouse-style rafters.

Kelsey.

Sam ran full-out toward the dressing rooms.

Kelsey inspected the shirt she'd picked up and took off her own well-worn top. She slipped an arm into one sleeve and lifted to get the new-to-her one over her head. No sooner was the garment covering her face than a click sounded beside her and the air shifted in the tiny room.

But I locked the door.

The top was tight, and she was stuck. A body brushed against her, the door clicked shut and a *shh-tok* filled the space.

That sound. I've heard it before. With Brock. It's a knife opening.

"Don't move." The voice was soft, low, meant only for her hearing. Chills slithered across her skin. She jerked and her elbow connected with flesh.

The intruder grunted. "Watch it. And get that shirt on. We're leaving. Together." Cold steel brushed her belly. She sucked it in. Looking down from under the shirt, and ignoring the blade at her middle, she focused on the man's feet. *I have to get out of here.*

Her brain decided and her body followed without conscious agreement. She whipped the top up and off and tucked her body away from the blade. Using her maximum force, she slammed the hand holding the top down on the man's wrist, twisted the top around the blade and shoved. She punctuated the action with a scream.

"Get out!" She hollered, praying that Sam was close. Not pausing, she stabbed her fingers toward the man's eyes, and hit glasses.

Damn that didn't work.

She curled her fingers around the frames and ripped the glasses off his face, dragging the nail of her forefinger over his skin at the same time. Dropping the glasses, she wedged against the wall, turned her hips and tucked up one leg. Channeling her fear and anger, she kicked out, hitting him just above the gut. *Thank goodness my brothers taught me to fight.*

His breath whooshed out.

"Bitch."

At least that's what she figured he said as he thudded against the door. The cheap lock set gave under the force, and he lurched backwards out of the cubicle.

She glanced into the store. Sam charged toward her. The man gained his footing, one hand to his face in a gesture she'd seen before.

"You'll pay for that." His snarl swirled around her.

He launched toward Kelsey, was jerked back.

Sam held him by the collar. "Oh, no you don't." He shoved hard and flung the man off to the left where he stumbled into a rack of ladies' slips and hit the floor in a tangle of red, white and pink.

Fists raised and pulse pounding in her ears Kelsey launched after the man. *I'm going to beat the snot out of this guy.*

· · · · ·

Sam caught Kelsey around the middle stopping her in mid-flight. "Easy, slugger." He ran a hand up her bare back and reached a narrow band of fabric. She was wearing only a bra.

There was no time to comment. The man gained his footing, pulled a red and black lace slip off his head and bunched his fists. Sam shoved Kelsey behind him and prepared to do battle. Before he could engage the man, someone brushed past and stepped between them. The gray-haired lady from the front counter came to the rescue.

"Don't move." She hefted a baseball bat, rested it on her shoulder and took the stance. "Give me a reason to smack you. How dare you come in here and harass the customers."

Sam grinned. Obviously it wasn't her first time up to bat.

Without looking back she continued. "You okay, dear?"

Kelsey edged around Sam. With one hand at her throat, she looked from the man to the bat and back. Visibly swallowing, she nodded. As if realizing the woman couldn't see her, Kelsey answered. "I'm fine."

Sam put a hand on her shoulder, and his body reacted to the touch of skin on skin. "You might want to find a shirt," he said. A fierce half-naked woman could sure turn a guy on.

Kelsey blushed. "I'll do that."

"Can you hold him?" Sam asked the clerk. The woman nodded and gave the bat a partial swing. "I got him. Call the police."

The man who'd just entered the store came running over. "I'll help," he said.

Sam pulled out his phone. He eyed the man. What was going on?

He wasn't buying the guy as a pervert. Attacking a woman in broad daylight in a visible location wasn't a random act. The man was targeting Kelsey. His assessment of escalating danger was smack on.

He could call Parker.

He snapped a photo of the guy and dialed 911.

"I'm at the Thrift Store in the Dartmouth Shopping Centre," he said. "A woman was attacked in the dressing rooms. The manager has him cornered with a baseball bat. Send help." And before the operator could ask a question he cut the call.

Fully clothed in jeans, shirt and jacket, her purse once again slung over her shoulder, Kelsey joined him. Sam scanned her toe to head and met her gaze. She raised both eyebrows and, blowing out forcibly, pushed back straggles of hair.

Wide eyes, pale lips – she's shook up.

He glanced at the price tag on his jacket and ripped it off, calculated what Kelsey's garments might have cost and doubled it. He pulled two twenties out of his wallet. "We can't stay," he said to the manager.

"The police will want a report," the woman said, maintaining a stance that would have put Casey Jones to shame. "Missy here should file charges."

"Can't be helped," Sam said. "I'll put forty dollars on the till. That should cover what we're taking."

"No problem. That's lots. Sure you don't want change?" This woman was not easily flustered.

A siren wailed somewhere up the street. "No time." Sam grabbed Kelsey's hand and raced for the door. "Thanks," he shouted over his shoulder and headed for the truck. By the time the police car pulled up, he had the key in the ignition. Driving slowly, he gawked as if he had no idea why the police were there.

The officers sat in the car, one of them calling in their status. They'd be in the store in a moment. Sam turned out of the lot and headed toward the Macdonald Bridge. Another crime scene deserted.

Kelsey stirred, shifted her feet around the pot now settled on the floor. "I know that man," she said.

Sam jerked. "What?"

Her arms, still clutching the purse, twitched. "He's the man who chased Frank." He barely heard her over the truck engine and road noise.

What was she saying? He glanced at the traffic and changed lanes to navigate the triangle of streets. Chased Frank? He shot her a glance. "Are you sure?"

She nodded. "He's the one who chased Frank."

Sam's stomach soured. He pulled over, stopped and reached for his cell phone. *You left two, make that three, crime scenes and you're worried about distracted driving.*

Kelsey turned her wide eyes toward him. She clenched and unclenched her fingers on the purse. "He had a knife."

"HAD a KNIFE?" Sam's hand froze at the edge of his pocket. What was she saying? He left the phone and put his hand on her arm. "He what? When?"

She pressed a hand against her middle. "He pointed it here." She closed her eyes and, if it was possible, paled further. "But I took it."

Sam drummed his fingers on his thigh. Good Lord, she took the knife away. She socked him and charged out ready to beat on him. Her adrenalin levels must have been through the roof. He focused on her pale cheeks and droopy eyes. Aftershock.

That explained her disjointed answers. He reached in the back and pulled out a blanket, tucked it around her and found a bottle of water.

"Here, drink." He held it to her lips. She opened her mouth and he poured in a bit. A trickle missed and ran down her chin. She pulled her arm from under the blanket and wiped. Her chin dry, she took the bottle and tipped it up, chugging the water.

What else should he do? Candy? Or was it diabetics that needed candy? Never mind. It might help. Reaching over her, Sam opened the glove compartment and pushed papers aside. A bag of gummy bears lurked in the bottom. He pulled them out, peeled a couple off the glued-together mass and held them out. "Eat these."

Kelsey lowered the water bottle and took the candy. She popped it into her mouth and chewed. Sam drummed his fingers again. He needed more details before he called Parker. Resting an arm on the steering wheel and one along the seats, he checked out the rear window. He finished his inspection and leaned toward her, his arm extended so he could touch her hair.

"Are you going to be okay?"

She opened her eyes, sighed with her whole body and nodded. "I'm fine."

*What am I saying? This isn't the time to pretend I'm okay.
Someone just tried to kill me. Well, kidnap me.*

"Can you tell me what happened?" Sam's voice drifted into her
thoughts.

She shivered. *No, I don't want to think about it.* She told him
anyway, detail by detail.

"You tossed his glasses and gave him the scratch?"

She nodded.

"And the knife? Where did it go?"

She released her grip on the purse. "I put it in here." She
unzipped, shoved her hand in and pulled out a shirt. The sharp edge
pressed against her palm. She shifted her grip and held it toward
him.

He took it, flipped back the corner and exposed the knife.

Kelsey's inners quailed, her skin shrank and her heart hit double
time. She could have been killed.

"And I lied," she said through clenched teeth. "I am NOT fine. I
am cold and tired. I am scared and confused. I'm a frigging
accountant, somebody's sister, a church-going-ladies-aid girl and
I've had it. On top of that, damn it, I'm bloody hungry." She
pounded her fist on her leg. "I want out of this mess. NOW."

Sam rested the backs of his hands against the bottom of the
steering wheel and cradled the knife in its wrapping. *Slashed throats.
Knifed bodies. A knife like this one could do all that.* Not one like
this, but this actual knife could have killed people. And there it sat.
In his hands. In his truck. He cleared his throat. Still could not speak.
He swallowed hard, and his neck muscles relaxed. She had every
right to want out.

"You are either gutsy or crazy," he said, feeling the tremor in his
voice ripple through him. He shouldn't be this emotional. But he
was. And there it sat. He bent to the side and put the knife under his
seat. That man must have followed them from Lil's house. He'd
been inattentive, relying on cursory visual inspections. Nausea roiled
in his gut. *And I missed him.*

But what about Kelsey? She wanted out. But out meant she could
end up somewhere they'd find her. Even Parker's safe houses might
not protect her if the mole started digging around. If only they could

pinpoint the mole.

"I could use coffee," Kelsey said. "Black and hot would be really good." She swiped both hands over her face. "That might help." Hands tucked under her chin, she tilted her face toward him. "Then we can decide what to do."

Was she reneging? "Are you sure?"

She nodded. "I understand I can't safely walk away, even if every nerve in my body is screaming at me to do so."

She's staying.

Sam grinned. Coffee he could do. He combed his memory. *Right. The Tim's is just a block from the bridge.* He merged back into the traffic, made a left and another left and came up behind the Tim Hortons. No drive-through.

"I'll be right back," he said. Coffee sounded like a damn fine idea. His stomach added a note. Okay, he'd get food too. The smell of that stew was making him crazy. He stood by the truck for long minutes, checking the area, noting the vehicles. The man might not have been alone. Someone might still be following them.

He entered the shop, checked the few patrons and found them absorbed in conversations or newspapers. *From here on I need to be as paranoid as Frank.* He pointed to two croissants with egg salad middles and placed his order. *Frank. Where is he?* Back in the truck he handed over Kelsey's coffee and a croissant and settled his drink in the cup holder.

"You said he wanted you to go with him?"

She held the brown cup with both hands, inhaled and sipped. "Yes." The word came out on a deep exhale and an aura of contentment settled around her. "Thanks. I needed this."

Sam opened the egg salad sandwich and ate. The food eased his stomach and the hot coffee realigned his fractured nerves. Would the food and coffee do the same for Kelsey?

"Kelsey, I'd let you leave right now if I believed you'd be safe."

"I know. I know. But right now I am wishing I'd stayed in Alberta."

Sam grunted. "Hindsight," he said, knowing she'd fill in the rest.

"So you'll hang in here?" he asked. "For now?"

"Yes."

Sam nodded slightly, pleased. "Let's figure this out," he said. "The first question is why did the man want to kidnap you? It only makes sense if he knows Frank is your father. But how would they figure it out? Would your public records," he said around a mouthful of food, "connect you to Frank?"

"I don't think so." She dabbed the corner of her mouth with a napkin. "The birth certificate I always use shows my parents as Will and Susan Maxwell. I found the old one, the one with Frank as my father, in a box from the attic. I checked into the adoption and name change process. The old certificate should have been returned or destroyed." She retrieved her cup. "I don't think there's any other way to figure it out. It was a private adoption."

Sam huffed. "Unless someone had mentioned it."

She turned, her croissant held in front of her, and gave him a deer-in-the headlights stare.

"Who knew?" he asked.

"Brock," she said. "He's the only one back home who knows Frank's name."

"Henry," he said. "He knows you're Frank's daughter."

"Frank," Kelsey added, her voice shaking, "and you. That's everyone."

"Call Brock," Sam said. "Ask him if anyone has called or if he mentioned it to anyone."

"But he wouldn't."

"Just do it."

CHAPTER TWELVE

Frank perched on the oak stump, elbows on his knees and his hands dangling. Someone cut the tree down since his last visit. He missed the shade, regretted the passing of one more landmark. Repairs and paint rejuvenated the fence behind him. The building at the back of the asphalt parking area showed similar upgrades. It was the one decent place he could get a room for cash, no questions asked. If Theodore was still in charge.

Vi came around the corner and he stood, watching her cross the asphalt. She hugged him and they stood for a moment, drawing strength the way they used to. Safety in numbers. She stepped back and took in the changes.

"Is Theo still there?"

Frank shrugged. "Might as well find out." He led the way to the building.

The door no longer creaked to announce their arrival, but a tinny bell replaced it. The man seated behind the desk stood, looked over and grinned.

"Frank. As I live and breathe boy, it that you?" He came around the end of the counter and pumped Frank's hand.

Theo. Thank goodness.

Not waiting for the obvious answer, Theo hugged Vi. "Girl, you are looking younger by the day." He stepped back and shook his head. "What on earth brings you two back here? I heard you'd moved up in the world, with apartments and jobs and all that fancy life."

Frank grinned. Things changed but people didn't. It was a good thing too. "Good to see you too, Theo. We need a room. The usual system?"

Theo looked to the door leading to his quarters. "Well, the missus says I have to register folks. But who's to say what name is what?" He winked.

"You have a missus?" Vi laughed. "Well I'll be damned."

Theo blushed and, raising his eyebrows, threw out his hands. He returned to the alcove behind the counter and turned a notebook toward them. Then he spread one hand over the open page. "No, it's not right. I owe ya one, Frank." He reached back and plucked a key off the board.

"What about the missus?" Vi asked.

Theo grinned. "She's the reason I owe Frank one," he said. "He sent her along here one year when she needed help. I guess I helped 'cause she's still here."

"Roxanne?" Frank asked. "You married Roxanne?"

Theo laughed and patted his belly. "Darn tootin'," he said. "Next to you, she's the best cook I ever met. And," he winked again, "she's a darn sight better lookin'."

Frank preceded Vi up the narrow staircase to a room at the back of the house. Theo gave them what over the years they'd jokingly called the bridal suite. It was the only one with a private bathroom.

Heat met them at the door. Dust motes floated in air stirred by their entry. Sun filtered through surprisingly clean windows. Roxanne had certainly influenced the place for the better. Frank shut the door, took off the oppressive coat and perched on the edge of the bed leaving the lone chair for Vi.

He leaned forward and the envelope in his waistband crunched. He pulled it out. Damn thing. He snorted. The expression that came to mind was more trouble than it's worth. But until Sam saw it, he had no idea of its worth.

Vi pulled off her turban and ran her fingers through hair that came to life in a curly mass around her head. She removed her poncho and folded it. With a sigh, she sank on the chair and put her head back.

Frank waited.

After a time, she lifted her head, squared her body on the chair and clasped her hands in front of her. "Story time, Frank."

Frank drew a deep breath. He could tell her what happened. But why it all happened, he still wasn't sure. "It started with Lem," he said.

She leaned forward. "Lem Ritcey? From billiards night at Henry's?"

"That's him. His nephew-in-law is, was a policeman. Now he does special security work. He needed to find someone working at *The Mingle and Touchdown*."

"Why on earth for?"

"Girl, if you are going to interrupt every two sentences, I'll never get this story out."

Vi sank her fingers into her curls and sighed. "Sorry, I'll be quiet." She looked up and laughed. "Just like old times."

Frank chuckled, started again and walked her through everything that had happened.

He finished and picked up the envelope. "They want what's in here." *And they want me dead.* "They want it badly enough to kill for it."

Vi took the envelope and dumped the contents on the bed. She examined several of the documents and picked up the resume. "But everything on here, except the name, could be you. Even the bloody home address." Her gaze met his. "How?"

Frank sighed. "Remember how in the beginning, they paid us in cash. Back when I washed dishes and you bussed the tables?"

"Yes."

"Do they still pay you in cash?"

She shook her head. "No way. I want to be on the record for Canada Pension Plan and Old Age Security." She examined his face. "You mean you still get cash?"

Frank nodded. "Yes. And since they own the apartment building, they take my rent money in cash once a month. The utilities aren't in my name."

"You mean, you are not on record. Like no address, no bank. . ."

Frank hung his head. "That's about it. No income tax records, no medical coverage. Nada." He'd been a fool, so blinded by his worry of watchers and God knows what. And the fact that he'd never considered he'd live long enough to worry about pensions.

The set-up suited him. Unfortunately, it suited his employer even better. They'd used him to create a file they'd sell to the highest bidder. And some criminal would get off scot-free. He lifted his head and held up a hand, one finger pointed. "Don't say it. I've screwed up." And now, the only thing he wanted was to live and spend time with his daughter. If it was too late, he couldn't blame anyone but himself.

· · · · ·

Kelsey did need to call Brock. Her phone had been off for ages. Wrapping her croissant in the napkin, she slid it onto the dash. She rummaged in her purse and found the phone. Text alerts flashed at her. She scanned the messages. Brock was trying to reach her.

"Trying to reach you."

"Where are you?"

"CALL ME BACK. URGENT"

Her gut sank. Was it just Brock being dramatic? She pushed the speed dial. No, Brock didn't do dramatic.

"Where the hell have you been?" Brock's voice boomed into the truck. "Where are you?"

"Busy," she said. "In Halifax."

"You coulda left the phone on. Or sent me a text. Some guy called me. He asked how to reach you. He said you flew home days ago. I've been frantic."

"Well, I'm still here. He must have been mistaken." *Or misleading you to get information.*

Don't be silly.

It isn't silly, it's real.

Danger, danger. Oh, God, her head was going to explode.

Brock's deep breath whistled through the phone. "Okay. Are you okay?"

"Yes," she said. *Unless the bad guys catch me.*

"When ARE you coming home?"

"I'm not sure." She paused. "Listen, who called? And what did you tell him?"

"Kel, you're not telling me everything. I can sense it."

"Brock, I'll tell you everything later. Right now I need you to tell me about that call."

"Damn, Kelsey. . ..."

She summoned her best big sister intonation "Brock."

"He didn't give a name. The call was blocked. I told him I didn't know where you were."

"Did he ask about why I was away? Or about my name?"

Brock hesitated. "Your name?"

"My other name."

"No."

"Did you tell anyone about what we found in that box?"

"Not a soul," Brock said. "On my honor as a cowboy. I told no one."

Relieved, Kelsey looked at Sam. At least one source was secure.

"Thanks, Brock. Look, don't tell anyone, no matter who they say they are. Not friends, not family, not the police. . ."

"THE POLICE! Oh god, you're in trouble aren't you?"

"Brock, it's okay. I'm with, um, a law enforcement guy. I'll be fine. You can talk to Sam Logan. If he calls, he'll say he has three things. Okay?" She didn't wait for an answer. "You watch your back. Love you." And she disconnected.

Cold fear and hot anger mashed in her chest. She rested her hand on her leg, her fingers still wrapped around the phone. "They called my home. Sam, I need the rest of the details. It's the least you can do."

He nodded. "Yes. You're right." He flipped his fingers against his leg. "I'm just not sure where to start."

"At the beginning?"

He crossed his arms and took a deep breath.

His phone chirped and relief crossed his face. "I have to take this," he said.

She opened her mouth to protest.

He held up one hand, answered the phone with the other.

"It's Parker."

Kelsey clamped her mouth closed and glared. He was not getting out of an explanation.

· · · · ·

"Logan here," he said.

"I'm surprised you're still answering your phone." Parker's tight tones did not bode well.

"We had an incident at the Dartmouth Thrift Store," he said.

"And who is WE?" she asked.

He swore silently. He'd forgotten she didn't know about Kelsey. "I have someone with me," he said. He needed to find the best way to put this.

"And might that be one Kelsey Maxwell?" she asked, sarcasm lacing her tones.

How did she find out? "Ah, yes."

"The same Kelsey Maxwell from Bolton, Alberta who was born Katya Binks and is the daughter of Frank, a person of interest, a possible suspect and a missing man?"

"How did you find out?" he blurted.

Her very audible puff of breath curled through the phone. "Homicide got a package in the mail. Old photos. Did you know people actually used to write on the back of their pictures?"

A rhetorical question. He didn't answer.

"Mr. Logan," she said, her voice icy. "What else are you not telling me?"

Mr. Logan? Wow, she's really ticked.

He didn't want to tell her anything she didn't already know. He had no idea who might have access to her phone lines and her information. "Ah, have they been to Lil's house yet?"

"Oh yes. You're O for two here, Logan."

"I got you to send someone."

"Listen, Cowboy, this isn't the Wild West and even though you are no longer officially law enforcement, you understand the drill. Travis always said you bent the rules. Well, Mister Logan, one of those bent rules may be shaped like a boomerang. It's come back to smack you."

"Sorry, Parker. It was a need-to-keep moving situation. And even then, someone followed and attacked Kelsey. Actually, it was an attempted snatch."

"And let me guess. You didn't hang around and talk to the police on that one either."

"The manager had the guy in custody. Little guy, missing his glasses, scratch on his face," Sam said. "I'll send you his picture. And you want to hold on to him. He's connected and he wields a knife, if you get my drift."

"Hold on." Rustling sounds told him she was covering the receiver. He still heard her issuing orders to find out about the Thrift Store. Her troops dispatched, she returned to the conversation.

"On top of that, Logan, some taxi driver called in after the appeal from the police. He said he dropped a couple off only blocks from *Henry's Bar and Pool Hall* early that evening. The descriptions match you two."

He should have known that taxi was a risk.

"So Mr. Logan, and Ms. Maxwell, if you're listening," she said, her voice rising, "the boomerang has turned. You are BOTH wanted for questioning in all matters. Get your butt in here, Logan, and straighten this out. OR ELSE. You have two hours before I'm scheduled for a meeting with homicide." She slammed the phone and the crash echoed in the cab of the truck.

· · · · ·

Two hours?

"She didn't leave us much time," Kelsey said.

"No kidding. We have to find Frank."

Before the killers do.

"And we need to secure that file and the book."

Damn Frank for running off with it.

"And we need a warrant for the third floor at *The Mingle*." He needed to get to his computers for that one.

Way too much for one man to do in two hours.

"Is she right?" Kelsey asked. "We'd be safer in the police station?"

"Huh! Tell that to the recently departed Dr. Alan Zinck," he said.

"Right." She furrowed her brow. "The witness who was killed in custody?"

"That's the one," he said. "He was a plastic surgeon who got into gambling debts. They made him pay them off by giving major facial reconstruction to high-paying criminals. He short-circuited and killed someone. Greg nailed him for it last summer."

"How did they get to him, if he was in jail?"

Sam gripped his forehead with thumb and forefinger, massaged his brow and dropped his hand to the wheel. "That's the crux of the problem. They are one step ahead of us every time."

Kelsey chewed her lip. "That inside help you mentioned in the shoe store?"

He nodded. "Has to be. That's why I don't tell Parker any more than I have to. We have no idea how high up the mole is."

He whipped out his phone and started punching buttons. "I can get that data to Parker. She'll have to move fast on it, but it's worth a shot."

He typed furiously, hit send and started again. Finished with the second text, he pocketed the phone and started the truck.

"Who'd you text?" she asked. "You need to keep me informed. You agreed I have a right to know why they want to kidnap me. Remember?"

Sam headed for the bridge. "My Ottawa contact, Jeff Brown.

Computer genius." He grinned. "Even better than me, although I'd never tell him. We work together, and he's linked to my computers. He can get Parker the information she needs for a warrant. And I told Parker the information is on the way."

"And we're headed where?"

"Hope Cottage," he said and tossed the token into the bridge gate. "We'll deliver the stew and ask if Frank has been there."

She raised an eyebrow.

"I remembered where I'd heard the name," Sam said. "I overheard Vi teasing Frank. They used to meet there for lunch, back in the day when he was still living free."

Kelsey shook her head. "You need to go back to the beginning and explain all this so I can make sense of the pieces."

They thumped over a bridge plate. "Okay. The investigation started with Dr. Zinck." He glanced at her and she nodded. "Once they caught him and figured out what he'd been up to, they realized they also needed to eliminate the paper side of the organization."

"Okay – by paper do you mean the fake documents?"

"Exactly." Sam said. "Turns out that organization has been around for a few decades. We're not sure how long, but we found tidbits. There were people who disappeared and were never recorded dead. When criminals using the missing persons' names died, the ruse came to light. They had a good thing going. And a port city is a great place to hide comings and goings. The group branched into the facial makeovers when new facial recognition software became prominent."

"And then they recruited the plastic surgeon, Dr. Zinck." Turned sideways on the seat, she leaned toward him. "Enterprising of them."

He grunted. "The police got very little from Zinck. They'd kept him on a strictly need-to-know basis. But there were some before and after files he'd kept complete with pictures. Enough to get the investigation rolling."

Sam shoulder checked and merged into a line of cars. "Greg formed a special unit and started compiling data. We're under contract to the police. With every man we apprehend, we retrieve another piece of the puzzle. My job, along with the Ottawa man, is to build a picture from the pieces." He grinned, "As an independent finder, we have more leeway for data collection."

"Humph. You mean you hacked where you shouldn't?"

"That's not technically the correct term, but in common vernacular, yes."

"What exactly did you, um, find?"

"A maze of information. Zinck was originally recruited in Toronto, but the markers pointed to Halifax as the hub. We profiled the organization and in the end, we narrowed it to three major companies, or groups of companies."

"Including *The Mingle and Touchdown*?"

"Yes. They are just one company in a group that charts like a twenty-legged octopus."

"I don't understand how Frank got involved in all this."

"Have you heard that premise – six layers of separation?"

"Yes. It supposedly takes six contacts to reach anyone you need."

"That's it. As it was, it only took three to find an insider at *The Mingle*. Greg's wife's uncle knows Frank."

"And Frank was working at *The Mingle*."

Sam inclined his head in agreement.

"And who are Greg, his wife and her uncle?"

"Greg Cunningham. We trained at the Calgary Police Force together. Devon Ritcey is his wife and they have a new baby, Grace. Lem is her uncle and Frank's longtime friend." Sam stopped, reversed the truck and parallel parked. "We're here," he said and turned off the engine. "Hope Cottage."

· · · · ·

"I'll be back," he said and opened his door.

"Hold it." Kelsey put a hand on his arm. "Frank is my father. I have a legitimate reason to look for him. You, on the other hand, might come across as police." She raised an eyebrow and tipped her head. "Don't you think?"

"I hate it when you're right." His smile softened the complaint. "Come on then."

Grinning, she joined him on the sidewalk and stood aside so he could retrieve the stew. "I'll let you carry the pot," she said. "It'll make you look useful."

She pretended to miss the glower he gave her as he got the pot.

They stood side by side for long minutes, looking at the cottage-style building, its fresh paint and two tiny gables. "Nice place," she said.

"Ah huh." He inclined his head to the few men lingering on the lawn. "We missed lunch but it won't be long before supper time."

She nodded. "Guess we should go in." Her nerves skittered under her skin. Frank used to come here for meals. Back in the day, Sam said, when he lived free, a not-so-subtle euphemism for living on the streets. How would these people remember Frank? As a drunk? As a person? She sighed. Possibly they wouldn't remember him at all. She started up the walk. Time to find out.

She hesitated at the door. Did you knock at a soup kitchen? She looked to Sam for an answer, but all he did was shrug his shoulders. She opted for knocking.

After a several minutes, the door opened. "Not time yet," a bald man said. His gaze settled on the pot, sans towel, in Sam's hands. "Ah. Sorry. You've brought us food." He stood back and let them in. Sam held out the pot.

The man took it, but frowned. "Usually it comes cold and in plastic tubs," he said. "We're not set up to return the pots."

"No worries," Sam said and wiped one hand on his jeans. "You can keep it. Lil doesn't need it back."

The man smiled. "Lil. She's one of our regular volunteers." He juggled the pot and extended a hand from under it. "Bernie."

"Hi." Kelsey shook his hand. "I have a question."

"Hang on, let me put this in the kitchen." Bernie turned away.

Kelsey took in the large pass-through window that fronted what appeared to be a gleaming modern kitchen. Off to the left the room opened into an eating area. Everything was neat and tidy.

Bernie returned. "Now, you have a question."

"I'm looking for my father," Kelsey said. "I learned he used to come here."

Bernie's face took on a guarded look. "We don't give out information on our clients."

Kelsey smiled and put a hand on his arm. "I understand. But I'm at a bit of a loss on where to go next. His name is Frank Binks."

The flicker in Bernie's eyes told her he knew Frank.

"My name is Kelsey Maxwell, but I was born Katya Binks," she said and pulled her purse forward. "I have a copy of my original birth certificate, if you'd like to see."

Bernie held up a hand. "No, that's okay. Frank's not a client these days. He's one of our volunteers." He looked at the floor, scrunched his mouth to the side. "But he was in here at noon. Vi joined him." He looked at Kelsey. "I must say, I was surprised to see them come for a meal."

Kelsey's hopes rose. "Do you know where they went, where they might go?"

Bernie shook his head. "Have you tried *The Mingle*" he asked.

It was Kelsey's turn to shake her head. "No luck."

Bernie scratched his chin. "Sorry, that's all I know."

"Thanks," Kelsey said. "It was worth a shot. If he comes in, tell him I'm looking for him, would you?" About to reach for one of her business cards, she caught Sam's slight head-shake.

He took her arm and urged her toward the door.

"What's he been up to?" Bernie called after them. "You're the second person looking for him."

"What?" Sam turned back.

"A little guy and a taller middle aged man were here. They said they needed to find Frank. Something about Frank would be fired if he didn't get back to work."

"When was that?"

"Yesterday before lunch. I mentioned it to Frank. Seemed to shake him up."

"What did you tell the men looking for Frank?"

"Nothing. At that time there was nothing to tell."

"Keep it that way, would you?" Sam said. "We don't want Frank to get hurt."

Bernie cocked an eyebrow at that, but he nodded. "Sure, no problem. Wouldn't have told you guys except for Katya here." He smiled at Kelsey. "You have Frank's eyes. Not too many around with that shade of green."

"Thanks," she said and led the way back to the truck.

She buckled in and stared straight ahead. "Now what?"

Sam pulled his seat belt across this body. "Lem," he said, "he's our next lead."

· · · · ·

Sam pulled out his phone and dialed. It rang through to voice mail. Damn. He tried the house phone in Caleb's Cove. It rang six times, and he slid his finger over the off button ready to disconnect.

"Hello. Lem's phone, Jackson here."

Sam avoided the hang-up. "Jackson. Sam here. Where's Lem?"

"Just up to the Marina, checking his cruiser for tomorrow. He's set up to pick up two packages."

"You mean?" Had Frank contacted Lem?

"Yes, you can stop looking in that direction. We have them covered."

"So you're with Henry?"

"Guard dog, that's me."

"I need to ask him if he told anyone about Frank's newly found relative."

"Hang on." The phone thudded. Sam waited. "No," Jackson said. "But the men who visited him took a photo album off the desk. There were old pictures in it, photos with names and dates on the back."

So that's what the old coot was muttering about. The pictures. The same ones that ended up in the hands of the police.

Sam glanced at his watch. In thirty minutes, every police unit in the city would be put on the alert to pick him up. If he and Kelsey stayed with the truck, they were sitting ducks. Not too many shiny black dual-ies in Halifax.

Lem has a boat, Jackson has skills and Caleb's Cove can be isolated. The thought dropped into his head.

Quickly he ran through the recent events, bringing Jackson up to date. "We need a plan, a sting operation. Talk to Lem. Give it some thought. I'll be in touch. And if you see Greg – tell him too."

"Who's Jackson?" Kelsey asked. "And what is he to the rest of you?"

"Jackson is Devon's big brother, so Greg's brother-in-law and Lem's nephew. He's ex-forces – special ops. Good talent. He's the third partner in the Caleb Cove Security Agency."

"Oh my, your group even has a name." Kelsey crossed her eyes. "I'll never keep all those people straight."

Sam chuckled. "Once you meet them, it'll be easy."

His phone interrupted.

Damn Parker? What does she want now?

He answered. "Did you buy me more time?"

"No. But you need to know what happened at the Thrift Store."

"I know what happened. I was there, remember?"

"Not for the final act. Between when you left and the uniforms arrived, the man got away."

"What?"

"Do you remember another man in the store?"

"Sure. He came and helped the clerk keep watch on the little guy."

"Some help. He was WITH the little guy. You were no sooner out the door than he offered to take over bat duty. When the clerk agreed, he bopped her with it and the two men took off out the back door."

Sam swore. Now there was one irritated killer on the loose. "The clerk?"

"Horrid goose egg on her head. But he didn't cut her throat at least."

"Not lucky," Sam said. "Kelsey kept his knife."

"She WHAT? You two are a walking nightmare. I want that knife."

"It's under the seat of my truck," Sam said. "Wrapped in cloth. You'll get it."

"I'd better, and damn soon too. On the up side, we got photos off a nearby camera and we have an APB out on their vehicle. If they keep it. I'll text you the info. But watch your six. They found you once." She didn't need to voice the rest of that sentiment. "Another good reason to get in here. And if you have any idea where Frank is, he'd be better in protective custody too."

"You mean like Dr. Zinck?"

"Rub it in, why don't you," she said. "We're wise to them now. We can do better."

"Maybe," Sam said. "Maybe not. What have you found out about the mole?"

Silence greeted his question.

A phone rang in the background.

"Hang on," Parker said, "I need to take that."

She was on the other call for several minutes. He could hear her voice but not what she was saying. And then she was back.

"Your computer buddy emailed me that information. He was quick about it too." She paused and Sam's senses tingled. "I got the warrant. The officers went in about twenty minutes ago." She stopped again. The woman was queen of pregnant pauses.

"The place was closed, the staff locked out when they got to work this morning. Everything above the restaurant level was cleared out."

Sam swore silently and fluently, pinching the bridge of his nose to counter his frustration. He looked at Kelsey. She was watching him intently, no doubt seeing the displeasure on his face.

"And Sam," Parker said, "Eric Chappell was found in the empty third floor space. And you can guess it. He'd been sliced ear to ear. He's been dead for at least forty-eight hours."

Crap almighty. "So he wasn't our top man," Sam said. "And now that file and record book plus Frank's eye witnesses testimony are all the evidence we have."

"You got it."

The dishwasher dead near Africville Park.

Dr. Zinck in the back of the van.

Eric on the third floor of The Mingle.

The little man and his sidekick were eliminating witness or punishing anyone who screwed up. That man didn't want just the evidence, he wanted Frank dead.

"By the way," Parker added, cutting into his silent analysis. "I'm heading into the meeting now. By the end of it, your information will be with every law enforcement personnel in the city. You might have half an hour before you're on the wanted list."

At least she didn't say the province – although that is probably a given.

Sam looked at Kelsey. If they turned themselves in, she might or might not be safe. If he was at the police station, any chance to corner the Knife Man killer could evaporate. And if that happened, their quarry would win.

"I need more time." He hung up.

He'd have to ditch the truck soon. But he'd find a hidey-hole first, one that would delay the finding of the truck and give them time to disappear. He also needed to contact Greg and Jackson. If they could lure the little man to the island, they could get him. No police, no opportunity for the mole to sidetrack events. For his money, it was the best way to go. He started sending out texts.

CHAPTER THIRTEEN

Almost supper time. Sam picked up his phone and dialed. A deep voice snapped an answer. "Jackson."

"You got the texts. You talked to the others?" Sam said. "We need to finalize. Where are folks and what's happening."

"Big bridge opening festivities tomorrow. Good and bad." He didn't need to explain that cover was good, potential innocent victims not so much. "Most of the crew is on-island. We're set up with decoys and traps."

"Good. This guy is twisted. We have to be ready for anything. Has Greg stopped being Daddy long enough to review that notebook?"

"Yup. Not only is there a list of people vested with new lives, but there's also a hit list of people who got in the way. We found a camera disk with pictures of his kills. Jeff started searching and we found news reports matching several of the bodies. Unsolved murders." Jackson paused. "Even gave me the creeps. This guy is proud of his work."

"And Frank, he's okay with the decoy plan?"

"Yup," Jackson responded with his uncle's vernacular. "His only stipulation is that Vi and Kelsey are safe and out of the action."

Sam grunted. "We'll do our best."

"That's what I told him." Jackson cleared his throat. "Lem's been in touch with Frank. Water-ferry time for him and Vi. Your Ottawa friend is ready to salt the data mines. Text him any particulars that you want leaked."

"Takedown location?"

"That, friend, is the wild card. Lem has to come into the marina with the cruiser. You need to be on that tour bus. Everyone arrives about one at the boat slips. The worst case will be a showdown at the marina. If we are able to execute all steps, we'll shift it to Lem's house. One risk is the target showing up early in Caleb's Cove. But we'll deal with it. By the way, the bus leaves Pier 21 at nine tomorrow morning and arrives here about one pm. Be on it."

Great, a bus tour and lunch at Peggy's cove. He and Kelsey would be sitting ducks for four hours. Four hours of stewing, watching his back and hiding his weapons. "Yippee."

He heard Jackson laughing as he disconnected.

Sam sighed and pocketed the phone. "We have shopping to do, darlin'. We are going sightseeing in the mornin.'"

Kelsey cocked her head and frowned. "What the heck are you talking about – and why are you talking like that."

Sam grinned. "You'll see."

He turned down a one-way street, ducked through a narrow ally into a parking lot and exited on a street headed back the way they'd come. The truck lurched and rocked, and Kelsey bounced and jerked.

"Watch it."

"Sorry," Sam said. "Our two hours were up twenty minutes ago, and that was a black and white in the other lane. I'd put money on there being an all-points bulletin out on us. I think we evaded detection this time, but there will be others. Time to ditch the truck."

· · · · ·

Kelsey planted her feet flat on the floor, aligned her ankles, pressed her knees together and folded her hands in her lap to the point of pain. The truck rocked over a curb jostling her, tossing her against the seatbelt. They headed into a lane that was old, rutted and deserted.

Sam leaned forward, his head turning from side to side as he checked the back of the ancient, three-story houses. Most had been converted to apartments. Laundry hung on several balconies and all needed paint.

"What's your plan?" she asked, no longer able to tolerate the silence in the cab.

"Hidey-hole slot," he muttered. Suddenly he applied the brakes and snapped the truck into reverse. In one smooth sweep he backed into a lot behind a dingy brown house. Palming the wheel, he maneuvered in between a dumpster and an old panel van. "This will have to do." He shut off the engine and reached for the keys. His fingers wrapped around them, he stopped and let his hand fall away.

"Damn," he said. "I hate to leave her behind." He sighed. "No choice."

Kelsey gathered up her purse, and reached for the door. "I can't get out," she said. "We're too close to the dumpster."

Sam turned from rummaging behind the seat. He settled his Stetson on his head. "Get out this side." He pulled papers from the glovebox and she glimpsed a pink slip.

She waited. Sam disconnected a key from the key ring leaving the others in the ignition.

"You're not taking the keys?"

"No, and not locking it either."

He went on before she could ask why. "How much room is there in that shoulder bag?" He pointed at the purse.

"Lots."

Sam reached under the seat and pulled out the knife. He made sure the fabric was tightly wound around it and handed it to her. She took it gingerly, zipped open the side pocket and put in the knife. She pushed it to the bottom and hid it with a tightly rolled shopping bag and a small cosmetic case.

Sam got out, pushing the door wide.

Kelsey twisted, passed him the purse and got up on her knees. She crawled over the gear stick into the driver's seat. Sam reached for her, grabbed her under the arms and pulled her out, swinging her feet to the ground.

"I could have managed," she said, fixing her shirt.

He grinned. "I know. But I just needed to be macho for a moment."

A dark note tinged his flirtatious words. Before she could figure it out, he scooped her purse up and handed it to her.

"I need one more thing," he said, and took off the denim jacket. He held it toward her and she took it. What was he up to?

Sam flipped the lever on the seat and tipped the back forward. He opened the crew door, knelt and leaned in between the seats. Kelsey peered over his shoulder, watching his progress.

A metal box was mounted under the seat. He used the small key he'd taken from the key ring and unlocked it. The lid, which was actually on the bottom, fell open. He reached in and brought out a gun.

"Oh," Kelsey said. "A. . . ."

He raised a hand silencing her. A holster followed. Sam rose, sat on the truck floor and donned the holster, slid in the gun. He stood, took back his jacket and put it on, adjusting it over the gun.

"We're ready." He closed the truck doors, adjusted his Stetson and stepped into the lane.

Kelsey stood between his shiny black truck and the rusted-out panel van. He'd left the keys in the ignition and the doors unlocked. "Aren't you afraid someone will steal it?"

Sam turned, rested a hand on the truck's hood. "That's the plan, sweetheart." He splayed his fingers on the black metal and looked so sad Kelsey felt tears gathering in her throat. The men back home relied on, took pride in and treasured their trucks, the way cowboys of the past felt about their horses. And Sam was a Western boy.

His car, his phone, his apartment and now his truck left behind. "Diversion," she said.

Sam nodded. "If this truck goes out and about, the law will be all over it. I can only hope they capture it intact and I can retrieve it from impound when this is all over."

"You're sure this is the best way?" Kelsey went to him and put a hand on his arm.

He nodded. "Remember those outcomes I mentioned, back at my place?"

She nodded. "One is Frank ends up dead." She drew an uneven breath. "And we end up in Witness Protection."

Never see my family again. How could I stand it?

Sam put an arm around her shoulders and held her. "I'm so sorry you walked into this mess."

She sniffed back threatening tears. "Option two—we could end up dead along with Frank." She felt his nod.

She cleared her throat. "Looks like our only option is to corner the bastard and end this."

Sam stepped back and cupped her chin. "That's my girl." He planted a quick kiss on her forehead. "Come on, darlin'. Let's go play tourist."

· · · · ·

Sam pulled the brim of his hat down against the morning sun glinting off the harbor. His boots thudded along the pier-front boardwalk. Kelsey, sunglasses settled on her face, strolled beside him, her hand tucked in his. Bacon, eggs and toast accompanied by copious amounts of coffee left him with a mellow feeling. Although the breeze was fresh, the sun warmed his shoulders. Under different circumstances, it would have been a fine morning.

Ahead of them, a multi-level cruise ship towered behind Pier 21. Clusters of tourists strolled along the boardwalk in both directions. Sam and Kelsey took the walk that brought them around the building toward the tour buses. Resplendent in red, blue and yellow, they lined up waiting to reveal the wonders of Nova Scotia to willing passengers.

"Caleb's Cove Tour?" he asked a driver standing in front of a deep blue bus sporting a picture of Peggy's Cove.

The man nodded, and Sam flashed the code on his phone screen. Jeff had purchased the tickets online and forwarded him the barcode. The operator scanned it with his little gun reader.

"Leaving in five," the man said. "Find yourselves a seat."

Chattering tourists already crowded the bus. Maps and flyers and cell phone screens showed the proposed route and the day's events. Kelsey led the way down the narrow aisle, found two seats near the back and they settled in.

Sam wedged into the aisle seat, stretched one leg along the outer edge of the forward seat and tipped his head back. The cash-only motel they'd stayed in hadn't been a restful spot. "Wake me when we get there," he murmured to Kelsey and pulled his hat over his eyes. He might not sleep, but he needed to at least rest for what might lie ahead.

The bus slowed and Sam leaned forward as much as he could in the high-backed bus seat. His hat pushed back, his hands dangling between his knees he watched the beach area go by. They were on the final approach to the new bridge linking Dane's Island and Caleb's Cove to the mainland. White beach stretched along the curve. Tiny waves curled and fizzled against a darker line of damp sand at the water's edge. A lone gull circled. Driftwood and minor debris speckled the otherwise smooth stretch.

Around him, passengers gathered their belongings, ready to get out and stretch their legs. The bus rocked, lurched once and stopped. The hydraulics hissed and the door eased open. The driver stood, turning to face them.

"Everyone out – there are ceremonies here and then we'll go across the new bridge and into Caleb's Cove. Food, washrooms, photo ops." He edged back to let folks access the steps.

A white haired lady put up her hand. "Isn't it Caleb Cove?"

The driver grinned. "Depends if you are reading the map or talking to a local."

Kelsey hugged that darn purse to her middle. Sam put a hand on her arm. He wanted to be last one off the bus. He had checked everyone when they made the Peggy's Cove stop, but he still didn't trust everyone on board. Jeff had leaked their destination, but supposedly not their transport plans. At the moment, Sam didn't trust digital anything.

Staying alert and close to Kelsey seemed like the prudent thing to do. No telling when or if the killer had intercepted the messages. He could be anywhere, even already at the Cove.

Outside, their fellow passengers straggled in bunches toward a bandstand and music. The islanders, or the tourism folk, had pulled out all the stops. There was even the requisite Nova Scotia bagpiper although they weren't in Scottish territory.

With an arm around Kelsey's back, he urged her along the rear of the crowd forming a semicircle at the bandstand. He found a position on the edge of the group, a spot that would be front and center in the crowd when they turned toward the bridge. Once the officials cut the tape, Sam planned to be in the middle of the pack making the first trek across.

The piper stopped and the speeches began. Sam listened with one ear and scanned the crowd, the officials and the welcoming committee on the far side of the bridge. Wayne Harris, owner operator of the Marina and café and the unofficial mayor of the Cove, made the final speech. Holding a huge pair of mock scissors over his head, he led the way to the wide blue and green ribbons stretched across the bridge access.

He shared the honor with Mrs. Gerber, one of the oldest residents of the island. The crowd clapped and cheered and surged forward carrying Sam and Kelsey with them. Wayne fell into step on the far side of Kelsey and caught Sam's gaze.

"Any sign of them?"

Sam did a double-take. "You know?"

Wayne inclined his head. "CCSA employee," he said, establishing his connection to the Caleb Cove Security Group. "Greg filled me in."

Sam nodded. "Any sign of trouble here?"

Wayne shook his head. "Head up the slope on the far side," he said, "and off to the right. Jackson's there. He'll get you to the Marina." He glanced at his watch. "If the plan is working, it's soon time for Lem to arrive at the Marina. I'll be along as soon as I can."

A man spoke to him and Wayne turned away, smiling and answering questions. "Yes, there's a picnic spread in the middle of town. Lots of food, no cost. Please enjoy."

Great, bloody friggin' great – tons of people wandering in the street and looking for pictures along the boardwalk. How on earth would this takedown play out? Would the man even show up?

Sam climbed the short, steep slope up from the bridge. They planned to lure the killer into a position favorable to them. But would it work? At the top of the slope, he located Jackson Ritcey leaning against his vehicle.

Black clothing, black SUV, black sunglasses. He looked every inch the ex-special ops guy he was. Jackson was a good man to have at your back. He saw Sam and Kelsey and pushed to a standing position. Sam's energy whirled and settled on him like a cloak. For good or bad, it was almost show time.

· · · · ·

Kelsey sat in the back seat of Jackson's SUV and peered ahead to the waterfront community of Caleb's Cove. A treed area gave way to fields and a well-kept stretch of road. Small buildings, replicas of fishing shacks, lined the area between road and water. Between the buildings she got glimpses of boardwalk. People were everywhere, carrying packages, eating ice cream, sitting on benches, taking photos out over the harbor. So this was Caleb's Cove. *My birthplace.*

Her attention shifted back to the men. Jackson stopped long enough for a young man to pull back a barricade before edging forward into a parking area. *The Marina Café* sign labeled their location. Jackson shut off the vehicle, pulled out the keys and tossed them in one hand.

"Let's walk," he said. "We can scout the area before Lem gets here. He picked up Frank and Vi at a private dock near Dartmouth. He'll bring them into the end berth. He can't take his boat into the shallower water at his own dock so we'll transfer them to a dory and shuttle them across the harbor to Lem's dock. Greg has it fitted out with a motor."

Greg? Right. Greg and Jackson were co-owners with Sam in the private security company based in Caleb's Cove. Sam and Greg went back to police training in Calgary and Greg and Jackson, a local, were brothers-in-law.

"Are there dory races?" she asked.

"Yup. There are. And see all those boats out on the water? Best camouflage going."

"The area is pretty open," Sam said, turning full circle.

"Can't help it. Unless we transported them in the trunk of car or a panel van, they'd be seen by someone. This time of year, everybody sees everybody. Best thing that could have happened is doing this at the same time as the festivities. The more strangers coming and going, the less likelihood of anyone pinpointing Lem's activities."

Jackson, like Sam, scanned the area non-stop. "Besides, we want them to be visible enough to lure the guy and at the same time we need to make it look like we're hiding them. For all intents and purposes, it will look like we have them holed up at Lem's."

Sam ran a hand down the back of his head. "What are the odds the man will show? He could be here already in some disguise and mingling with the tourists. He could be an avid sailor and heading here by water. Not knowing is a huge risk."

"Two if by land, one if by sea or something?"

Sam returned Jackson's grin. "I suppose. Where's Greg?"

Jackson jutted a chin toward the water. "Out there in that gaggle of boats."

"And Devon and baby?"

Kelsey struggled to keep the cast of characters organized in her head. *Devon is Greg's wife and Lem's niece. The baby, Grace, is only a week old.*

Jackson looked up. "They were in the apartment over the café. Gwen and Wayne don't live there anymore, but it's a good vantage point to watch the festivities. Gwen and Jude are with her."

Sam's explanations ran in her head. *Wayne and Gwen own the café and marina. Their son is almost two.* She was starting to keep them sorted out.

"They'll be there or over at the house." Jackson turned and pointed southwest across the main parking area. "They bought the old Manse about six months ago. And Devon has Greg's gun." His half-grin came and went. "Don't tell anyone official." He sobered. "No reason for anyone to bother them though. Our man wants what Frank has. And, given the profile we have on this guy, he'll be out for revenge. He takes pride in eliminating those that cross him."

Kelsey shivered. She'd crossed him. In the Thrift Store she'd bested him. Did he want her dead? Sam looked back at her. Did he share her fear? He'd accosted the man as well.

"Let's go." Jackson left the truck and led them between the café and a marine museum. A boardwalk ran along the waterfront joining the café and marina with the shops. Sun warmed Kelsey, breezes cooled her and voices ebbed and flowed, muted from the land, sharper off the water.

The boardwalk wound out of sight on the left but ended off to the right just beyond the boat slips and parking lot. Small tables dotted the patio. Longer plank tables laden with food skirted the parking lot. Young wait-staff flowed in and out of the café replenishing trays. Tantalizing odors drifted on the air. She sniffed and her stomach rumbled.

An ice cream cart pulled up beside them and she turned.

"Cones anyone?" A cheeky teen asked. "On the house for you guys."

"Hart," said Sam. "How's it going?"

"I passed my driver's." Hart grinned. "I can drive legally now." He filled a cone and handed it over. "And I won the junior dory races this morning." He bent his arm in a classic muscle man pose and flexed his biceps.

"This is Kelsey." Sam introduced her. "Hart is Jackson's stepson."

"What flavor, Kelsey?" Hart served up her chocolate cone and handed a walnut special to Jackson.

"Head back that way, would you?" Jackson jutted his chin in the direction away from the boat slips. "And buzz me a 911 if you see anything out of the ordinary."

Hart sighed. "You always try to keep me out of the action."

"Go," Jackson ordered and watched Hart leave before turning to scan the harbor. A boat rounded the left prominence. "There they are," he said. "Eat fast, folks. Duty calls."

He pointed off to the left where buoys held a rope taut in the water. "As planned, we've scheduled a diversion. The senior men's race is set to start as Lem reaches the docks," Jackson said. "The

race generates a lot of cheering and yelling. Should work as cover."
He turned toward the jetty.

Sam put a hand on his arm. "Just a minute." He scanned the area
in all directions.

"Kelsey," he said, "can you watch our backs? You've seen the
guy."

Kelsey stopped, reminded that in spite of all the makings of a
lazy day celebration, they were stalking a killer. Or being stalked.

She blinked, focused on a door in the back wall of the café.
"Yes." She pointed. "I can see in all directions from there and keep
my back to the wall." She rummaged in her purse and brought out
the whistle Brock had given her for safety. "If it's serious, you'll
hear me."

Sam grasped her hand and squeezed. "It'll all be over soon."

She smiled at Sam and tilted her head at Jackson.

He pointed to a dark-haired waitress just leaving the building
with a large coffee pot. "That's Kim," he said, "my daughter. If you
need anything, ask her."

Kelsey nodded and headed for the wall, reassured to be among
friends.

· · · · ·

Sam followed Jackson along the bobbing jetty, flexing his knees
against the slight rise and fall. The marina was full. People lingered
on several decks, but most boats bobbed empty on the rolling waters
of a calm ocean. Jackson stopped one slip from the end and waved a
hand at the sloop tied there.

"Greg's new toy," he said. "Bought it off Sheldon's estate after
all was said and done. We can check it out while we wait for our
arrivals."

The slim, white sloop, sails stowed, rocked in its berth. Sam ran
an appraising eye over it. If he were looking at a horse he might have
an informed comment or two. But a boat? All he could say was it
looked slim.

He swung his gaze past Jackson and focused on a larger boat in
the midst of the row boats. "Cruiser approaching." He continued his
scan to include the rest of the busy water scene. "The starter has his
gun raised over at the race site. The plan is coming together."

Moments later, Sam caught the rope Lem tossed him and helped
edge the cruiser into the slip. He couldn't tie it, but he could guide it.

Jackson took over, made some expert loops and twists around a post. The crack of the starting gun cut the air, and the cheering and hollering of the crowd swept over the harbor. It took all his concentration not to turn and look. But he needed to focus. Hopefully everyone else was watching the race.

On the outer edge of the slip, a dory pulled up and the skipper grabbed the post on that side. Sam took a good look. It wasn't Greg – it was Wayne, his pseudo-mayoral duties completed and the café in other hands. The man got around.

Wayne winked. Two people wearing hats and sunglasses, exited the cabin cruiser, stepped to the planks and scurried to the dory. Wayne shoved off, pulled the starter on the outboard and chugged away. The dory wove through other craft, zigzagging across the harbor toward Lem's private dock.

"Pull, pull, pull." The enthusiasts urged on their favorite rowers. Sun twinkled on the swells. Sam straightened, shoved his Stetson back and scanned the scene. All looked calm. No uneasy prickles alerted him to a watcher. They'd executed the transaction unnoticed. One more step successfully completed.

He extended a hand to Lem. "Good job," he said. Lowering his voice, he kept talking as he gave the older man a guy hug. "Why was Wayne in the boat? Where's Greg?"

Lem laughed and slapped Sam on the back. "Good to see you too," he said. He bent to tie the stern moorings. "Change of plans," he murmured. "Greg already picked up Frank and Vi – before we rounded the point. They're safe."

Sam planted his hat. "Okay, then. So who did we just transfer?"

Jackson came up behind him. "My wife and your buddy, Jeff Brown."

They turned and walked up the center planks toward the café and Kelsey. If they thought a slight variation in plan was needed, he was good with it.

"I'll give you a ride," Lem called after him. "We'll head to my place."

Sam shoulder checked and gave a wave. The hook was set.

· · · · ·

Kelsey lifted her purse strap over her head and put down her purse. She washed her hands. The transfer at the end of the dock appeared to have gone well. Now they would wait. Sam had not told her the full plan, or if she'd be allowed to be there, but he knew what he was doing. He'd better. It was her father they were using for bait. Her gut grumbled. Sooner or later, nervous stomach or not, she'd have to eat.

She gave the washroom one final inspection, picked up the purse and stepped into the hall. A short man with thick hair, a straw hat and a flowered tourist shirt blocked her way. She sidestepped. He matched her.

Short. Glasses. Scratch on his face. Oh oh. What is he doing here?

She took a step back. *He should be headed for Lem's.* Why had she put away her whistle?

He held up a hand and put a finger to his lips. "Shush," he said and reached under his jacket. "I'm not alone and a lot of people could get hurt, including you." He frowned. "You were not a nice lady. Taking a man's knife. Really, my dear."

His mouth turned up in a smirk. "Lucky for me I keep a spare." He pulled a long, wide-bladed knife from under the jacket draped over his arm. He touched the tip to her solar plexus. "And no funny stuff. I won't underestimate you a second time."

"Move, carefully." He pulled her up beside him and poked the knife in her side. "I'm going to keep this under my jacket, but it'll be ready and I'm a lot stronger than I look." He laughed. "I'd find it easy and pleasurable to drive it under your ribs and into your heart." He poked harder.

She flinched. Flexed her wrist and tested the weight of her purse at the end of its doubled up strap. Dare she swing at him? Maybe not right now. They reached the end of the wall dividing the washroom from the main dining area.

He looked around the wall and pulled her into the main café, hustling her toward the reception desk and the street door.

Kelsey glanced back. The room was dismally empty. There were people beyond the patio doors. Most were watching the races. No one looked in. *I have to help myself.*

"Don't even think it," he said and shoved the knife tighter against her body. He pulled her into the small entry, removing her from any line of vision from the main room. She hung back. When the man opened the door and stuck his head out, she released the double-looped purse strap. The purse dropped to the full length of the strap and dangled a mere inch above the floor.

The man leaned out, and she gave the purse a gentle swing letting it fall the final inch to the floor behind the door. Someone would find it. *Sam will know, he'll come looking for me.*

The act of defiance gave her hope. She needed to leave the best trail she could. But she couldn't be dropping things every few minutes. Irritating this man wouldn't be wise.

Tracking. She'd heard her father discuss it with the boys often enough. The slightest mark or change in the usual could help, if someone could read the signs. She squared her shoulders. All she could do was leave the best trail possible. The rest was up to Sam.

And then the man pulled her out the door. She glanced down, stepped off the slab and ground her foot on the grasses. Two markers. She could do this. She must do this. Her life depended on it.

· · · · ·

Sam stepped onto the patio proper and looked for Kelsey. She wasn't at her post beside the door. He ran his gaze across the back of the building and the patio. No sight of her. He expanded his visual search and strode toward the building. She must be inside.

He entered the café, blinked to adjust to the dimmer light and looked. No Kelsey. He stood aside to let a waitress pass. It was Kim. "Did you see the brunette with the big purse?"

"Hi, Sam." Kim glanced over her shoulder. "Sure. Kelsey, right? She asked for the washrooms."

How did these kids know everyone? Sam's tight gut relaxed. Washroom breaks he could understand. Sometimes when you gotta go, you gotta go.

He headed for the corridor to the washrooms. She must still be in there. He leaned against the wall, head back, one foot up behind him. Phase one done. Frank and Lil were transported to Greg's property out on the point. The decoys, Jackson's wife, Nancy and Jeff Brown, would enter Lem's house and leave later as themselves.

Sam opened his eyes. Where was Kelsey? Surely she should be done by now? He rapped on the women's washroom door. "Kelsey? Are you okay?" There was no answer. He tried again. No response. He pushed the door. "Coming in," he called.

His voice echoed in the tiled room. Both stall doors stood open, no feet showed. No Kelsey. Sam's gut sank. Where was she? He whirled around, pulling out his phone as he went. He punched the one-button call for Jackson. "We have a situation," he said tersely. "I can't find Kelsey."

He ran through the empty café and burst out the door. Kim and Lem stood off to one side. He ran to them. "Kim, how long ago did Kelsey go to the washroom?"

She stopped mid-sentence and turned to him, glancing past him toward the building as if expecting to see Kelsey there. "A few minutes." She puckered her forehead and looked first at the tables and then at the docks. "I was carrying out the squares," she murmured, "and Lem had just docked." She pointed at the waterfront.

Good Lord, that was at least ten minutes ago.

Jackson joined them. "What happened?"

"Good question," Sam said. "Kelsey went to the washroom and never came back."

"And you're sure. . ."

"Yes, I looked."

Jackson's gaze went up. "The apartment. She might be with Devon and Gwen." He hurried toward the door. "I'll check. Sam you take the boardwalk – ask Hart – get him looking. Lem – you and Kim search the crowd. She has to be here somewhere."

God, Sam hoped Jackson was right. But Kelsey didn't know Devon or Gwen, didn't know about the apartment. How would she end up with them?

He took off at a run, scanning all faces, peering at every long-haired brunette in sight, even if they weren't dressed in jeans. He didn't find her. He came up behind the ice cream cart. "Did you see Kelsey?"

Hart, squatting to give a toddler a cone, looked up at Sam. "You mean since. . ."

"Yes, in the last few minutes. Have you seen her?"

Hart shook his head, stood and handed napkins to the little guy's mom and turned. "What happened?"

Sam pinched his lips together. Huffed. "Good question. She's gone."

"Shit," Hart said under his breath. His face paled. "Not again."

"What's that mean?"

"Just a flash of déjà vu," he said. "Back to when Kim was

kidnapped last year."

Cold chills ran over Sam, and his heart missed two beats. Kidnapped? Had they misjudged? Had their man snatched Kelsey while they were executing their elaborate plan?

Hart put his hand on Sam's forearm. "Hey, relax, Sam. It was just a flashback. Doesn't mean Kelsey was kidnapped. She'll turn up." He snapped down the lids on the cooler bins in the cart and flipped over the sign on the front. *Closed.* "Come on, I'll help you look. You take the parking areas and the street. I'll go up the boardwalk. We'll find her."

"Be careful," Sam said, his gaze already searching the walkers along the street.

"No worries." Hart hustled off.

Fear building inside him, Sam continued his frantic search. Kelsey would not have wandered off. He knew it, didn't want to admit it, and refused to accept the worst until he was forced to.

His phone rang. Keeping his gaze on the ever-shifting crowd, he answered. "You found her?"

"No," Jackson's voice was sharp. "And the women and babies are gone too. They're probably together. You know women and babies."

No, he didn't know women and babies. But if it meant Kelsey was safe, he'd take the concept. "Okay. We still need to find them. If they are together, it'll be easier to see them. Keep in touch."

Five minutes later, he'd run the entire length of the main drag and found no sign of Kelsey or Devon and Gwen and the babies. He stopped running, turned in a full circle. There were no people beyond his position, no cars on the road. Where the heck did they go? Into the bushes?

Sam jogged toward the café, fear escalating with every pounding step. Jackson, Lem, and Kim waited in the dining area. Outside, the meal was almost over and workers carried in empty platters but took no full ones out. Through the windows, he could see the crowd thinning as people moved off. The day's festivities were ending.

But no Kelsey. Only grim faces staring at him. Jackson toyed with a pink baby bootie. Oh god, did that man have Devon and little Grace?

CHAPTER FOURTEEN

"Found the babies and moms," Jackson said in a hurry. "Jude was fussy so Gwen took him home for his nap. Devon and Grace went with her."

Thank goodness. If the man took the babies. Unthinkable. But they still didn't have Kelsey. He counted faces. One searcher missing. "Where's Hart?"

Jackson shook his head. "He checked in. Now he's over at the blockade. He's checking everyone going out and noting the cars they get into. He'll ask folks if they saw Kelsey."

Sam's gut contracted. The teen's suspicions were true. "He got her," Sam said. "We need to be looking in cars leaving the island. We need to search the island." How could they do it all? The wooded areas provided hiding. The boats and the now open bridge provided escape routes. *All those people milling around and leaving for home. Perfect cover.*

His innards cold, his head pounding, Sam faced the others. "We have to face it. Our carefully laid plan has backfired."

"Take a breath," Jackson said. "We know this man wants his trophy book and even more, he wants revenge. Even he can't think that retrieval of the material will stop the investigation. But looking at his kills, his photos, his carefully hand-printed list of days and times and the supposed sins of the victims, he NEEDS revenge. I don't think he'll leave the island. Not yet."

Sam closed his eyes and focused. Objectivity, he needed a good dose of it. Kelsey was there because of him, because he'd foolishly assumed he could keep her safer than Parker's plan to put her in a safe house guarded by officers. *Hubris. It'll bite you in the ass every chance it gets.*

He lifted his head, looked into their worried faces. "Okay, let's start where we saw her last and walk through this. Kim, did you see her come into the building?"

"She was inside when she asked about the washrooms. I think she went straight there."

Sam looked around, counting doorways. "Everyone was using the patio door? Right?"

Kim nodded. "The main door," she pointed to the front of the café, "is locked."

"Did you see anyone else come into the café?" Sam kept his gazed fixed on Kim. One set of questions at a time.

"No, but I was busy. Anyone could come in while I was in the kitchen or out at the tables."

"We need to talk to the other servers." Sam lifted his chin in Jackson's direction.

"On it," Jackson said and patted Kim's shoulder before he headed outside.

"The other doors are internal. She's not in the ladies' room. Lem, take a look in the men's." Sam looked around. "What else is there? Am I missing anything?"

She pointed as she spoke. "There's the front desk and that little hall that blocks the view of the front door. There's the kitchen, through there, and it does have an outside door. The one used for bringing in supplies. And there's a walk-in cooler."

"Who's in the kitchen?"

"Two cooks. Want me to ask if they saw her? Or anyone who shouldn't be there?"

Before he could answer, Lem came back. "No one in the Men's," he said, "and no sign of any disturbance. I double-checked the windows in both washrooms. They're locked."

Jackson returned. "No one remembers anyone coming in or asking for the washroom. But they were all busy and their backs were to the door." He shook his head. "Damn, all these people played against us."

"No time to rethink it now," Sam said. Regret was a useless emotion. Didn't stop him from feeling it. "Jackson, check the kitchen and talk to the cooks."

Lem headed for the front door, stepped out of sight behind the partial wall. "Sam," he called. "You need to have a look."

Sam joined Lem and bent to examine the lock. "It's been jimmied," he said. "Someone came in this way." He ran a hand up the wall not quite touching it. He checked the strike and knelt to see the floor and threshold. His gaze shifted, taking in the full area. And he saw it. Kelsey's purse. He'd know that suitcase-sized bag anywhere.

He picked it up. "She went out this way," he said. "She dropped this. She never lets it out of her sight willingly."

Jackson returned from the kitchen. Sam shook his head and in spite of the fear tingeing his thoughts, a small smile played around his mouth. "She'll do what she can do to slow him and mark a trail." A shiver engulfed him, and he met Jackson's gaze.

If the killer realizes it, he'll retaliate. Neither of them voiced the thought.

Sam reached for the door, stayed his hand at the last moment. The man was a professional killer. He probably didn't leave fingerprints. But they should try. "We need Greg," he said. "And whatever gear he has."

Jackson snorted. "After that hurricane incident, he laid in a lot of supplies, law enforcement type of supplies. He has a kit." Jackson stepped away and pulled out his phone. His voice rumbled as he brought Greg up to date and requested his presence at the café.

"This changes the plan," Sam said. "Our trap isn't going to work. But someone needs to guard Frank. If Greg is coming here and Wayne is at Lem's house, there's no one watching him." He looked at Jackson and raised an eyebrow."

"I'm on my way," Jackson said. He walked shoulder to shoulder with Sam across the room. Kim and Lem brought up the rear.

Lem cleared his throat. "Do you think he'll contact us?"

Sam paused. "If he can figure out how. We all have secure cell phones."

"My house phone is listed," Lem said.

"The café phone number is listed as well." Jackson glanced at Lem and Kim.

Sam picked up on the glance. "You two stay here," he said. "If he calls, Lem, you handle it. Kim, you get on your cell and call me." He took her cell and programmed in his number.

Jackson dashed off. Sam watched him go. *We need more manpower.* Everyone was doing something. Even Hart was watching the barricade asking folks if they'd seen Kelsey They were stretched thin.

Well, then, get moving. Nodding at Lem, he headed for the front parking lot and the outside of the door. He slowed and scanned in a grid pattern. Just off the side of the single-rise concrete step, a grassy patch caught his attention. Sam knelt and looked. Someone had ground their foot on it. He touched the broken stems and raised his fingers to his nose. *Fresh marks, moist stems and pungent odor. This is new.* Resting one arm on his leg, he stayed squatted and checked the road in both directions. Still no sign of Kelsey.

· · · · ·

Frank paced the floor in the fancy kitchen at Greg's estate. The boy had bought the place when it went up on auction. Had plans for summer camps on top of the security business he and the other boys were running. Frank heeled around and headed toward the windows, stopped short. He and Vi were to stay away from windows.

For the first time in over a decade he yearned for a shot of whisky. Or for the mind-numbing effect it might have. His nerves didn't like their plan. Not for himself, but for Vi and Kelsey. Especially Kelsey. Sam better have her in a safe place.

Vi entered the kitchen. "We could have lunch." She headed for the cooking area and started opening doors. "There's canned food."

"Not hungry," Frank said and went to stand beside her. He hesitated before putting an arm around her. "I'm sorry you got dragged into this. I'm even sorrier about Lil."

Vi turned into his embrace and buried her face against his shoulder. "Can't be helped, can it." A sob shook her. "But why did they have to kill Lil?"

"Do you think Kelsey. . ." He'd finally told Vi about Kelsey being his daughter, Katya, and his past in jail. Good woman that she was, she'd hugged him and kissed his cheek.

Now, once again, she tightened her hug. "Sam and the others will keep her safe."

Frank nodded but his shoulders refused to relax and his brain rejected the assurance. A bad, bad feeling settled in his gut. Like the feeling he'd had the day Susan left and took his baby away. That time his drinking and temper were his undoing. His actions had driven them away.

This time, he'd done it again. Thanks to his actions, even though they were well-intentioned, she could end up in danger. They'd figured out that she was his daughter, and if they found her, they'd use her against him. He groaned. He couldn't stand to lose her again.

·····

Kelsey, because of the knife and the people around them, allowed the man to drag her through the crowd. The lunch over, people milled about, heading away from the parking lot and toward the waterfront. Others swarmed onto the street and headed back toward the makeshift parking area on the far side of the barricade. A few people wandered south toward an old church and a store whose sign announced it to be the *Caleb Cove Emporium.*

Kelsey and her captor joined this last group.

Where is he taking me?

She tried to make eye contact with anyone she could, wiggling her brows and crossing her eyes, hoping they'd remember, and if questioned tell someone.

What does he plan to do?

One older couple hustled off to the side when she gave them her fisheyes.

Does he have a car down here?

A little boy looked up at her. She stuck out her tongue and crossed her eyes again. He started to giggle. Kelsey felt the man turn toward her and she quickly averted her face, lowering her eyes.

They passed the store and the church-turned-gift store. There were cars both places. He didn't turn in.

The old Manse was next. Standing well back from the road, it was boxed in on one side by the church and separated from the graveyard by a high fence. Further along she saw only fields and woods. No more houses. She checked the road. No cars.

"In here," he said and guided her onto the driveway beside the Manse. He hustled her along until they passed a hedge hiding them from the street. He glanced around, pulled her behind it. Kelsey gulped and put a hand to her neck. Was he going to slit her throat?

The man shifted his grip from her elbow, knocking away her hand and replacing it with his own. Forcing his thumb and forefinger in under her jaw, he made her tip back her head. The knife came out from under his coat. He held it close to her and trailed it up her belly and between her breasts. She closed her eyes. *This is it? Oh Sam, I'm going to die.*

Sharp and cold, the knife blade pressed high against her cheek bone. Pain trailed down her face and ended at her jaw line. The man chuckled. "A little something to remember me by," he whispered. "If in fact you end up alive."

He shoved and she stumbled back, her eyes flying open. She saw red on the blade he pointed at her and raised a hand to her face, feeling the wet slick of her own blood. *I'm alive.*

She turned and ran, tears joining the blood on her face. She leaped onto the step and pounded on the door. *Oh God, please somebody be home.* A corner of her mind acknowledged the irony of evoking God on the doorstep of the Manse. She pounded again, feeling the pain in her fist mingling with the pain in her face as her hand connected with the wood.

"Help me, please help me." She looked back. The man leered at her. What happened? Why did he let her go?

· · · · ·

Sam started forward. Stopped. Should he go up the road with the crowd or down past the few buildings leading to the open stretch before Lem's property. He paced across the parking lot, still undecided. *And if they doubled around to the boardwalk?* NO, one of them would have seen them if they went down the boardwalk. He rubbed his head and quieted his gut. *Make a freaking decision. Kelsey's life depends on you.*

And if he made the wrong one? If she died? How could he face Frank? Sam's breath caught in his chest. What would he do without her?

A couple passed, nodding to him as they went. A little boy followed, stopped in front of Sam and cocking his head crossed his eyes and stuck out his tongue. The mom turned and caught him at it. "Joey, cut that out, it's not polite."

"But that lady did it." Joey protested. "And she did this too." He waggled his eyebrows. "She was doing it to everyone." He was almost in tears. "Why can't I do it?"

Sam knelt by the boy. What grown-up would be making faces? *It's Kelsey. Has to be.* Tangible hope exploded through him. "Joey, it's okay." He held a hand up, palm out toward the mom when she moved to interfere. "What woman? Where did you see her?"

Joey scrubbed the back of his hand across his nose and turned. "Down there," he said, pointing a grubby finger toward the store. "She made faces, but that man didn't. He looked mean. She stopped when he looked at her. Was she being bad?" He tipped his head and looked to his mom for an explanation.

"No," Sam said and stood. "I'm looking for that lady," he said to the woman. "What Joey told me is really important. Please don't scold him."

The woman gave him an odd look and pulled Joey against her. "Okay." Suspicion tinged her voice. "Come on, Joey, let's catch up with Daddy." She took the boy's hand and hurried up the street.

Striding down the street, Sam flicked his focus from person to person. He pulled out his cell. "Greg, I think they went toward Lem's. Can you let the others know?"

He was running by the time he reached the store. Had they gone inside? Did the man want more hostages? He checked in the store. Business as usual. Kelsey and her captor were not there.

At the church-cum-gallery, he asked about them. Kelsey and her captor hadn't been there. That left the Manse and, further down, Lem's place. But if the boy just saw them, they should still be on the road. The road was vacant.

Sam made another phone call. "Jackson," he said, "you said Gwen and Wayne are living in the old Manse?"

"Yes," Jackson said. "Why?"

Gwen took the baby home for a nap and Devon went with her.

Jackson's optimistic words rang in his memory. Sam's breath stopped, his eyes closed and despair washed over him. "We have a problem."

CHAPTER FIFTEEN

The door opened under Kelsey's barrage of pounding. She fell forward. A pair of arms reached for her and pulled her inside.

"Close it," Kelsey gasped. "Close the door."

She put out a hand and steadied herself on the wall. A short-haired brunette stared back her. The woman didn't hesitate. She reached behind Kelsey, slammed the door and locked it. A plumper blonde woman joined them.

Both women looked from Kelsey, to the wall and back. Oh god. She'd smeared blood on the wall. The women didn't even flinch. They got on either side of Kelsey, hustled her along the hall and into a kitchen. The brunette settled Kelsey in a chair. The blonde hurried away.

"What happened?" The brunette's voice was gentle.

I wouldn't be that calm if a bloody women burst into my house.

"Kidnapped," Kelsey said. "He has a knife." She raised a hand toward her face but the woman stopped her.

"How did you get away?"

Kelsey froze. "He let me go."

"What's your name?"

"Kelsey." She started shivering. "Kelsey Maxwell."

"Shock." The woman called out. "Bring a blanket."

She pushed Kelsey's hair off her face and tipped her head to look at the cut. "That explains things. Who was the man?"

"The killer. The guy with glasses. The guy who wants. . ."

"Frank and the paper work. I got it."

Kelsey shook her head. How could this woman know that?

"Devon," said the woman. "I'm Greg's wife."

Kelsey looked over as the blonde returned.

The woman raised one hand from under an afghan. "Gwen," she said. "Wayne's wife."

Kelsey started to cry. They were friends. They understood what was going on, or at least they knew who she was. She sniffed hard, took the tissue Gwen offered her. "Call Sam," she said. "He'll be looking for me."

Devon held up her cell. "Already on it."

Gwen wiped Kelsey's cheek, dabbing carefully along the cut. "It's not deep," she murmured. "Here, hold this while I find the butterfly strips." In moments Gwen applied butterfly bandages along the cut and Devon finished her call. They escorted Kelsey to the living room, settled her in a recliner and wrapped the blanket around her.

Devon looked at Gwen. "Tea," she said, "hot tea and sugar. Give me a hand would you." The women left.

Kelsey closed her eyes, felt the heat from the blanket soak into her. The last fifteen minutes swooshed by like a movie running too fast. She opened her eyes, shaking off the memory.

Why did he let me go?

· · · · ·

Sam stared at the phone and applied his entire supply of reserve to staying put. He wanted to run to the house, to see Kelsey. But Devon's information raised his risk hackles. Why did the man take Kelsey, threaten her and then turn her loose? And why turn her loose at Wayne's house? Goose bumps slithered up his spine and prickled his throat stealing his spit.

His phone rang again. Lem. Sam answered.

"He called." Lem's voice was low, choked. "He turned Kelsey loose."

"Yes, Devon called me."

"Where are you?"

"Beside the church, looking at the house. What's the missing piece here?"

"It's not pretty. Take a look around the foundation of the Manse? Can you see anything out of place?"

Sam moved to the tree by the end of the drive. He started his inspection at the door and front step. A gray lump peeked out from the concrete ledge around the landing.

"Gray putty," he said to Lem. "At least I'm hoping it's putty." He scanned the front of the house. At the front right corner another gray bump peeked from under the edge of the siding. "There's another one."

Lem swore. "He wasn't bluffing."

Sam's innards echoed fear. "Explosives."

"Yup."

Three women, two babies and what looked like enough explosive to create a hole the size of Halifax Harbor. A near impossible situation.

"How did he manage that?" Sam couldn't believe it. "How did he know where to put it?"

"Remember the bait your computer buddy leaked? My guess is our quarry came straight to Caleb's Cove. Given the computer skills in his organization, he probably has more information about any of us than we have on him. At least the personal information."

Sam clutched the back of his head. This was his fault, his plan, his screw-up. All the guy had needed to do was get the lay of the land. When he'd seen the women and babies, he must have felt like he'd hit Christmas.

"And the explosives?"

"Not that hard," Lem said. "If he had them ready, planning to use them out where Frank is, all he needed to do was fasten them to the house. Wouldn't have taken him more than a few minutes."

"Did he have any demands?" Sam asked.

"Not much," Lem's tone was sarcastic. "He wants his trophy book if you can believe it. And he wants Frank Binks. He said the book and Frank or the women. We can choose. And Sam, he says he's watching and that all the usual caveats apply. If we try to disarm, get the women out. . ." his voice trailed off.

Sam shut down his emotions. He couldn't afford to allow them free rein. He needed rescue mission mode. "Call the others. Have them meet us at the church. Don't tell them on the phone but ask Jackson to bring Frank, and Wayne to bring the trophy book. Who runs the store in the old church?"

"Jackson's wife, Nancy. She's a calm one. You can explain the full details to her."

"Right. I remember her." Sam rang off, turned on his heel and dashed for the church.

"Nancy," he said approaching the counter where she was pricing souvenirs. "We have a family emergency."

She looked up, took long seconds to gaze at his face and paled.

"We need to close and ask folks to head north, up past the marina."

She chewed her lip, looked past him to a family with three little girls and nodded. She quietly but firmly cleared the room, pointing folks up to the café before asking. "What's up?"

Sam filled her in. "Listen, go up to the café – keep people from coming this way. Tell them anything. Is there a volunteer fire department?"

She nodded. "But half of them are already with you."

"Get the rest, quietly. Be ready just in case. Is there any Emergency Medical Safety?"

"Jackson's the medic," she said "And Hart's been training with him. And one of the fire volunteers is EMS in Bridgewater. If he's at home, I can get him."

"Get them ready," Sam said. "But keep things undercover. At least with all the folks around, the guy shouldn't notice people heading into the café. Now go."

Nancy gave him a quick hug. "You can fix this," she said. "You've got great helpers." And she was gone.

It felt like forever but was probably less than fifteen minutes before the others arrived.

"Fill them in," Sam said to Lem. Lem repeated the information. "And I went up the bush trail and took a look at the back of the house." He held up a pair of field glasses. "There's another one of those bundles at the far back corner." He waved an arm. "Diagonal to the one at the front. The back door is also decorated – and that one looks like it's rigged to go off if anyone opens that door."

And there they stood. Six men including two fathers, a couple of uncles and good friends. They faced the total destruction of three women and two children they all loved.

And Kelsey.

Nausea swamped Sam and, hyperventilating, he bent and rested his hands on his knees.

"Timing?" he asked Lem. "Did he have a plan?"

"He said he's watching and that he'd call once we're here. He took my cell number." Lem stood by the window, his back to the room. Only the thick undertones in his voice betrayed his emotion. Silence hung on them like the shrouds of the dead. Sam wanted Kelsey back so ferociously it frightened him as nothing in his life ever had. *Do the others feel the same?*

A noisy inhale and a huff cut the air. Lem turned. "All right, you bunch of lily-assed youngen's, let's figure out how to save them."

Jolted, Sam snapped to attention. This was his operation. He'd better smarten up. "Jackson, do a perimeter check on this building and take the field glasses and see what you can see at the house." He did not have to tell Jackson to stay well back. Thinking rapidly, he dispatched the others to reconnoiter everything within three hundred feet.

· · · · ·

A phone rang, jarring Kelsey out of a light doze. She dragged the blanket with her, struggled out of the chair and headed to the kitchen. Devon raised a hand to Kelsey and activated the speaker mode on her phone.

"Devon," Sam's voice carried into the room and sent tendrils of hope through Kelsey. "There's a big problem. I'm going to tell you straight out. But first the three of you need to suck in your guts and brace for bad news. I need you thinking and planning. If we're going to figure this out, we need to have detailed information about that house."

"Sam, what are you trying to tell us?"

"The house is rigged with explosives."

"So, we need to get out."

"Not that easy. If you try that, the whole place could go up."

Kelsey met Devon's gaze, felt Gwen stiffen beside her. A baby's cough echoed from the baby monitor. A sun mote floated past Kelsey's gaze.

"What are you doing about it?" Devon's terse voice restarted time.

"Jackson is finding out about the explosives. He has training. Wayne and Greg have gone on a reconnaissance mission to see if they can locate the bad guys. We don't know if the knife man is alone or not."

"There are two of them," Kelsey said. "He said he'd hurt a lot of people if I didn't cooperate."

"Thanks, Kelsey, good to know," Sam said. His voice broke and he cleared his throat. "Frank's up in the attic checking our visuals and making sure we are alone in the building. At the moment, I'm talking to you. I need your help."

Gwen and Devon moved closer to Kelsey, nodding even though Sam could not see them. "Anything," Devon said. "What do you need?"

"You and Kelsey go upstairs," Sam said, "and look out each window. Do your best to stay out of sight. You're looking for people, parked cars or stacks of materials, anything and everything. Look for places you think someone could hide and still see the house. And Gwen, check your basement for the safest location possible. I don't want to scare you girl, but you're looking to create a bomb shelter." He hung up.

Kelsey dropped the blanket.

Gwen tugged her shirt.

Devon pressed her lips together.

"Is this real?" Kelsey asked.

"Think so." Devon tilted her head.

"Oh God," Gwen said.

And suddenly they were all in motion. Gwen flung open the basement door. Kelsey raced after Devon through the front hall and up the staircase. They took a front room each.

Kelsey stared out. The road ran past the front, open fields lay on the far side and beyond that was the ocean. Directly to the left, she could see the parking lot and the front of the church. Beyond was the store and diagonally across from it the Marina. She raised her gaze to the sky and started her inspection.

Think hunters. Where would Dad and Brock hide?

Roof tops, upper floors. The third floor attic windows in the store building. The church tower. Trees. All locations would work for a clandestine watcher.

Kelsey returned to the hall. Both babies were asleep in one room and Devon tiptoed in to check on them. Kelsey entered the master bedroom and slid into the corner beside the window. The curtains here were heavier, wider, blocking her view. Cautiously, slowly, she managed to get a line of sight. The graveyard encompassed her entire vision field. Most of the tombstones faced the street. Looking across the area, she could see between the rows. Directly behind the house, each stone blocked its own small patch. Here and there, extra-large monuments created black holes in the vision range. Too many places to hide. She went into the hall and followed Devon downstairs.

How can we escape a blast? What does the killer want in exchange for not blowing us up?

She stopped, one foot on the last step, one hanging in the air and a hand gripping the newel post. *He wants Frank.* Tears clogged her throat and clouded her eyes. *And Frank will do anything to save us— to save me.*

· · · · ·

Sam cleared the counter in the middle of the converted church. He found a roll of packing paper Nancy used for shipping packages and rolled it out, taping it flat. He sketched building locations and nodded to each man as they returned. He positioned Lem in the front foyer to watch the street. The entire time he reined in the monster roaring in his head and ignored the voice yelling at him to storm in and rescue Kelsey.

Jackson returned. "How bad is it?" Sam asked. His logic reinforced that the best way, the only way, to stop the killer was to work as a team.

"The primary explosives are at the back corner of the house. Bushes partly obscure the area. There is no line of sight to most of the graveyard from here. I didn't see any wires running away from the house, so I'd say the man's using a remote detonator." He set down the field glasses.

"The back door has a trip switch, but the others will require a remote trigger. He can't watch us and all of the locations at the same time."

"Kelsey confirmed two men. At least that's what the knife man told her."

"Damn." Jackson muttered. He grabbed up the field glasses. "I'll do another check. He has to be somewhere."

Sam gave him a clipped nod and lifted his chin as Frank came out of a small side room.

"We're alone in this building," Frank said. "Didn't find any extra wires, there's no basement and a peaked attic space, but no way to see out from up there." He waved his bug detector. "And no devices. Near as I can tell, we've a clean space that way. Biggest problem is the lack of view to the rest of the graveyard and back of the house."

Sam stilled his thoughts. Bit by bit they would narrow the options. They'd see a movement, hear a sound and they'd get the bastards. Hanging on to that belief was critical.

Greg returned. "I checked all three floors in Marta's building. No one's hiding and, looking at the dust in the third floor, no one's been up there recently. Marta knew all the nooks and crannies. If there was anyone there, she'd have found them. She said nothing was out of order, set her alarm and locked up. She has one kick-ass alarm system. If anyone tries to get in there, we'll know about it. I think for now we can rule out the store."

"Where is she?"

Greg nodded toward the road. "She went to the café with the others. The EMS van pulled in up there and parked out of sight."

Jackson nodded. "Good. They'll be ready."

Ready for what? A chill coated Sam's skin. Those explosives might blow the women to smithereens. He blocked the idea, tapped his finger on the drawings. "Not many other places left for them to hide," he said. He marked an X on the far diagonal corner of the old Manse. "The field and the road area are too open, no cover. My guess is that whatever they've planned will be mounted from the graveyard."

"Did anybody get a visual on either man?" he asked. "Or any evidence of where they might be hiding?"

"No."

"Nothing."

"Not a whisper."

The answers were unanimous.

"There's a vent in the attic at the house," Lem said. "We had to get bats out of there one year. It's only held in with a few screws. A person could get a really good view from there."

"Good. The best option is for one of us to get into the house." He looked around the group. "Too risky though?" They nodded agreement.

"Second best plan, we'll get more Intel from the women."

He shook his phone. "I've lost connection. No bars."

The others all checked their phones. "None here either," Wayne said. "What happened? I have great connection at the house and we're not that far away."

"Jamming," Jackson said. "They are using a jammer." He met Sam's gaze and the tension in the room went way up.

"I suppose the upside is that the explosives won't be triggered by phone." Wayne said.

Sam shook his head. "Doesn't matter. They can turn off the jammer whenever they want. We're screwed."

"Hold on, fellas," Frank said. "It's not all bad. Get over the loss part and think. You boys have used surveillance equipment. The range on those things, especially black market stuff here in Canada, has a maximum of two hundred feet. Most don't top one hundred. So we've just narrowed the options for their location."

"Quite possible," Sam said. "Unless they set it up and moved their position farther back."

"Too many trees farther back," Lem said, "and the land drops into the swamp. Unless they're up a tree, they'd lose sight of the house. And the trees are bushy and stunted."

Sam drew a circle on the map, marking the new approximate perimeter. Bit by bit they were narrowing the options. His phone rang. He checked. Bars.

"They have the blocker off," he said and circled his hand. "Call Devon," he urged Greg, "we may only have a few minutes." He answered. "Logan here."

"Saw everyone arrive, saw you checking things out. You know I'm not bluffing. And I know you have who and what I want."

"Bully for you. Just remember," Sam said, "if the women and children are harmed, we'll hunt you and find you. Be sure of it."

"Sure, sure. But you're going to do what I want and they'll be fine. Have a little faith. That building was a church wasn't it?" The man laughed. "Now, give that book to Frank Binks. He's going to walk slowly out the back and along the path toward the house. Behind the house is a gate to the graveyard. Give him your phone, and tell him to stop when he's through the gate." The caller hung up.

Sam relayed the information and looked at Greg. "Did you reach Devon?"

Greg nodded. "But all I got was they have a shelter in the basement, and Kelsey has a rifle she says she can use."

Wayne nodded. "It was in the gun safe in the bedroom."

"But can she really use it?"

Sam shrugged. "She's a rancher's daughter. It's quite possible."

Ragged, loud noise ripped through the room. They all jumped. Sam swore. "What the heck is that?"

Lem looked at Frank. Frank nodded. "Phone," they said simultaneously.

"How," Greg asked. "We checked. The phone line was cut."

The jangle came again. They all headed toward the sound.

Sam rooted behind a counter and pulled out an old black unit with a circular dial.

Lem started to laugh. "The last clergy we had kept an office here. His wife had that direct line put in to reach him. Answer it, Sam. It's the women."

· · · · ·

Kelsey climbed the rickety pull-down stairs to the attic in the old Manse. When she reached the top, she lay on a beam and reached down. Devon handed her the rifle.

"Go," Kelsey said. "Get in the shelter."

Devon, her head tilted back, sighed. 'Good luck," she said and turned away.

She'd need luck. She hadn't fired a rifle in two years. She could only hope it was like riding a bicycle and it all came back to her. Frank was about to follow the killer's instructions. There was no other long-range gun available and definitely no other vantage point as good. It was up to her.

The air vent at the back of the attic overlooked the yard. She had tools, the gun, ammunition and prayers. She could only hope it was enough. Walking on two joists, she balanced her way to the vent.

As reported, the old-fashioned slatted vent was held in place with screws. Securing the gun, she checked. Slot heads. She chose the right end on the Multi. *Lefty loosey.* She started on the screws. Luck was with her. Two screws actually came out in her hand as soon as she started turning them.

In minutes she was ready. Now, she needed the little man with glasses to underestimate her once again. As long as he didn't look up, way up, she'd make this work.

She found a solid footing, propped the gun on the casing and peered through the scope. Wayne had said it pulled slightly to the right. She looked at the grasses and trees. A minimal breeze blew straight back. No noticeable crosswind. *Please let me remember.*

Sam's advice rang in her ears. *Aim for the chest. It's the biggest target. If you go wide you have a better chance of hitting at least part of his body. If you aim for a limb and miss, you could miss him altogether.*

She sucked air, blew out through her mouth. *Calm. I need to stay calm.*

The logistics in place, her emotions took over. Could she actually shoot a man? Waiting was the hardest part. Only two months ago she'd never heard of Frank. Less than a week ago she'd met him for the first time. Those moments swirled in her head, and she remembered his tears, his words. *I'm his little girl. I have to do this.*

A squeak rang in the air. The gate. She looked. Frank, his hands held up on either side of his head, the book in one, Sam's phone in the other, stepped into the graveyard. *My father. My flesh and blood. His life is in my hands.*

She alternated between looking at Frank and keeping an eye on the cell phone. Sam figured they'd turn off the blocker to call Frank. She'd have momentary connection. She held her finger over the preset button to Jackson's phone.

The bars lit up, she pushed the button.

Sam's phone rang outside and Frank brought the phone to his ear.

Her call clicked on an open line. Sam answered.

"I can see all the way to the tree line," she said. "No movement straight out or toward you." Again she scanned to the left, the area least visible from the old church, the area facing the explosives. A movement caught her eye. "I see him," she said. "He's behind the biggest monument."

Below her Frank headed toward that monument. The phones went dead. Kelsey dropped the phone, shifted her position and tracked Frank. He placed each foot, marching in slow motion as they'd planned.

Acid backwashed from her stomach and burned her throat. Sam figured they'd blow up the house no matter what because the killer needed a diversion to escape. Her presence on the third floor might save her or kill her. *Depends on the size of the blast.*

Devon and Gwen were in the shelter with the babies. Fortunately, solid concrete walls framed an old coal room. Located in the back corner of the house, it was away from all the explosives. The mothers and babies were as protected as possible with a sturdy table surrounded by mattresses as extra protection in the middle of the room.

Kelsey brought her gaze and her mind back to Frank. So much hinged on his performance. A few feet before the monument he stopped, brought one hand to his chest and dropped to one knee. His fake heart attack.

She heard a voice but couldn't discern the words. She could only guess Frank was being instructed to keep moving. She leaned as close to the hole as she could, scanning the very edge of her vision field. Through a gap in the fence, she saw what she sought. A prone figure crawled commando style toward the far side of the graveyard. But Greg's progress was slow. Would Frank's act buy enough time?

Would Lem and Sam be able to disarm the charges at the front of the house? Was the other man watching? Did they have to turn on the phones to activate the charges? So much to consider.

Focus. Your job is to watch Frank and keep him safe. She stilled her breathing and steadied her hands.

A kafuffle on the periphery of her vision told her Greg had found the other man. Sounds on the main floor told her that someone had breached the perimeter and was headed up the stairs. *The front explosives must be deactivated.*

She pulled her full attention to her task, keeping her gaze on Frank but allowing her peripheral vision to watch the area immediately around him.

Her former captor erupted from behind the monument.

Her phone blipped.

The man grabbed Frank by the hair and tilted his head back. He raised his knife arm. The sun glinted on the blade.

Kelsey squeezed the trigger.

The splat of the bullet, the jerk of the man's body, the tumble of both men to the ground played out in the echo of her shot. In the aftermath, an explosion shook the house. Kelsey toppled, one hand sinking into insulation and her shoulder landing crushingly on a joist. The gun spiraled out the opening.

Ringing filled her ears. A sharp shape dug into her stomach. Dust assaulted her nose.

Kelsey groaned and shifted.

The pain lanced through her. Pain meant she was alive. She gasped, opened her eyes.

The babies. Oh, my God, the babies.

"Kelsey." The faint call penetrated the ringing in her ears, a hand touched her shoulder.

"Sweetheart, can you hear me. Are you okay?"

"Ah. Ooh" She found solid purchase for one hand and pushed back, turning her head.

"Thank God." The voice, louder now, came attached to a face, a body.

"Sam?"

"Right here. Don't move. There's help on the way. We need to check you for injuries."

"Sam, I need to move. Something is digging into my gut."

"Hang on, Sweetie." His hands started at her heels and worked up her body and finished with her scalp.

"I can move," she said, "and everything bloody hurts. No numb spots. That's good, isn't it?" She found purchase on a second joist and pushed with both hands, ending up on all fours. "That's better." The culprit causing her belly pain was a brick, one of several dislodged from the chimney. At least they hadn't fallen on top of her. Sam held out a hand and she took it, allowing him to help her up.

She moved each limb, found all her parts working. She looked at Sam and tears started. "Oh god, what happened?"

Sam tucked an arm around her. "Come on, watch your feet. Let's get out of here." He guided her through the settling dust, down the ladder and into the hall.

"Greg got the second man," he said as they went. "Jackson and Lem were able to disable the charges at the front corner and front door. The only ones to go off were at the back."

They reached the hallway. Pictures slewed on the walls, dust and plaster billowed from the master bedroom, the room below her attic position. Sam escorted her toward the main staircase. "Most of the damage is in this corner of the house."

"The babies," she managed to say before descending into a coughing attack.

"Wayne went," Sam said. Below them, Greg charged through the front door and headed for the basement stairs.

The sobbing wails of a toddler and the mewling cries of an infant drifted up from the basement. *Alive. Babies that cried were alive.* Tears welled in Kelsey's chest and tight relief gripped her solar plexus.

In the kitchen, debris slowed their progress and a breeze flowed in through a hole in the wall.

"The coal cellar." Kelsey's voice rasped. "It's near the front."
Was it far enough away from the blast for safety?

Moments later, Wayne exited the stairwell, his son on one arm,
the little boy's face pressed against his shoulder.

Gwen, streaks of dirt marring her features, trailed behind. She
had one hand hooked in her husband's belt. She grinned even as
tears traced tracks through the dust on her face. "We're all fine."

Greg and Devon followed them up the stairs. Greg held his infant
daughter with one arm and his wife with the other, so tightly aligned
they came through the doorway abreast.

Devon met Kelsey's gaze and nodding, gave her a thumbs-up.

Kelsey turned to Sam, buried her face in his shoulder and wept
hot tears of relief.

And Frank?

Shock receded, pushed back by the echoing memory of that
gunshot.

She sniffed, pulled back and whispered in Sam's ear. "Where's
Frank?"

He held her away and turned her toward what was left of the
backdoor. The step was gone, the door was gone, the frame hung
crookedly, but a man looked in at them. *Frank.*

Blood spattered his clothing, his hair stuck out in all directions,
but he was grinning. He met her gaze. "Not my blood," he said and
swiped at his shirt front.

Kelsey pulled away from Sam and knelt in the door opening,
putting out a hand to her father. Tears ran down her face.

Jackson appeared behind him. Kelsey sought his gaze.

He gave a curt nod, looked toward the graveyard and back. "He's
alive," he said, "worse luck."

Relief washed over her. *I didn't kill him.* She nodded and huffed
to stop more tears.

Frank took her hand in one of his and extended the other toward
Sam. "Well then, boyo, gives us a boost would you?" His Henry-
Newfie impersonation broke the tension.

Laughter swelled into the existing puddle of tears. The volunteer
fire department arrived and was greeted by a dirty-faced, bloodied
group, laughing the shaky, thank-God-I'm-alive laughter of
survivors.

CHAPTER SIXTEEN

Sam pulled into the café and Marina parking lot, stopped and turned to look at Kelsey. "I'll pick you up after the meeting," he said and smiled. "I'm sure you and Frank still have lots to talk about."

She paused with her hand on the door. "No doubt. We've done a lot of catching-up-on-details type talk, but we're edging into reasons and feelings. It's not easy for Frank. He lived so peripherally for so long." She looked into the distance. "It's been enlightening for me. When I started looking, I was shocked after learning about Frank. And angry my parents had lied to me."

She took a deep breath. "Over time the balance changed." She tilted her hand. "Like a teeter-totter. Finding Frank became the more important goal. In the end, it was what truly mattered. And I realized my family is still my family. I CAN have it all."

She laughed and opened the car door. "I'll be here when you get back."

Her phone chimed out the *Friends in High Places* tune. Sam laughed. "Brock," he said, "he seems to sense when we're in the car."

He watched her face as she put the phone on speaker. "Brock, how's it going?"

"Great," he said. "Your plane comes in tomorrow, doesn't it. At seven?"

"That's right," she said. "You'll be there to meet me?" She grinned at Sam.

"Darn straight," Brock said, "we'll all be there, even Dad."

Tears welled in her eyes. "Thanks, Brock. See you then."

Sam reached over and wiped her tears. "They missed you."

She nodded. "But they managed just fine." She stood and looked back. "See you in a bit."

Sam watched her enter the café and, turning the car, headed for

Greg and Devon's estate. The Bockner Estate, as the locals called it, had a local history and a personal one for Greg and Devon. The events involved the previous estate owner, the now dead Dr. Zinck, and a dory rescue at sea.

Jackson's car was already parked in front of the house beside a jeep Sam didn't recognize. He must be the last to arrive. He headed around the side, hopped onto a deck and reached the private door to Greg's office. Inside he found Greg, Jackson and Wayne already seated around the circular table at the far end of the office along with Jeffrey Brown.

The room, as much games room as office, occupied the entire side of the main floor. Oak floors, solid beams and a huge fireplace created a club atmosphere. The wide maple desk opposite the fireplace was flanked by computers and office equipment. The best of both worlds as far as the men were concerned.

"Pull up a chair," Greg said holding out a sheet of paper, "and have an agenda." It was the first official meeting of the *Caleb Cove Security Agency* in two months.

They whizzed through the basics and got to the reports.

"Dick Harett," Sam said, referring to the knife-wielding killer they'd apprehended, "is recovering under lock and key. The gunshot caused substantial damage but it is isolated to his shoulder. His house has been dissected." He tapped the table. "This fellow is a classic. How he's stayed under the radar for three decades is amazing. What's good for us is that he's compulsive about many things, including record keeping."

"On that front," Greg added, "there are paper records of kills, fake IDs and other criminal activities. The officials want it all digitalized for cross referencing. They are practically salivating at the possibility of catching criminals who have been under the radar for years."

Sam huffed. "They have their work cut out for them. How will they ever find the manpower?"

Greg grinned. "They're hiring outside experts, consultants to do the computer work." He picked up a folder and waved it. "Contracts are in here. CCSA got the deal." He plopped that folder on the table and picked up another. "And your cohort, Jeffrey Brown, is joining us full time." He nodded toward Jeffrey. "He'll be overseeing the project."

"Thanks, Greg. It'll be a challenge entering all that data and creating macros and logarithms to sort them. But, no worries, I love a good challenge."

"Welcome aboard, Jeff," Sam said. The others added their greetings.

Sam coughed. "We also found the leak in the police department. Dick has a twin sister. She was a personal assistant to high-ranking officers. She's been there for decades and as a trusted, high-level support staff could access secure files."

Jackson snorted. "Not anymore, I hope."

"Are they taking any action against Kelsey for shooting the man?" Wayne asked.

Greg shook his head but it was Sam who answered. "There was an investigation, but the general consensus is that the circumstances warranted the action. And the man is still alive." Murmurs of relief and support rolled around the table.

They all consulted their agendas and looked at Jackson. "We have a contract to provide security for a big concert coming up next winter in Halifax," he said. "I've started screening for staff but I'll be counting on you boys to do your part."

Sam sat back and looked at Greg. "Well, my friend, it looks like your plan is working. We have one case successfully wrapped up and more contracts on the table. *Caleb Cove Security Agency* is in business."

· · · · ·

Kelsey stood in the entry of *The Marina Café*, letting her eyes adjust to the darker light. Kim came towards her, smiling.

"Hey, Kelsey. You're looking good." Kim hugged her.

"Frank's back by the windows," Kim said and led the way.

Frank stood to greet her, hugging her solidly before letting her sit.

His gaze searched her face. "Still can't believe it sometimes," he said. "You are so like your mother and yet so much yourself. And you're here."

Kelsey parked her purse on a spare chair and grinned. The absolute delight Frank showed in her presence warmed her every time she saw him. *Total acceptance*.

"How's Henry?" she asked.

"Good," Frank said, "real good. He's selling his bar. Said this was the last straw. The company that's wanted to buy the land for years is still interested." He grinned. "The old goat is hedging, making sure he gets a good dollar from them."

A silence, not quite comfortable, but not totally awkward, settled around them. Kelsey fiddled with her wrapped cutlery. Frank hitched his chair forward.

"How are. . ." They started in chorus.

"You first. . ." Again in sync.

They laughed. Frank pointed. "You first."

"Just going to ask how you're doing?"

Frank nodded. "That's my question too." He paused. "I'm doing fine. Vi and I have been talking, you know, real talking." He smiled. "'bout time I guess." He tipped his head at Kelsey. "Your turn."

She touched her face. "My doctor says I won't have a scar."

"Good, good."

"I have a job offer here."

Frank's smile lit his face. "Really? You'll stay?"

She nodded. "I'm going home to Alberta for a visit, but I'll be back."

Frank's eyes filled with tears. "I missed you all those years. I missed so much of your life." His chest heaved. "But I figured it was best. Your mother said it was best for you." He slid his hand across the table and touched hers. "All I ever wanted was for you to be happy and healthy."

Kelsey's throat clogged. She cleared it. "I'm happy, Frank. You did good. I was raised right and I have brothers and a Dad." She stopped. How did she say this? "But the way you make me feel, the way you accept me, I missed that. No one else makes me feel as loved as you do."

She tugged the napkin off her cutlery and swiped it across her nose. "Oh darn, damn tears."

Frank sniffed hard. "Thanks, my girl, you just made my day." A crooked grin creased his face. "Heck, you just made my life."

They looked at each other, tears clouding two pairs of gray-green eyes.

"Say," Kelsey said, "did you used to take me on the Halifax-Dartmouth ferry?"

Frank laughed. "Every chance we got, kiddo, every chance we got. You loved standing in the front with the wind in your face."

"I remembered," she said, "I used to dream about it." She blew her nose. "Can we do it again sometime soon?"

Frank nodded. "You bet. Every chance we get."

· · · · ·

Celebrations were finally in order. Weeks of planning and organizing and a visit back to Alberta over, Kelsey surveyed the room. Sam stepped in behind her and wrapped his arms around her middle. "Happy?"

She smiled even though he couldn't see her face. Soft light glowed over the decorations, the white bells, the large cake and the colorful dresses of the women. The men, including Brock and her Dad, clustered at one end of the room, beer glasses in hand. Every darn one of them had discarded their ties and jackets and rolled up their sleeves as soon as the Justice of the Peace said, "you may kiss the bride."

Across the room with Grace in her arms, Devon swayed in that side-to-side Mom-rocking motion. Jude toddled unsteadily after his father. Chatter and laughter filled the room and drifted out on the night air.

Frank turned, caught Kelsey's gaze and, cocking his head with a smile, raised his grape juice in a salute. Beside him, resplendent in a flowing dress, Vi grinned at her.

"About time he made an honest woman of her," Sam murmured.

Kelsey nodded. "It seems surreal," she said. "Here I am back in the house where I was born, a witness at my birthfather's wedding. I have two dads, a new stepmom and," she paused, "a whole new circle of friends."

"I know Greg talked to you," Sam said. "And I know what he asked. Will you stay?"

"Yes," she said. "I'll stay." She turned toward him and patted his cheek. "Greg's job offer was too good to refuse. Happy?"

Sam grinned and wrapped her in a hug. "Absolutely."

About the Author

Mahrie wrote her first mystery book at age eight and the handwritten copy of *Mystery on Tancook Island* still exists. Pursuing an education, a husband and kids and a busy career overtook her writing for many years. During that time, she read copiously, studied writing craft and shared her learning in workshops, conferences and courses.

She always kept writing, publishing non-fiction, short stories and poetry as Mahrie Glab. She has now come full circle, returning to writing mystery novels, this time with a touch of romance. Her first *Caleb Cove Mystery* was released in February 2014.

Mahrie is a member of Alberta Romance Writers' Association and a graduate of Calgary's Citizen's Police Academy and Private Investigation 101. She lives north of Calgary, Alberta with her hubby and a cat named Kotah.

www.mahriegreid.com

www.facebook.com/mahriegreid

Made in the USA
Charleston, SC
22 March 2016